THE CHEF AND THE COUNTESS

The Duke's Bastards
Book 2

by

Karyn Gerrard

ARE YOU SIGNED UP FOR DRAGONBLADE'S BLOG?

You'll get the latest news and information on exclusive giveaways, exclusive excerpts, coming releases, sales, free books, cover reveals and more.

Check out our complete list of authors, too!

No spam, no junk. That's a promise!

Sign Up Here

www.dragonbladepublishing.com

Dearest Reader;

Thank you for your support of a small press. At Dragonblade Publishing, we strive to bring you the highest quality Historical Romance from some of the best authors in the business. Without your support, there is no 'us', so we sincerely hope you adore these stories and find some new favorite authors along the way.

Happy Reading!

CEO, Dragonblade Publishing

PROLOGUE

Northern England
December, 1898

CELIA GILLINGHAM, COUNTESS Winterwood, the wife of Carlton Gardiner, the Earl of Winterwood, was acutely aware that this day was inevitable. Her husband, a man of sixty-five, had been ailing for the past six years, his health deteriorating with each passing week. Sitting outside the sick room, her hands folded in her lap, waiting for the doctor's verdict, she couldn't help but wonder about her future. *What will become of me?*

It was rather selfish to think of such while Carlton fought for his life, but Celia could not help it. Every time she raised the subject during their marriage, Carlton dismissed her concerns regarding her future with a wave of his withered hand, stating all was as it should be, whatever that meant. She wished now she had taken firmer control, demanding to see his solicitor and be shown the documents—if any existed. Not that a married woman could make such a request. Celia would possess more legal rights if she were single instead of married, a fact that she found profoundly unjust and disheartening. She had no idea of just how much a husband could legally control a woman, especially when it came to finances.

Sitting alone in the shadowy hallway, Celia admonished herself for allowing a topic as imperative as her future well-being to slide. What *would* she do? She had no family except for her Aunt Etta, the Countess of Darrington, and they had not been in contact for years. Celia still harbored a lingering hurt over her arranged marriage and the fact that when it counted, her aunt did not stand up for her. But then, the countess's husband, William Buckingham, the Earl of Darrington, was not a man to refuse. There was something entirely sinister about Uncle William. And her loathsome cousin, Troy Buckingham, Viscount Shinwell, was worse. These earlier experiences left her with a deep mistrust and uncertainty about her future.

At least the past few years had been peaceful. Life in Marshall Meadows, a small hamlet in Northern England near the border with Scotland, meant isolation and a quiet existence. Especially now with snow blanketing the countryside. By the end of January, travel would become nearly impossible until spring. It gave her time to read and lose herself in fictional adventure and romance. Perhaps Celia had become too impassive and, because of it, she had stopped asking questions about securing her future. Well, that and Carlton had categorically refused to discuss it. The realization of her complacency filled her with a sense of urgency and regret, a burden she could not shake off.

As the door creaked open, the doctor's solemn expression told Celia all she needed to know. The room was filled with the acrid scent of illness and the faint crackling of the fire in the hearth. *This is it, then.* Celia sat by Carlton's bedside, a feeling of sadness washing over her. After all, he was her husband and, after a fashion, a friend.

"Forgive me, forgive me," he muttered, his head tossing to and fro on the pillow. Sweat ran in rivulets down his pale, hollowed cheeks.

"Forgive you for what, Carlton?"

"He'll look after you. He *promised* me."

Celia's blood chilled. She had heard those words before—from her uncle on the day of her arranged marriage. "Whom are you speaking of?"

Carlton coughed, and saliva dribbled from his mouth. "My heir."

The shock of that declaration hit her hard, reverberating

through her nerve endings. This was the first time Celia had heard of an heir. Carlton had entered into marriage for the specific reason of begetting an heir, and they had tried for the first five years of their marriage. At least, that was the reason he gave. Alas, she did not become pregnant. Soon after that, Carlton became ill.

"To your earldom?" Indeed, he had to be mistaken. It was the sickness talking. What else could it be? He hadn't been well for years. The fever must have affected his mind. Celia knew deep down they should never have traveled to London last month. He'd taken a turn for the worse as soon as they arrived home.

"My late cousin's boy. We haven't written much." Carlton started coughing again. "He said he will look after you. It is the way of things."

The way of things? Celia did not like the sound of this. "What do you mean? What about your will?"

Carlton shook his head, struggling for breath. "None— recent."

After more than a decade together, the revelation of an old will—a will that might not include her—left Celia in a state of shock. As a countess, wasn't she entitled to a living from the estate? But that provision was from a bygone era, when aristocrats had tenants making money and paying rent. A feeling of dread crossed her soul. Then annoyance rose within her. Celia did not get angry often, hardly ever, but there was no holding back her rising aggravation.

"How could you? How could you not tell me of an heir? You lied when you said you needed an heir!" Celia's sense of betrayal was overwhelming, a sharp pain that pierced her heart. She was tempted to grab and shake him, but what would be the point at this juncture? He had lied all those years ago regarding the title. Celia had even felt sorry for him and agreed to marry him—not that she had much choice. The depth of his duplicity left her feeling utterly deceived.

"I wanted *my* heir," Carlton wheezed. "I did not want my

cousin's boy to have it, but it's his now. Forgive me."

No, she would *not* forgive him. For once in her life, fury overcame any compassion. "What's his name? Where is he?" Carlton's eyes closed. This time, she did shake him, though gently. "Do not die on me yet. Not until you explain how you could be so thoughtless and selfish. I thought we were friends. I thought you cared for me, at least a little."

His eyes popped open, and his milky gaze slid toward her. "His name is Franklin Gardiner. From Canada. I wrote him two months ago. Here. Now." Every spoken word was an effort.

Celia's mind spun from the multiple tumultuous revelations. The anger vanished, and a deep hurt took its place. "You knew you were dying and never said a word. That's why we went to London, so you could make arrangements. Oh, Carlton. How could you do this to me?"

"I went to see a doctor for a second opinion. Did not. Want. To worry you." His breathing grew shallow.

Holy crow. Celia was in a fix.

"The heir will look after you. He *promised.*" Carlton gasped as his gnarled fingers wrapped around her wrist. "You were good to me."

Perhaps too good. "You appreciated my company and care. But not enough to legally secure my future or be truthful. Instead, you placed me in the hands of a stranger." Celia shook off his hand. "You failed me. You neglected your basic duties as a husband and a friend." Celia snorted. "I failed myself. After being handed off to you by my family, I should have insisted on legal guarantees. But I was nineteen; what did I know? I became too content and comfortable with my life."

"Forgive," Carlton gasped. "Please."

Forgiveness would be the decent thing to do, but just as she started crafting a response to do so, Carlton began coughing, sputtering, and gasping for every breath until he grew still.

The doctor entered the room, stood by the bed, and felt for his pulse. "He's dead."

He was gone. It happened so swiftly. And with it, her life as she knew it—swept away with a raspy, rattled final breath. She felt another twinge of sadness at Carlton's death. But it was mixed with uncertainty and resentment.

"Mr. Frankin Gardiner is waiting to see you in the library, my lady."

Celia whirled around to find Patrick, the footman, standing in the doorway.

Well, the second cousin didn't waste any time. He'd traveled here to claim the title and everything that came with it. Standing, Celia smoothed her gown and headed downstairs with as much dignity as she could muster. When she entered the library, a tall, thin man turned to greet her.

Franklin Gardiner looked to be in his thirties. He was not homely as such but certainly not handsome—much like Carlton. His expression remained neutral and guarded. "Countess, I am Franklin Gardiner. How is the earl doing?"

"Dead. Not five minutes ago," Celia replied flatly.

"My condolences," he said, giving her a slight bow. "I did not know the earl. I was born and raised in Nova Scotia, Canada, but my late father remembers him from when they were younger."

He acted polite enough, though somewhat distant. She would do the same. Celia motioned toward the leather chairs by the fire. "I had no idea Carlton had an heir. To say I am shocked is an understatement."

"I would imagine so, my lady," he murmured as he sat across from her. "I have met with the late earl's solicitor, Mr. George Sanderson, since my arrival here last week. He found me a room across the Scottish border at the inn in Lamberton. It is only a few miles from here, but a difficult journey overall."

Celia did not reply, as she could not participate in polite conversation. She was still in shock.

Gardiner cleared his throat. "Well, then. I will get straight to the point. The will is over twenty years old, but Mr. Sanderson says it is valid. I am to inherit the entailed country estate." He paused. "And I'm to inherit this cottage."

Yet another shocking blow. Where could she go? They rented a modest town house during their first five years in London when Parliament was in session. After that, they stayed exclusively in Marshall Meadows. Celia's mouth quirked. "Which leaves me homeless. Carlton said you would look after me. He made you promise. Correct?"

"That is so, my lady. I met with the earl three days ago in his sick room. He said you were not to be disturbed."

More secrets. No one told her of the visit. What did they do? Smuggle Franklin Gardiner through the servants' entrance?

"How convenient that you arrived a week before his death and met with the solicitor. Did it occur to any of you to update his will before he died? To inform me of your arrival?" Celia's voice remained steady, but the intensity of her emotions was palpable, threatening to break her resolve.

Mr. Gardiner bristled. "My lady, I tried to reason with my cousin during my visit. I told Mr. Sanderson I would do so. The solicitor himself tried many times in the past few years to convince the earl to update his will, but he would have none of it. Two months ago, Mr. Sanderson sent me a cablegram stating I should come at once to get the estate in order before the earl died. Mr. Sanderson has copies of our trans-Atlantic correspondence if you wish to see them."

Celia sighed. "I did not mean to cast aspersions on your character, Mr. Gardiner, but surely you can understand my frustration at being left out of these discussions. However, I am at fault, too. I should have insisted that my future was secured years ago. So, where does this leave us?"

"Alas, my lady, there is not much wealth attached to the earldom," Mr. Gardiner continued solemnly. "There hasn't been for many years. As it is, I must sell this cottage and the land. It is not entailed, you see. I will need that money to support my wife and two sons. The move here alone will cost a pretty penny." His financial burden was evident in his grave tone.

Wife? Which meant Celia—

"I believe that makes you the dowager countess. 'Celia, the Dowager Countess of Winterwood,' the solicitor told me. I am unfamiliar with all the rules regarding the aristocracy, although Mr. Sanderson mentioned that you're entitled to an income from your dowry."

The news of her new title left Celia momentarily speechless. "There was no dowry." Her blasted uncle never offered one, the skinflint.

Mr. Gardiner tsked. "Oh, my. The solicitor said there was no record of one. I had hoped that was a mistake in bookkeeping. You see, there are no tenants to collect rents from, and because of the primogeniture, entailed properties and the goods therein are now mine as the heir. And the late earl left me his investments, which, I am told, are barely enough to live on."

It took a moment for this shocking information to digest. "So I am to have nothing, then."

"I promised the late earl and intend to keep it, my lady," the new earl replied firmly. "There will be a yearly payment of forty pounds a year. The first payment will not be until next year on this date, but I *am* prepared to give you ten pounds now so you can comfortably travel to London. It is all I can spare at this moment. My travel here cost more than I thought, and I have yet to make arrangements to sell my home and possessions in Nova Scotia and pay for travel for my wife and sons. But you do not want to hear of my travails. Mr. Sanderson tells me you have an uncle and aunt, the Earl and Countess of Darrington. Surely, you can stay with them until the estate is sorted."

Celia's mouth dropped open. "You cannot be serious. Forty pounds a year?" It was a good income, and most people would kill to have it. But after all she had endured, this was all she would receive?

Mr. Gardiner stiffened. "I can show you the books, my lady. There is no spare money. As it is, I will have to cut back on the staff and sell some of the earl's belongings. And I am told the country estate requires extensive repairs."

He wasn't wrong on that fact. Celia had only been there twice, and it was a decrepit and drafty manor house situated on a desolate hill in Sussex. Oh, she was in a pickle. To wind up back at her aunt and uncle's place?

Blast Carlton! Celia immediately felt terrible for cursing a man not even in the grave, but he had left her with nothing. Not even her dignity. But she must keep her head and act rationally.

"I would like to see the books and meet with Mr. Sanderson. I cannot believe I am not entitled to more than that. I am—was—the countess. We were married close to eleven years."

"The late earl should have made provisions for you, my lady. It was not well done of him. Your husband came from a genera-tion where wives were not a factor in wills and other documents regarding inheritance. It is why he would not brook any argument concerning updating the will." Mr. Gardiner paused and met her gaze. "Societally speaking, I am not under any obligation to give you anything at all. We are not blood-related. But a promise is a promise. We will do this legitimately, draw up papers, and the like. I will even include a provision that if the investments improve, I shall raise the yearly stipend to reflect that."

Celia eyed the new earl. She did not appreciate the blood-related comment. It sounded as if it were Mr. Sanderson speaking. Could he cut her loose with no support? She didn't know much about the ins and outs of inheritance but was aware that the laws favored men in all ways. Celia started laughing—she couldn't stop. It was either that or cry. To live as a widowed dowager in reduced circumstances, depending on the whims of her estranged aunt and uncle—and a stranger from Canada—was too much to bear.

At the age of thirty, her life was over.

CHAPTER ONE

Early January, 1899
London, England

CELIA STOOD SHIVERING in the front hallway, awaiting her aunt and uncle. Uncle William finally came toward her, with her cousin, Troy, Viscount Shinwell following close behind.

"Good afternoon, Uncle. Cousin." Celia said cheerfully. "It has been a long time. How nice to see you both!"

"I received no word of any visit," Uncle William said, sniffing haughtily.

Celia glanced down the hall. "Where is Aunt Etta?"

"Away. Gone for months."

The trip to London from the Scottish border had been long, tedious, and even precarious. She'd been held up in Yorkshire for several days because of the snowy weather, depleting her funds to a perilously low level. And now, arriving in the city to find her aunt was not home? The crushing disappointment overwhelmed her to such a degree that Celia was ready to collapse from fatigue. "Where is she?" she whispered.

"Your aunt is wintering in Italy," her uncle said.

What would Celia give to be lounging about on a sunny, sandy beach right now, drinking champagne cocktails, and reading a book?

"Won't be back until the end of March," her loathsome cousin added, a self-righteous look on his face.

"Why *are* you here?" Uncle William demanded. "Where is your blasted husband?"

"Winterwood is dead. He left me nothing." Celia looked about the hallway where the coachman had unceremoniously dumped her two trunks. She had dragged the things for hundreds of miles. It was all she had left in the world, and that was not saying much.

"That wretch. Always was a penny pincher," Uncle William groused. "So I am expected to take you in, am I?"

"It would be appreciated," Celia snapped. "We *are* family." She rubbed her aching temple. "I'm sorry. It has been a harrowing journey. I am exhausted and hungry, and I have caught a chill. I would be grateful if you could put me up until I make other arrangements."

"How grateful?" her cousin leered.

Uncle William punched Troy's arm, making him wince. "Enough of that. You can stay for a week. Baldwin will show you to the upper-level guestroom. At dinner, I expect you to answer my questions. And do not assume my servants will wait on you constantly. They have enough duties to attend to."

Celia sputtered. "A week?"

"We can negotiate for a longer stay. We will discuss it more at dinner."

Negotiate? She had very little money left of the ten pounds given to her by the new Earl of Winterwood. With Aunt Etta away for the winter, what options were before her? Her aunt was her only blood relative. There was Corrine and Selena, her recently reacquainted school friends. What a burden to place on them when neither was in a happy marriage. In Corrine's case, she may already be in the process of obtaining a divorce from Baron Addington.

Baldwin picked up her case. "The footmen will bring your trunks. If you will follow me, my lady."

Baldwin had been the butler when she'd come to live with her aunt and uncle after her parents' untimely deaths. For three years, she resided here, from age ten to thirteen, until Uncle William had sent her away to school. She'd stayed at Miss

Langston's Finishing School for Girls until age nineteen, when Uncle William had stopped paying the tuition—and her marriage to the much older Earl of Winterwood had been arranged.

"It is good to see you, Baldwin," Celia smiled.

He nodded, a slight smile curving about his mouth. "And you as well, my lady."

As they ascended the stairs, she asked, "Baldwin, where is my Aunt Etta?" She wanted to see if her uncle and cousin were telling her the truth. Of course, they could have instructed Baldwin to lie. But Celia doubted the butler would tell falsehoods—they had always treated each other respectfully.

"I heard Italy, my lady, but she may travel to more than one Mediterranean country or district. Your uncle would know more about it."

The butler opened the door, and Celia stepped inside. This certainly was different from the room she had lived in before. It was small, dusty, and looked more like a servant's room than a guest's.

Beggars cannot be choosers. Or so the saying went. Celia was too tired to argue.

"I will see all is tidied tomorrow, my lady." In a lower voice, he said, "I do apologize for the choice of room. But the earl said to place you here."

"It does not matter. All I need is a bed." The room was blasted cold, which would not help with the permanent chill overwhelming her. There was no fireplace in the room, either. "I hate to ask, but is there any way someone can bring me something hot? Tea? Soup? Anything?"

"I will see what I can put together." Baldwin glanced about the room. "I will see that a brazier is brought to the room, my lady, as well. And an extra quilt. It may not come all at once, for I must do this without the earl and viscount knowing." He lit the large gas lamp, and illumination filled the room.

Celia managed another smile. She had always liked Baldwin and had always been polite with him. Now, he was paying back that esteem in return. "Thank you. Anything you can arrange will be most welcome."

Bowing slightly, he left the room. Celia kept her coat on and plopped onto the bed. Shivering, she pulled the quilt over her. She must have fallen asleep because the next thing she knew, she was shaken awake.

"My lady," a woman whispered.

"How much time has passed?" she asked groggily.

"You've slept for two hours, my lady," the maid said. She held a tray, and the aroma of chicken soup and fresh bread filled her senses, making Celia's mouth water.

Celia sat upright, her back straight, as the maid placed the tray on her lap. "Mr. Baldwin had the footman bring up a brazier an hour ago. If you don't mind me saying, my lady, it's a disgrace the earl put you in here. It's a servant's room! The last one to stay here was a scullery maid about five years ago. Shameful, it is." Her words resonated with Celia, making her feel less alone in her predicament. She nodded as she shoved spoonfuls of hot soup into her mouth.

"Mr. Baldwin added lavender seeds and orange peel to the coals, my lady, so the smell from the brazier will be sweeter," the maid continued, her voice carrying a note of empathy. "On the chair is an extra blanket and another quilt. I also opened the window a crack to allow air circulation."

"Thank you—what is your name?"

"Jane, my lady."

"Thank you, Jane," Celia replied kindly. "And thank Baldwin for me. I'm very grateful."

"I wound the clock on the wall. It's the correct time, my lady. The earl says you're to join him and the viscount for dinner at seven. I'll come at half past six to wake you."

Celia glanced at the clock. It would give her another three hours of much-needed sleep. "Jane, I hate to impose, but when you come, could you please bring ink and paper? I have pennies for the post. I need to send letters to my two friends."

"I'll mention it to Baldwin, my lady. Good gracious, you finished the soup and bread already. I'll take the tray."

Celia snatched the mug of tea. "I will keep this to sip on. Thank you again."

Exhaustion was covering her in waves, but Celia forced herself to stay awake, taking large gulps of tea. With that and the soup, warmth spread throughout her at last. Draining the last of the tea from the mug, Celia pulled the quilt over her, curled into a ball, and fell asleep.

Baldwin escorted her to the dining room promptly at seven. "While you are dining, I will dust and tidy the room, and ensure fresh coals are added to the brazier," he whispered as they approached.

"Thank you," Celia murmured. "You are most kind."

Neither her uncle nor her cousin stood when she entered.

"Sit there," her uncle grumbled, pointing to the chair opposite her cousin. Typically, Troy gave her an ogling look that made her skin crawl. Celia must make a point of asking Baldwin if the bedroom door locked. Her reprobate cousin was three years older, and when they were younger, he had tormented her to such an extent that her uncle had felt it necessary to send her away to school. When she was twelve and her cousin fifteen, Troy tried to get into her bedroom late at night—and more than once. Celia inwardly shivered. She had hoped her cousin would be married and out of the house by now. But what intelligent woman would have him? Well, one who someday wished to be a countess, Celia reasoned.

The footman served the fish course, and Celia was tempted to take two portions of the salmon but restrained herself. She had to remember to eat slowly.

"How is your room?" Uncle William asked, smirking.

"Why, it is lovely, Uncle. Thank you," she replied brightly, her voice steady and her gaze unwavering. Celia would not give her uncle and cousin the satisfaction of seeing her displeasure. They thrived on others' misery. She remembered that much about them—two peas in a pod. But she would not be another victim in their game.

"About you staying here—" Uncle William began.

"I need to contact two friends of mine," Celia interrupted. "Baroness Addington and the Duchess of Barnsdale. As soon as I can arrange it, I will leave." She looked him squarely in the eye. "Aunt Etta will not appreciate you treating her niece in such a shabby manner."

"Addington? Do you not receive London newspapers in that God-forsaken place?" Uncle William boomed. "Addington was murdered nearly three weeks ago. Shot by a criminal with a notorious reputation. But that is not the worst of it. Baroness Addington has already remarried and to a lowly policeman. The bloody cheek of it. I hear they are off on an extended honeymoon and will be gone for months."

Celia dropped her fork on the plate, and a small piece of salmon bounced across the tablecloth. "Murdered?" she whispered—and Corrine gone for months? Celia's heart sank. While she was glad her friend found happiness—and no doubt the man Corrine previously mentioned had caught her attention—it meant Celia had lost one possible place to stay. It was selfish, perhaps, to think of her travails when a man had been murdered, but survival remained of paramount importance. The news about Corrine's marriage blew Celia's hopes of finding a safe haven to pieces.

"Not many options left, eh, Cousin?" Troy smirked. "And Barnsdale? What have we heard about the duke, Father?"

Celia kept her expression neutral. She hurriedly finished eating the fish as the footman had reentered to remove the dishes.

"First, tell me why Addington was murdered?" Celia asked. Her uncle must be telling the truth about this, as it could be easily verified.

"Who knows? The papers never said," Uncle William replied between forkfuls of salmon. "The villain is in prison. That is all I care to know." He ran a piece of bread through the remaining dill sauce and stuffed it in his mouth. Drops of the sauce dribbled out of the corner of his mouth. Watching her corpulent uncle eat always made her stomach churn. "There is an heir, so your friend is no longer a baroness. And since she remarried, she's no longer a dowager."

"She is now part of the middle class," Troy spat. "How droll. Well, the policeman's wife can't assist you. And neither can the duchess."

Uncle William chuckled as another footman entered the room. The footman offered her uncle a platter of sliced roast beef. He speared four slices and put them on his plate. The footman moved toward Shinwell.

"Your duchess friend is not in London either," Uncle William continued as he cut his roast beef. "The prevailing gossip states that she and the duke have been separated for over a month. Barnsdale is holed up in his residence—not because he misses her but because he is ill. At least, that is the story being put forth. I don't know why he married that woman. She's as cold as a dead fish laying on ice in a costermonger's cart."

Celia's heart sank further. "Where did the duchess go?"

"Who knows? And more to the point, who cares?" Uncle William replied as he shoveled potatoes and meat into his mouth.

It was hard to believe that almost a month and a half ago, the three of them shared tea at Corrine's, reigniting their friendship with promises to write. Celia had left London the next day and had every intention of writing, but Carlton's health had spiraled downward every day until he died. There had been no time to craft a letter. And if her friends had written to her recently, she hadn't received the letters before she departed.

When the footman came to Celia, she slid four slices of roast beef onto her plate. Hang polite dinner manners. When the vegetables came around, she scooped significant quantities onto the pile of meat.

Her uncle snorted. "Enjoy this meal, Celia. It will be the last one you have in this room. If you wish to stay beyond the week, I will require a fee to be paid each Sunday. When I think of the money I dispersed on your behalf over the years for clothes and meals, and later that blasted expensive tuition, you owe *me*."

"Couldn't be bothered to pay a dowry, though," Celia muttered as she speared a piece of roasted potato with her fork.

"No, not after the money I already spent. Winterwood wanted a young virgin to give him heirs. You could not manage that either, I see. As to the fee, I will require five pounds. Every week." Her uncle gave her an arrogant smile of triumph, for he knew full well she could not afford it over the long term.

Celia laid her knife and fork on the table, then exhaled. "I will not pay such an outlandish amount. Please give me my aunt's address so I can write to her and tell her about my predicament. If she says I can stay, you will allow me to visit here in a proper guest room until she returns from her trip. If she says no, I will leave. Until we receive a reply, I will stay put. I am a countess. You cannot treat me this way."

Uncle William pounded his fist on the table. "To the devil with you! This is my house, not your aunt's! I will dictate the terms, not you. And you are a dowager, less than nothing!"

Celia met his cold stare. It gave her a pull of satisfaction that her uncle's face was mottled and purple with rage. Perhaps she should not be poking the fat bear, as it were, but Celia was past caring.

"But I am still referred to as a Countess of Winterwood. If you treat me ill, I will let society know how horribly you are treating me. I seem to remember you value your reputation within the peerage. You probably use it as a shield to hide something more nefarious." Celia knew of no such thing, but she would not leave this room without shooting a few salvos.

Uncle William threw his napkin to the floor and stood so suddenly that his chair toppled. "Get out of this room before I squeeze the life out of you."

Her uncle's tone dripped with venom and danger. Maybe she'd hit the nail on the head. Celia rose, took her still half-full plate with the utensils, grabbed pieces of bread and roast beef, tossed them on her plate, and marched toward the door. She stopped by the sideboard and took fruit, cheese, and biscuits. Celia turned toward her uncle and cousin, giving them a radiant smile. "Thank you for the lovely dinner. I enjoyed it immensely!" With her head held high, she flounced from the room.

It was quite an overly dramatic scene for the butler and footman to observe, but Celia might need them as witnesses later. Holding her food plate tight against her chest, she hurried to her room. Her situation here was undoubtedly precarious. But where could she go? Who could offer her assistance?

WILLIAM PICKED UP his chair and sat on it as rage boiled his blood to dangerous levels. His doctor had told him not to become over-excited because of his high blood pressure. "Get out!" He yelled at the butler and footman. "And close the blasted door!"

The servants rushed from the room, securing the door behind them.

Troy sliced the asparagus into small pieces. "I thought you told me never to show your cards, emotionally speaking?"

"That mewling bitch! I never liked her, even as a child. Always so blasted cheerful. But your mother insisted we take her in. Now, how in the devil can I get rid of her? Throw her out in the snow? Your mother will make my life a living hell if I do."

His son was right; he should never have allowed that termagant to goad him into an angry response. But when she mentioned "using his reputation as a shield to hide something more nefarious," it rang a little too close to home.

Unknown to almost everyone, William Buckingham, the Earl of Darrington, led a double life. Known as Billy Buck on the streets among the criminal elements he associated with, he'd started a smuggling operation after his marriage to Etta, as it became clear that he didn't have enough money to live comfortably. Gradually, he expanded into handling stolen goods and other underworld dealings, making additional criminal connections. William had taken to the felonious life as if it were second nature.

He glanced at his son, stuffing food into his mouth. He was a good-looking lad but lacked specific attributes, including decent table manners. Troy had recently learned about some of William's underworld dealings, but not all of them.

"When did you ever care what Mother thinks? You do as you please," Troy shot back.

"What goes on between your mother and me is none of your affair," William grumbled. The sad fact of the matter was that deep down, he still loved Etta—as much as he was capable of loving. William had been genuinely hurt when she had announced her departure for a months-long tour of the Mediterranean. Not that he would ever show her how much he still cared. It angered him afresh when he considered their past argument over his plan to marry Celia to Winterwood. Things between them had never been the same after that. It was all her bloody niece's fault his marriage faltered! However, this recent cold front was due to Etta's continued exasperation over their son's insufferable behavior. Blast it, the woman blamed him for the boy being a shiftless gadabout.

"I know of a way to get rid of the bitch, Celia," Troy said as he gulped red wine.

"Oh? Enlighten me."

"I owe a gambling debt to a certain person in Spitalfields."

William slammed his fist on the table. "I told you to halt that blasted gaming. It shows a decided lack of character and control. I cannot afford to keep bailing you out of debt!"

"Easy, Father. You will pop a vein in your head if you keep exploding. And I only owe a few hundred pounds instead of a few thousand. And I *have* cut down. I hardly ever partake in games of chance any longer. They're starting to bore me. Anyway, this debt concerns cards at The Crowing Cock."

William's brows furrowed. "Isn't that a brothel?"

"Not for several months. The owner has turned it into a respectable restaurant by day and a card-playing pub by night. I say we drop my cousin off there and have her work off the debt."

William laughed heartily, then sobered. "It *is* a fascinating notion. But that practice went out with men's high-heeled buckled shoes and powdered wigs. Indentured servitude is illegal."

"Since when do you care what is lawful? Besides, the owner will never agree to it. But from what I know of him, he won't turn Celia into the streets. He feeds the poor, if you can imagine. Bloody do-gooder. Let him feed *her*."

All William's concerns regarding his wife's anger dissipated. Why should he care after the way Etta has treated him these past years, especially leaving him alone for the winter? Revenge took hold. Retaliation on a girl, now a woman, who had been a thorn in his side for years. And now the ingrate had returned with a begging cup in her hand?

"She must have money of her own," William ventured.

Troy reached into his side pocket and placed a sheet of paper on the table. With the tip of one finger, he pushed the paper toward William, who took it and read its contents.

"Forty pounds a year, and the payment does not start until next year? What is she living on?"

Troy reached into his pocket and dropped a small silk bag on the table. "There are four pounds and ten shillings in there. It is all that she had."

"How did you get this?"

Troy shrugged as he took another swig of wine. "I searched her room as she slept."

William's mouth dropped open in shock. "You rifled through her room—while she was sleeping?" Then his look changed to one of admiration. Perhaps his son was not a total loss after all. "Clever boy," he purred. "Well done. We must devise a plan to get her out of the house and to the East End. But what will stop her from returning here? I don't want her begging at my door."

Troy shoved the silk bag in his pocket. "I'll keep her money. She can't find her way here without coin. Also, I have another idea. A drop or two of chloral hydrate in her morning tea will make her drowsy and pliable enough for transport."

William's eyebrows shot skyward. "I don't want to know how you became aware of such a drug. Who is this pub owner in Spitalfields, anyway?"

"His name is Liam Hallahan."

CHAPTER TWO

"BEEFSTEAK, TABLE THREE!" Liam Hallahan yelled to the servers to pick up the meals from the prep table. He placed another platter of food next to it. "And table four!" The waitresses grabbed the plates and disappeared through the swinging door into the restaurant. Behind him, a young lad ladled stew into crockery bowls while another sliced Irish soda bread and placed it in baskets with pots of whipped butter.

Liam tousled the lad's hair when he finished cutting the bread. "Well done, Tommy boy. Is everything else done?"

"Aye, sir. The potatoes and carrots are peeled and sliced for tomorrow's stew and the chicken meal on the luncheon menu. Everything is in the larder and the icebox, just as you told us."

Since taking over the ownership of The Crowing Cock four years ago, Liam had made many changes, including closing the brothel upstairs six months ago. He had wanted to close it as soon as he signed the title transfer, but the transition from a dodgy, run-down pub into a respectable restaurant serving well-cooked simple meals for the masses had taken longer than Liam had anticipated. "It's one o'clock. Time for you lot to hie off to school."

The three boys ran to the back room they shared, gathered their books and coats, waved at Liam, and disappeared through the rear entrance. Why did he take in street urchins? Well, he knew why. Walter Henning, the previous owner of this place, had taken in Liam at age fourteen. Walter had changed his life for the better, taking in a near-starving boy who lived in a dark alley, giving him an education and a warm bed. Walter had saved his life. Liam never forgot that. There was another more important reason he took in these particular homeless boys, but Liam wasn't ready to make that public yet.

"Lamb stew, tables eight and ten!" Liam yelled.

Enya placed bowls of stew and baskets of bread on her tray. "That's it for the lunch crowd. The place is thinning out."

"Good. Once you see the tables cleared, help yourselves to whatever is left." Liam wiped his hands on a tea towel. Cooking, not to mention running this restaurant, was exhausting but also satisfying. It had become more of a success than he could have ever hoped—so much so that he would have to hire more workers soon. But until then, he would make do.

A commotion from the front of the restaurant caught his attention. Voices were raised in high-dudgeon and coming closer. The swinging door hit the wall with a bang, and a well-dressed man pushed a woman into the kitchen. The lady nearly tripped crossing the threshold.

"I am Viscount Shinwell and I'm here to settle my gaming debt."

Shinwell. Liam couldn't stand the man. He always made leering comments to Liam's female employees and acted like an all-round arse while playing cards. "The time to settle debts is when the pub is in operation," Liam growled. "Come back at seven."

"I am settling the bill now." Shinwell pointed at the lady. "My cousin will work off the debt. In any way you see fit. She's a tasty dish, if nothing else." Shinwell gave Liam a knowing, smirking look.

Liam swung his annoyed gaze to the woman. The lady cousin was petite—at least compared to Liam's towering height—with large, expressive blue eyes and golden-brown hair. She was attractive, very much so. And right now, she was giving Shinwell a look that could kill.

"What you are proposing is illegal," Liam growled. "Leave my place of business and take your cousin with you or I'll fetch the constable."

"I think not," Shinwell replied smugly.

"How dare you?" the cousin sputtered angrily to Shinwell. Then she looked at Liam. "I had no idea he was bringing me here for this. It is unconscionable." The last word was slurred. Was this woman drunk? She appeared to be in a bad way, which activated something within him. Although he wasn't sure what exactly.

Another man, probably the coachman, entered and dropped a carpet bag at the lady's feet.

"She has trunks. I will send them along later," Shinwell added, grinning.

Shinwell turned to leave, but Liam grabbed his arm. "The hell with this. Take your wretched family business out of here. I want no part of it."

Shinwell shook off Liam's grip. "I consider my debt paid."

"The hell it is!" Liam yelled.

Shinwell sprinted from the restaurant with his coachman right behind him. Liam did not dare chase him, as it would have caused a scene and spooked the remaining customers. Instead, he ran through the rear door, into the alley, and onto the walkway just in time to see the carriage heading down the street.

"Damn it! The fecker." He would deal with Shinwell later.

Infuriated, Liam stomped into the kitchen and found the woman leaning against the wall. Her expression showed complete shock, with an underlying appearance of weariness. Her eyes were glassy. The lady did not look well.

"Enya," he said to his head waitress, who stood in the kitchen with his other workers, looking stunned by the turn of events, "Take over. I won't be long." Liam turned toward the woman. "Come to my office." He held out his arm to indicate she was to go first. The lady stumbled, so Liam took her arm to steady her.

Once in his office, he pointed to the chair and closed the

door. He sat at his desk, facing her.

"Holy crow, I cannot believe he would do such a thing," the lady murmured.

"Well, he did. Shinwell is your cousin. We've established that much. Let's start with your name."

CELIA WAS STUNNED, utterly shocked, and dismayed right to the toes of her boots by her cousin's shameful behavior. She clutched her mid-section. She did not feel well and her head spun. How naïve of her to fall for Shinwell's story of going to the bank to give her a loan of ten pounds. Desperation made someone believe all sorts of things, she supposed. Did Uncle William know of the ruse? No doubt. Did they want to be rid of her that badly? *Unwanted. Alone in the world.* Just like when she'd been thirteen years old and sent away to school.

"My—name," she whispered. "Celia Gillingham." She wasn't about to throw around her dowager countess title or married name. Why bother?

"I'm Liam Hallahan. What about your family?" Mr. Hallahan asked.

"I have no immediate family My parents are dead. I have no siblings." Her extended family had never wanted her around, at least not her uncle and cousin. There was no way to write to Aunt Etta, as her husband and son had refused to share her aunt's contact information. Nor did Celia know of any acquaintances of her aunt as she'd been away at school for years. She would never think of Darrington and Shinwell as her uncle and cousin ever again. "And I have no money. Shinwell took what little I had left." She had discovered it just before they arrived here. Her loathsome cousin had made a point of telling her he searched her room while she'd slept. Knowing he'd been in her room when— she inwardly shivered. Shinwell returned her paper from the new earl's solicitor. It was not a legal document. So her uncle, knowing she had no money, saw an opportunity to be rid of her.

Things were dire, indeed. Perhaps she should write the Winterwood solicitor and inform him what had occurred, although she didn't hold out much hope. Still, perhaps they could spare a few pounds. Celia had been feeling so poorly since arriving in London that she never had a chance to finish her letters to Corrine and Selena. Perhaps the Duke of Barnsdale could tell her where Selena had gone. *One thing at a time.* Celia needed a place to stay before she did anything else.

"Your cousin is a despicable bastard, begging your pardon," Mr. Hallahan barked. Celia looked up and caught his gaze. He must be a whole foot taller than her and ruggedly handsome. With a name like Liam Hallahan and with that coal-black wavy hair and sky-blue eyes—an even lighter shade than hers—he had to be Irish. However, she couldn't hear much of an accent—just a hint of the Irish lilt.

"I agree. Despicable. In all ways." Celia's mind swirled in all directions. What would she do? "I have nowhere to go."

"Is there anyone I can contact for you? A friend?"

"I have two friends in London, but both are away, and I don't know how to reach them."

"Then I can fetch a constable."

The police? "What could they do? My uncle can legally toss me to the cobbles without a by-your-leave." Her insides rolled, she felt all at sea. "And stealing my money? There is no way to prove it."

"The police can find you somewhere to stay. A charity house or the like."

"Is such a place safe?" she whispered.

Mr. Hallahan frowned. "Probably not." He studied her closely, and his stare was mesmerizing, seemingly gauging if she told the truth. "Miss Gillingham, I'll not turn you out into the street. I have a room upstairs you can use until you figure out what to do next. It's not much, but it's warm and comfortable."

Celia was stunned once again. She gave him a warm smile. "Thank you. Your kindness is—"

Mr. Hallahan waved his arm dismissively. "I'm not kind. I remember what living on the streets is like, and a woman alone is in danger. You wouldn't last the night out there. The room won't be free. I could use a hand around here. You will not be paying the debt of that worthless cousin of yours, but paying for room and meals, and you can put some aside until you plan what to do next. Is that agreeable?"

What could Celia say? She was in a desperate situation. She didn't even own jewels to sell, only the cheap gold band on her finger. Celia would be lucky to fetch a few pounds for it. "Yes, that is agreeable. At least until I find a way to contact my friends. Hopefully, one of them will take me in. In the meantime, I appreciate your kindness."

He brushed aside her thanks. "Have you eaten lunch?"

"No. I have not." It was good that she'd piled her plate with food four nights ago when she'd dined with her uncle and cousin because she hadn't had much since. The earl had told the butler and the maid to stop bringing meals to her room yesterday beyond tea and toast.

"There is lamb stew."

"Mr. Hallahan, if I may, I would like to go to the room. I am more tired than hungry." And that was saying something. Honestly, the room was spinning and her eyesight grew even more blurry. Celia started coughing, then pulled a handkerchief from her wool coat pocket, and blew her nose. "Pardon."

"Are you sick?" Mr. Hallahan demanded. "Or perhaps you're drunk. You are slurring certain words."

"Drunk? No! Although I started feeling dizzy after tea this morning. As for a sickness, it's just a lingering chill. I recently completed a difficult journey from Northern England. I still have not recovered."

Mr. Hallahan growled with a deep rumbling that Celia imagined frightened most people. But to her, it was endearing somehow. She couldn't explain why and was too exhausted to delve into her reasoning.

Mr. Hallahan shot to his feet, opened the door, and yelled, "Enya!"

A young woman entered the office. "Yes, Liam?"

"This is Celia. Celia, Enya. Take her to the empty room on the left. She will be with us for a while."

Enya was pretty, with reddish-brown hair, a smattering of freckles, and brown eyes. "Come with me, Celia."

Celia opened her mouth to thank Mr. Hallahan, but he had already left the office.

"Don't mind Liam's gruffness. It's just his way. Here, I have your bag. Now, out through the rear door," Celia followed Enya outside, and a blast of cold wind slammed her, causing her breath to seize. "Someday soon, Liam intends to enclose this so we won't have to go outside to take the stairs. Here we are, up we go."

The wrought iron stairs were narrow, and Celia held on to the railing for dear life. Climbing the stairs took what little energy she had left. What was the matter? This seemed beyond a common winter chill. Enya opened the door, and warmth covered Celia as she entered the hall. She stumbled, and Enya grabbed her arm.

"Are you all right?" Enya asked.

"I am just exhausted."

"The warmth from downstairs, the ovens and whatnot, heats the upstairs nicely. We hardly ever have to light the coal stoves. Here we are." The room size immediately struck Celia. It was much more significant than the cubbyhole Darrington had stuck her in. "Now, the restaurant is not too busy at the moment, but during meal times, the din is hard to ignore. Even more so at night, when this turns into a pub and card gaming room. You'll get used to it. My room is across the way." Enya set her case on the floor. "Fresh sheets on the bed along with a wool blanket and quilt. There is an extra blanket in the wardrobe. Rest now. I'll see to your supper later."

"Thank you, Enya. I apologize for all this. My cousin—" Her voice trembled, and a knot formed in her throat. Emotion threatened to overtake her.

"There, there. No need to explain. I know what family can be like, as mine turned me out at fifteen. Don't give that horrid man another thought. You're safe. We look out for each other here. If Liam has offered you a haven, then you have no worries. He will not turn you out unless you give him a good reason. Be honest with him, work hard when asked, and all will be well."

Enya patted her arm, then departed, closing the door behind her. Celia exhaled shakily, determined not to break apart. All she wanted was sleep. Shivering from the chills wracking her body, she removed her wool coat and gloves and dropped them to the floor. She had bought them secondhand before leaving Northern England, along with the sturdy wool gown she wore—and it was a good thing she had. The garments had kept her warm these past weeks. She'd sold the few fancy gowns she owned in Yorkshire, where she purchased a scarf, gloves, a woolen hat, and other suitable traveling clothes.

Aching all over, she pulled back the covers and climbed into bed. Her teeth chattered as she tucked the quilt under her chin. Blast this chill that had nagged her for days! It teetered between 'feeling under the weather' to 'full-blown sickness' from one day to the next. All this accumulating tension was not helping, either. Nor was this nausea and the overall feeling of confusion, as if her mind were in a fog.

Shinwell had brought her here to humiliate her and anger Mr. Hallahan. He succeeded at both. It would be easy to curl into a ball and give up, but Celia was made of sterner stuff. This was a temporary bump in the road. She had options. There was always hope. No matter what happened in her life, Celia always managed to find a bright side of things. She would do so here.

The image of the towering Mr. Hallahan entered her mind. When had Celia seen a man look so decidedly male? Virility came off him in waves—those broad shoulders, those mesmerizing eyes. She smiled as she drifted off to sleep. At least she would have pleasant dreams.

CHAPTER THREE

IT WAS PAST seven when a knock sounded at Liam's door. "Yes? What is it?" he shouted. He sat in his oversized chair, eating a bowl of stew, trying to unwind. His night manager, Fiona, ran the card games and supervised the pub in the evenings. Liam was done for the day and did not appreciate being disturbed.

Enya stuck her head in. "Sorry. I knocked at the new girl's room. She didn't answer. I have stew for her. I thought you had better come with me to check on her. I may need your help."

He should have sent the stranger on her way, but he loathed the way her cousin had treated her. Also, she'd looked tired, weary to her fragile bones. Liam couldn't toss her to the cobbles. This was all he needed—to have some woman pop off in one of his rooms. Having someone die on the premises was terrible for business.

Liam shot to his feet and stomped down the hall. He rattled the doorknob and swung open the door. It banged against the wall with great force, but the woman hardly stirred. The room was in semi-darkness as the gas lamp was nearly spent, so Liam headed toward the wall sconce and turned the knob. The gas hissed as a yellow flame cast a dull illumination over the area. All he could see was a pile of blankets on the bed. She must be under there somewhere.

He strolled to the bed, clasped her shoulder, and shook her none too gently. "Wake up!" he barked.

There was no reply.

He shook her harder. "I said wake up."

Again, no response.

He placed his fingers against her neck. She was alive. Thank God for that. "Miss Gillingham!" he yelled.

The reply came as a soft moan. Then a sneeze.

Feck it all. Liam grasped the blankets and tossed them aside. Miss Gillingham was still wearing her clothes and shivered so intensely that Liam could hear her teeth chattering.

"You're sick!" he boomed accusingly.

"Only a little," Miss Gillingham sniffled. "I need rest—just a couple of days. Then I will be ready to work."

Liam rolled his eyes. This outsider could pass on her illness to the rest of his staff, then where would he be? "Enya, fetch Tommy."

Enya passed him the tray and hurried down the hall.

"Sit up. Can you?" Liam asked in a clipped tone, exasperated at this turn of events.

"I will try," the woman replied weakly.

Liam placed the tray on the dresser, reached into the mound of blankets and quilts, grasped her under her arms, and hauled her upward until she sat straight. His arms brushed against the sides of her breasts, and a jolt of desire shot through him, causing his heart to thump faster. Where in the hell had that come from? He swiftly released her and grabbed the tray.

"Pull the blankets over you." She did, and then he laid the tray on her lap. "Now, eat."

His commands were brusque to his own ears, but Miss Gillingham upended his routines. Besides, he was worried about her. She wasn't well, that much was obvious.

Tommy ran into the room. "Sir?"

"Get bundled up, lad. Go to 48 Gloucester Square and find Doctor Drew Hornsby. If he's not home, wait for him. Bring him here." Liam tossed the boy a coin, and he caught it. "Here's a shilling. Bring back the change, mind. Get along now."

Tommy departed, and Liam turned to face Miss Gillingham.

"I do not need a doctor, Mr. Hallahan—"

"My name is Liam. And you bloody well do, Celia. Besides, I can't have the staff getting sick. Do you follow?"

Sighing, she nodded as she took a spoonful of the stew and ate it. Then she took another. This wasn't some doxy or girl from the lower classes. Her mode of speech and refined manners showed that, as did the fact that she was related to a viscount, no matter how detestable. He noticed the plain gold band on her finger in the glint of light. "You're married?"

"A widow."

That readily explained her reduced circumstances. Now widowed, she was reliant on her family. Only they wanted nothing to do with her. The fact that Shinwell had dragged her here showed a decided lack of respect for Liam and his business, but more importantly, an absence of respect for his cousin. If there was one thing Liam could not abide, it was the mistreatment of women and children. He had witnessed enough of that while growing up on the streets.

He glowered at Celia. Sweat beaded on her forehead, and she was having difficulty eating. His concern for the lady ratcheted up another notch. Liam grabbed the wooden chair and hauled it over to the bed. He took the spoon from her trembling hand, dipped it in the lamb stew, and held it aloft. "Open. And eat."

She did as she was told.

"It's delicious," she murmured, giving him a sweet smile. The warmth from that ready smile arrowed straight to his heart, giving it a jolt. It was a reaction he had not expected.

"It'll chase away the cold." Liam offered another spoonful. When a spot of stew dribbled from the corner of her mouth, he gently wiped it away with the napkin.

Unshed tears gathered in the corner of her eyes. *Not tears— can't abide those, either.*

"Why are you doing this?" she rasped between spoonfuls.

"I feel you have had enough men treat you with disrespect

lately. I wasn't about to add my name to the list. Can you cook?"

The abrupt change in topic caused her to blink rapidly. "No. But I can learn."

"When you're well, you will start with scullery work. Chopping, slicing, or is that beneath you?"

⋙✳⋘

BENEATH HER? SHE was in no position to turn her nose up at honest, hard work. Celia closed her eyes as the body aches rolled through her like waves crashing against the shoreline. Logically, she understood she needed a roof over her head to recover from her traveling ordeal. Then, she could start to plan her next moves. If that meant she had to peel potatoes and chop carrots, then so be it.

"Not at all. I'll take on the work gladly. And gratefully." The warmth from the stew was welcome. "There was no need to call in a doctor. I'm not that sick. I do not want to cause you any extra expense."

Liam held up another spoonful of stew, and she took it. "He's an acquaintance."

"Living at Gloucester Square?"

"He's related to the peerage. His uncle is a duke," Liam scoffed, saying 'duke' as if it were offensive.

"You don't like peers?"

"I've got no use for them. Arrogant, bloody pillocks. Well, maybe not all, but most."

Holy Crow. Celia would be wise to keep her ties to the peerage under wraps, at least until he asked any further probing questions. Hopefully, he wouldn't, but if he did, she wouldn't lie about her life. Celia did not plan to be here long enough for multiple in-depth conversations.

Celia pushed away the spoon. "I can't eat anymore. Not now. Thank you."

"Fair play." Liam dropped the spoon on the tray, stood, and then took the tray away. "I'll leave you to rest."

He departed, closing the door behind him.

With a shaky exhale, Celia curled up under the covers. All she needed was sleep.

SHE WAS SHAKEN awake in what felt like minutes. Glancing at the wall clock, she saw that she had slept for an hour, which wasn't nearly long enough.

A man stood beside her bed. Tall, handsome, with golden blond hair, he pushed his spectacles up his nose as he regarded her. "Miss Gillingham? I am Doctor Hornsby."

Celia sneezed as she struggled to sit upright. The doctor placed his black bag on the table next to her.

"How long have you felt under the weather?"

"Just before I arrived in London close to a week ago." It seemed longer than that to Celia. "I had a distressing journey from Northern England. There were many railway delays, so I hired a private coach part of the way. It was freezing inside and out, and I caught a chill. I cannot seem to get warm." What a waste of money, too. The slow journey by carriage had depleted most of her funds.

Doctor Hornsby sat in the chair beside her bed. "It is plenty warm in this room. You do not feel it?"

The doctor's voice was pleasant but professionally distant. He also had an upper-crust accent. Of course, Mr. Hallahan—Liam— said the doctor was related to a duke.

"Not really, no." Celia sneezed again. This time, she was able to cover her nose with her hand. The doctor reached into his bag and handed her a laundered hankie. "I cannot accept that."

"I have plenty, made from sturdy cotton. Keep it."

"Thank you." Celia wiped her nose and hand, then tucked the handkerchief under the sleeve of her wool gown.

"Have you brought up any yellow or green sputum? Are you coughing steadily?" He pulled a stethoscope out of his bag. Celia knew what it was as she had seen it used on Carlton enough.

"No to both."

"That is good. Your sickness has not settled into your chest. We want to avoid that. Please unbutton your collar."

Celia did, and the doctor breathed on the chest piece, warming it before placing it against her exposed skin.

He listened. "Breathe deeply. That's it. Inhale, hold it. Now exhale. Cough for me. Well done." The doctor sat upright. "You have caught a cold or chill, as we call it, probably from your prolonged exposure to inclement weather and your less-than-perfect traveling conditions. If treated correctly, this infection will disappear in less than seven days." He felt her forehead. "Perhaps a slight fever. Body aches?"

"Here and there," Celia replied. "I also feel nauseated. That started this morning. My eyesight was blurred, although not so much now."

The doctor leaned in and looked into her eyes. "Any balance trouble? Confusion?"

"A little. But I feel strange, beyond the chill."

"Please open your mouth."

Celia did, and the doctor leaned in to examine her throat.

He stood upright. "Bed rest. You must stay hydrated with plenty of fluids. I believe you are over the worst of it. I predict you will feel much better in three days. I will stop by the day after tomorrow. I would suggest you remove your gown and any undergarments. You must be comfortable."

"Thank you, Doctor."

With a nod, he packed up his case and departed. Well, Celia was right. She had caught a chill. She felt worse the day after her defiant exit from Darrington's dining room. For four days after that, she hardly ventured from her room. The sneezing had been much worse then. With great effort, she stood, unbuttoned her wool gown, and undressed down to her chemise. Celia had no idea what garments her loathsome cousin had stuffed in the case. She opened it to find her clothes mashed into balls. Digging through, she discovered her flannel nightgown, pulled it over her head, and climbed into bed, pulling the covers over her.

Another knock at the door. "It's Enya."

"Come in."

The waitress entered with a tray and placed it on the table next to Celia. "A pitcher of water and a glass. You must drink as much as possible. Next door is a water closet for your use. Wrapped in the parchment paper are ginger biscuits if you get hungry. The doctor said you're to be left alone for the rest of the night." Enya opened the wardrobe and brought forth a wool blanket. After straightening the covers, Enya laid the blanket over the quilt. "There now. All cozy. Are you warm enough? I can bring another quilt."

Celia smiled. "You have all been so kind. I am warm enough, thank you."

"You're welcome." Enya turned the gas light to almost complete darkness, and left her alone.

The tears that threatened to spill earlier finally trickled down her flushed cheeks. Celia allowed it, but only for tonight. She would do all she could to recover and work for Mr. Hallahan and, as she did, she'd find out about her friends and try to discover her aunt's location. She would also write to the new Earl of Winterwood and his solicitor. Not all was lost.

Not when she had a tall, handsome guardian angel with gorgeous eyes and broad shoulders watching over her.

With a sigh, Celia wiped her eyes and pulled the blankets to her chin. All she could hope for tonight were more pleasant dreams of Liam Hallahan.

CHAPTER FOUR

Liam passed Doctor Hornsby a glass of scotch. After examining Celia, he'd come to see Liam in his flat. "You're sure it's not serious?"

Hornsby took the glass and sat opposite him. "As sure as I can be. How did she act when she first arrived? Confused? Loss of balance?"

Liam shrugged. "Aye, she slurred some of her words. I assumed she was drunk."

"Her pupils were dilated, and she complained of blurred vision and confusion. I did not smell any alcohol on her. In my medical opinion, she may have been drugged. Not enough to cause unconsciousness, but enough to make her biddable."

"As in easy to remover from her uncle's house?" The thought twisted Liam's insides and brought forth every protective instinct he had. He wished now he had given that arrogant viscount a thrashing.

"Yes. It's only a medical opinion, but one based in fact. Although I did not smell any alcohol, there was a faint pear odor. One drug has that characteristic—chloral hydrate. Thankfully, Celia Gillingham was not given enough to do any lingering harm. The worst of the effects have already passed."

"Bloody hell," Liam muttered.

"I'm curious," Hornsby mused. "Why call me in when there are plenty of doctors in the East End?"

Liam raised an eyebrow. "Have I inconvenienced you, Hornsby? I thought being part of this group meant we help each other out."

Doctor Drew Hornsby was Liam's recently discovered half-brother. Hornsby and Detective Sergeant Mitchell Simpson, the widowed Baroness Addington's new husband, had approached Liam a little over a month ago, claiming they, too, were the offspring of the notorious late Duke of Chellenham.

"Do you remember?" Liam continued. "You said the group would be called The Duke's Bastards and that we would assist those associated with the duke through a shared bloodline. To rise above the late duke's despicable legacy. To assist those less fortunate, whether in our immediate sphere or beyond. And especially to those Edward Cranston left to flounder: his own children. Or words to that effect."

Liam had found the argument compelling but had not been looking for a family connection. He'd gotten this far without one. Regardless, he had agreed to join. Hornsby was already assisting Liam by coming by once a week to offer medical care to the unfortunate people lined up before the restaurant opened to get a free bowl of stew. Hornsby and Simpson had their toff friends send along uneaten food from their aristocratic kitchens for Liam to reuse, either by giving it to the poor or selling it to his customers to raise money for his charity undertakings. He frowned. What had he done to contribute to this venture? Not much. He supposed assisting the woman upstairs would be a place to start. It certainly qualified as 'assisting those less fortunate, whether in our immediate sphere or beyond.'

"Call me Drew, please," Hornsby said, tearing Liam from his thoughts. "We have been acquainted long enough to move towards a more casual form of address. And yes, I recall speaking those words. I am glad to help you. Who *is* the woman?"

"Viscount Shinwell dropped her here. The repugnant bastard said she was his cousin and would work off his card gaming debt. I rejected the premise outright—it's illegal and it's obvious he was using it as an excuse to remove her from his residence. Celia Gillingham claims she is recently widowed and has no money. Now she's sick. I told her she could stay until she made other arrangements. And once she's better, she will help in the kitchen. The money she makes will be hers. Do you know Shinwell?"

Drew sipped his scotch. "No. It's too bad Mitchell isn't here; we could have the arse investigated. But I will send a telegram to my father, Viscount Hawkestone. He runs a sizeable progressive caucus in the House of Lords. He knows—or knows of—just about everyone. I'll ask him for any information regarding Shinwell and his family. He can send a response by train. It would be faster than by post. I should have an answer the next time I come."

"I would appreciate that—Drew." Liam frowned. "I'm still not sure why you want me in this venture. I haven't done much to contribute."

Drew raised an eyebrow. "Not done much? Before your restaurant opens, you feed the unfortunates of the neighborhood"

"Not every day, not any longer. As of the first of January, I'm closed on Sundays. Not for religious reasons, but because my staff needs a day of rest. I also changed Monday's hours as it's my slowest day. We open at two in the afternoon until six with a light menu. I still feed the poor on Mondays, only later, around one o'clock."

"Well, there you are. You have proven the point. I have been contemplating cutting back on my punishing schedule as well. A human can only do so much. You no doubt need the rest, too."

Drew wasn't wrong there. Liam was at the height of his vigor, but the constant fatigue was starting to take its toll.

"Not only do you feed the unfortunates of your district, but you have also taken in three apprentices—youths you found living on the streets," Drew continued. "The ladies who work with you, weren't they employed at the brothel before you closed it?"

Liam never liked that Walter Henning, the man who had

taken him in off the streets, had run a brothel above the pub. When Walter died and left the place to Liam, he'd first wanted to close it down. Unfortunately, there was not enough money to make the changes he required—like turning the place into a respectable restaurant during the day. The women who worked for Walter suggested they keep it running while he made the necessary renovations as long as they had a say in the new business plan and were part of it in the future.

And so, Fiona, Enya, Hannah, and June became his *de facto* business partners. He constantly consulted them over the physical reconstruction, menu ideas, staffing, finances, and the rest. June departed two months ago to get married, and while Liam was pleased she'd found happiness, he also could admit he missed her. He had known them for years, and as he told Drew and Mitchell when they approached him, he wasn't looking for a family. The people who worked with him were as close to a family as he needed—or wanted. Not that he would ever admit that to anyone.

"Yes. They have responsible positions in my business."

"Most business owners would have turned them out into the street. You did not. See? You are meeting the core ideology of The Duke's Bastards. 'To assist those less fortunate, whether in our immediate sphere or beyond.'"

"Why don't you have that embroidered on a cushion," Liam muttered.

Then Drew did the strangest thing: he laughed. Liam had never heard the self-contained doctor do so. He even slapped his thigh. "I needed that, thank you. My parents constantly tell me I'm too serious for my own good. I suppose the past is hard to shake."

Liam agreed, but the last thing he wished to do tonight was to start rooting around in his dark past or that of Drew Hornsby's. They had similar starts: a single mother living in poverty, on the run from Chellenham. *Aye, none of that.*

Liam stood. "I have supper for you to take home. Not only

are you far too serious, but your eating habits are atrocious, either by skipping meals or not eating properly. You have a standing order. When you come every Thursday, you will stay for a hearty meal—on the house. No argument."

Drew downed the last of his scotch. "And I will not refuse excellent food when offered. Thank you."

"How much do I owe you?"

"Nothing. As you said, we assist each other. Consider the food sufficient payment." Drew stood and reached for his doctor's bag. "I know many places that will take in Celia Gillingham, charity homes, and the like. They can assist her in getting back on her feet. Say the word, and I will make inquiries."

Liam already felt responsible for her. It didn't sit right with him to fob her off to some charity. Or maybe he should, since he'd had a physical reaction to touching her when assisting her to sit upright. "I'll mention it to her. Let's go to the kitchen. I've lamb stew, fresh Irish soda bread, and seed cake. We have to fatten you up, Doctor."

Drew smiled as he followed Liam down the hall. Liam glanced at the closed door to Celia's room. Was she resting comfortably? Was she warm enough? Did she have enough to eat?

Bloody hell. He was right. She was affecting him already.

CELIA OPENED HER eyes and stared at the wall clock. It was past ten in the morning. She had slept more than nine hours. Groaning softly, she struggled to sit upright. Once she did, Celia had a good look at the room. *A window!* She hadn't noticed that last night. Grabbing the bedpost, she forced herself to stand. Now fully awake, she could hear the noises from downstairs—muted voices mixed with kitchen sounds like pans and dishes being rattled about.

Celia inhaled, not that she could smell much with her stuffy nose. The unmistakable and enticing odor of onions and beef filled her senses. With careful steps, she made her way toward the window. Celia pulled aside the heavy draperies. The window was bowed with the sill large enough to sit on. Celia did precisely that, pulling her flannel nightgown over her legs and wrapping her arms around her bent knees. The street below was alive with activity, with people wearing fur-lined coats stopping to examine the costermonger's carts. The streets were filled with carriages, hansom cabs, horse-drawn omnibuses, and the odd automobile.

After spending the past six years in the barren wilds of Northern England, watching passersby and transportation vehicles was a pleasant change of scenery. She sat for the longest time, watching a woman in a brown wool coat and matching hat buy bread from one vendor and potatoes and carrots from another. The lady slipped her purchases into a wicker basket she carried. Then, the lady ducked into a drapery shop.

It would be easy to bemoan her fate. Instead, a smile crept across Celia's face. Not everything was hopeless. It could be worse. She could have perished during the journey to London or been tossed into the street instead of being brought here. Liam Hallahan could have kicked her to the cobbles as well.

The restaurant owner was sheltering her, and Celia would be eternally grateful. A chill tore through her, and she sneezed. She must locate the water closet and return to bed. So, she headed to the table and drank a glass of water.

Shivering, Celia opened the door and peered into the hall. No one was about. Where was the water closet located? *Right. Next door.* Celia held onto the wall and hurried as fast as she could. After she finished, she stepped into the hallway, and a wave of dizziness overcame her. Her legs trembled, and she wobbled. At that moment, she was swept up into strong arms, squealed at the sudden motion, and grabbed the neck of the person holding her.

"What are you doing out of bed?" a deep voice snapped.

It was Mr. Hallahan—Liam. She met his intense gaze. My,

but he possessed beautiful crystal blue eyes with long black lashes—and he had a small mole at the corner of his right eye. Celia had the urge to touch and caress it. She waved her arm toward the water closet. "I had to—you know."

He kept staring at her, not moving to put her down or take her to her room. How wonderful it felt to be held in his sturdy arms; he was as warm as a wood stove and as solid as—Celia wasn't sure what words to describe him. She trailed the tips of her fingers across his shoulder and partway down his arm. He was so muscular. And tall. He had to be three or four inches over six feet.

Liam strode toward her room. Celia had left the door ajar, so he kicked it open with his boot. She stroked his longish hair at the nape of his neck. So silky—what was she doing?

Celia pulled her hand away. *How shameless.*

Liam lowered her to the bed. "Doctor Hornsby said you're to stay in bed today. I'll fetch breakfast."

"Please don't trouble yourself. Someone can bring me porridge later when you are not busy—"

"I will bring it," he replied firmly.

Right. There was no arguing with this man.

"Cover up." He poured a glass of water and thrust it toward her. "Drink this."

Celia gave him a proper salute. "Yes, sir!" She smiled to show she teased him.

He stomped from the room. Liam Hallahan was obviously not fond of teasing—that was good to know. But she couldn't help it; he acted far too seriously—*such a grumpy man.* Celia pulled the quilt up to her chin and waited.

Not ten minutes later, Liam returned with a tray.

"It must be difficult in this weather to bring food trays outside and up the stairs," she ventured. "But then, I suppose, it's not something anyone does often."

"No," he grunted as he placed the tray on her lap.

"Holy crow. This is a veritable feast," she murmured, impressed at the fried eggs, ham, toast, and cheese. "Thank you so much."

Liam turned to leave.

"Wait, can you sit with me? I would love the company. I have had no one to talk to for weeks. Well, longer, really. Oh, do stay. Please." However, she had the notion that Mr. Liam Hallahan wasn't much for conversation.

Liam looked toward the door as if trying to craft an excuse to depart. Then he glanced at her. "A few minutes," he ground out as he pulled the chair over to the bed and sat on it.

Celia sliced into her ham. "The most inviting smells are coming from your kitchen. What are you making?" she asked brightly.

He pointed to the food. "It is cold?"

"Not at all." She took a sip of tea. "Even this is still warm. You must have sprinted up the stairs. So, what are you cooking?"

"Beef stew."

Carrying on a conversation with this man will be a challenge. "Is your restaurant open?"

He folded his arms. "Not until noon."

"Enya says your place turns into a pub and gaming room at night. How fascinating. Do you run that, too?" Celia took another bite of the egg. "This is delicious. How did you get the edges so crispy?"

"I cook the eggs in rendered bacon fat and baste the edges with a few drops of olive oil."

"Olive oil? From the Mediterranean? I didn't think it was used for cooking."

"Not so much here in Great Britain. Other countries use it. Olive oil gives the eggs crispy edges. The previous owner of this place used olive oil to lubricate the meat grinder. I cook the eggs on high heat and baste them with hot fat. That's the trick."

Celia smiled. So, to get him to talk—mention food. "How did you learn about cooking with olive oil?"

"I read it in a cookbook."

"Do you run the pub?"

"No. I have a night manager, Fiona. Her room is across the

hall. I'm finished work at six or sometimes earlier."

Celia could listen to Liam talk all day. His deep voice was rich, like decadent chocolate, with that barely-there lyrical Irish lilt. "Do you serve food at night?"

"No, not usually. If food is left from luncheon, we sometimes offer it."

Celia took a bite of toast. "That is very clever. Why waste food?" Celia pointed to the window. "Isn't it a glorious day? Look at that winter sunshine. There is not a cloud in the sky. I cannot wait to recover so I can go for a walk and explore—when I'm not working, of course."

Liam's eyebrows shot skyward. "How can you be so blasted cheerful?"

She met his gaze frankly. "Because it *is* a lovely day. I believe in positive thinking. Smile, and let people know you feel that way. Even at the most horrible times of my life, I tried to stay away from brooding thoughts."

He shot to his feet. "If you're done, I'll take the tray. Someone will come to check on you after the luncheon rush."

Celia's smile disappeared. "Oh. I had hoped you might visit again. You do take a break at some point, I assume?"

He nodded as he picked the tray off her lap. She had all but licked the plate clean.

"Why not come and chat?" she asked, giving him another inviting smile.

Liam looked at her incredulously, as if he couldn't believe she would make such a request.

"Maybe. Try to rest." Liam turned on his heel and departed, closing the door behind her.

Celia fluffed her pillows and lay prone, bringing the blankets and quilt to her chin. As she drifted off to sleep, images of Liam at a stove cooking her eggs filled her thoughts. What woman wouldn't want a handsome man making her a meal? She fell asleep with a smile on her face.

CHAPTER FIVE

C ELIA NEXT AWOKE when a knock sounded at the door. She sat upright and hurriedly tried to set her hair to rights. She must look a fright as she hadn't had time to do proper ablutions or wash her hair. How pleased she'd been to find a large clawfoot tub in the adjoining room to the water closet. When she recovered, a warm bath would be perfect.

"Come in," she said as loudly as she could.

A strange woman entered, holding a tray with a teapot and enamel mugs. "Good afternoon. My name is Fiona. I'm across the hall, in room three."

A jolt of disappointment shot through her. Celia had been hoping Liam would visit.

"The night manager. I *am* pleased to meet you. I'm Celia Gillingham." Her nose twitched, and she reached for the handkerchief and blew her nose.

"How are you feeling?" Fiona asked as she placed the tray on Celia's lap.

"Better. All that sleep has helped. I should start my duties, the slicing, chopping, and whatnot."

Fiona poured hot tea into the mugs. "Help yourself to milk and sugar." Fiona added milk to hers, then sat in the chair by the bed. "There is no rush. Liam says you're to wait until the doctor comes tomorrow."

"What a fascinating man," Celia murmured between sips.

Fiona smiled. "Who, the doctor or Liam?"

"Both. Why would Mr. Hallahan take me in?"

"Because that is what Liam does—he helps others. We use first names here. He has three homeless orphan boys helping in the kitchens—Timmy, Tommy, and Teddy. Yes, those are their real names." Fiona smiled. "We guessed their ages fall between thirteen and sixteen, although the boys claim not to know. They share a room in the back, work here in the mornings, and attend school in the afternoons. The boys are learning to read and write, although Tommy already knows how."

Celia's heart squeezed with compassion. "What a considerate thing to do."

Fiona took a sip of tea. "Don't ever tell Liam that. He has no patience with praise, giving or receiving."

Celia held the warm mug between her hands as she assessed Fiona. The woman was in her late thirties or early forties, with dark red hair and blue-green eyes. She had a lovely countenance and possessed a nice figure. "How long have you worked for Liam?"

Fiona smiled. "Since he took over ownership of this business four years ago. But we've known each other for much longer. We both worked for the previous owner. To change the subject, Liam told me what happened with your cousin. I'm sorry you were mistreated. Is there anyone I can contact for you?"

Celia shook her head. "My aunt is my only living blood relative and we have not had much contact these past years. Her husband and son claim she is wintering in Italy and they refused to give me the address. My husband died a month ago. He had not provided for me in his will. I was given ten pounds and told to leave the cottage. I arrived in London last week. My aunt's husband offered a room—for five pounds a week."

"The bloody cheek!" Fiona exclaimed.

"My aunt's son stole what was left of my money. Then he dragged me here." Celia sighed wearily. Recounting all this was depressing to the extreme. "The only other people I know in

London are two school friends, and I was told they are not in town. As soon as I'm recovered, I will seek them out because I don't believe the source of the information."

"I've noticed you don't refer to the men as your uncle or cousin," Fiona observed.

"I will never claim them as a family again. Even if I did locate my aunt and we reconciled, I could never stay there. But I refuse to dwell on it."

Fiona tsked. "It doesn't take much for someone to end up on the streets. I know. Experience one ill-fated circumstance or several smaller ones, and then—boom—you're homeless. It must have been quite a shock."

Celia nodded. "It was and still is. First, I must recover. Second, I must write a letter to my late husband's solicitor and tell him of my predicament. Perhaps he can assist me by sending money. Even a few pounds will help. I am determined to regain my independence and not be a burden to anyone."

"I'll try to locate some paper and ink for you. Can I bring you anything? Something to read? Are you hungry?"

"Something to read would be lovely. A cookbook, a newspaper, whatever you can find. And as far as food, I'm not hungry. I can wait until later."

Fiona patted her hand and stood. "Keep the tea; there's plenty in the pot. I'll see you later."

"Thank you," Celia smiled.

Fiona nodded and departed.

Celia yawned. *Tired again?* Well, that was the way it went when one was ill. She had undeniably witnessed Carlton sleeping constantly. She had asked the doctor about it, and he'd claimed that sleeping could be crucial to the healing process, although that hadn't been the case for Carlton. But it might be true for her illness.

After all their amiable years together, how could Carlton have left her without a home or money? Men were foolish and selfish creatures—at least, that had been her experience. But it didn't sound as if Liam fell into that category. Giving homeless boys a purpose? Her admiration of Liam ratcheted up a few notches. Celia wanted to know more about the intriguing Irishman and intended to stick around long enough to find out.

"WELL?"

Fiona closed the door to Liam's office and sat in the chair, facing him. "I believe she's telling the truth. She wants to write to her late husband's solicitor, inform him of her situation, and perhaps have him send her some money. Women are often left out of wills. It's not fair. If her late husband has a solicitor, the old bugger must have been part of the middle class at the very least."

Liam had solid principles and a soft spot for those in need, especially women like Celia. His own past experiences had shaped these ideologies, and he was always ready to help those who were struggling. What Fiona said was true. Most people couldn't afford solicitors, and most never made wills. That was a luxury for those with some status, money or not.

"I'm pretty good at judging when someone is lying—and so are you," Fiona stated, pulling him from his thoughts. "I believe Celia is sincere. I like her. She smiles readily, is pleasant to talk to, and is a good listener."

"I had the feeling she spoke the truth, but I wanted a second opinion," Liam muttered.

"Celia also mentioned two friends, but her uncle and cousin told her they were not in London. How would they know that?" Fiona questioned.

That is a good point. "I suppose they know the families. When she's feeling better, I'll question her more thoroughly."

Fiona chuckled. "You're hardly a detective with Scotland Yard. Too bad your friend, Sergeant Simpson, is away. Try to be polite and not bark at the poor lady. She's been through enough."

Fiona sobered. "When she does recover, what will you have her do?"

"She says she can't cook, so there are scullery duties, washing dishes, feeding the unfortunates, and the like. There's enough to do around here to keep her busy."

"Further proof that she came from the upper middle class. For example, wives of bankers and lawyers have cooks and housekeepers."

"I never thought of that." It made perfect sense.

"To change the subject. About the business hours—let's alter them further."

Liam raised an eyebrow. "In what way?"

"Cut them back for the rest of the winter. Everyone is exhausted, Liam, including you. The Crowing Cock has become more of a success than we ever imagined. Let's close the pub at one, instead of two. Maybe even midnight. Most of the gaming takes place between eight and twelve. We don't make enough after that to justify staying open. It will give us more time to clean and prep the area for the luncheon and teatime crowd the next day. I can show you the pub ledger regarding the earnings."

Liam sat back in his chair. "I believe you. Midnight it is. Who has outstanding accounts regarding the gaming?"

"Viscount Shinwell, 240 pounds, and Mr. Elliot Hartright, Esquire, 178 pounds."

Liam whistled. Those debts had to be collected promptly. "The men are barred until they pay. Make sure Bruce is aware." Bruce Shepherd was an ex-boxer who was taller and more muscular than Liam. Since hiring him two months ago, any rowdiness and requests for credit had fallen. "I will see about the debts this Sunday, and if I don't receive any satisfaction, I'll send Bruce. What about other customers regarding our new policy on credit?"

"The regulars are still given credit and pay within two weeks. Those accounts are up to date. A few newer customers have asked for credit; I said no, and there was no further argument."

"Good. What else?"

"We should cut the restaurant menu even more. Instead of offering three or four choices at luncheon, there should be at least two during the winter. Teatime has become very busy with ladies looking for sandwiches. We should offer them every day. Put Celia in charge of making the sandwiches. We can use leftover meat and other foods for the fillings."

"Maybe you should be the manager of this business instead of me," Liam grumbled.

Fiona laughed good-naturedly. "Give over. It was your idea to offer teatime delicacies."

"Only because of the toff food that's donated through Hornsby and Simpson's aristocratic connections."

"And look how popular it's become. You said you're making a profit in that area with that and the bakery items you buy from Mr. and Mrs. Eckley. We charge more, especially since you bought those three-tiered fancy stands and the extra china dishes. Tommy said he wants to learn to make scones since he's mastered soda bread. We can offer those as well. Tea and scones. They are a perfect pair. Tearooms are opening up all over."

"Anything else?" Liam said sarcastically.

Fiona chuckled. "I've been saving these ideas. I wanted to present them to you all at once."

Liam gave her a slight smile. "Maybe you should be running the restaurant, and *I* run the pub."

"You love to cook. You'd miss it. Besides, I like sleeping late and being out on the floor at night giving orders. Especially to men." She gave him a wink. "So, what have we decided?"

Liam counted off on his fingers. "We close the pub at midnight starting next week. We'll go with two options for luncheon starting tomorrow. We'll meet with Celia and plan the menu for teatime. I'll speak to Tommy about the scones."

"He's a good lad," Fiona said. "You never said where you found him—or the other two."

"I can't talk about it—not yet," Liam said. "It wasn't the best of situations, as you can imagine." And had far more personal implications than Liam was ready to acknowledge as yet.

"Then we'll discuss it another time." Fiona clapped her hands together. "Perfect. I do like it when everything works out."

"You mean when everything goes your way," Liam replied gruffly.

"We will have to consider staffing in the next week or two. I want to hire another muscular young man for the pub to serve drinks and help keep the customers in line. That will free up one of the young women to work during the day."

"We'll discuss it next week. Is that all?"

Fiona smiled. "For now. Did you have lunch?"

"No."

"You stay here in the office. I'll bring you a bowl of stew. Take some quiet time for yourself. I'll see that teatime runs smoothly. I have to check on the beer delivery anyway." Fiona stood, came around to where he sat, leaned in, and kissed his cheek. "I love you, Liam, like the younger brother I had always wished for. Never forget that."

Liam grunted in response.

"You can respond with more than a grunt," Fiona admonished gently. "We are alone, no one will know."

Liam took her hand, the one resting on his shoulder, and kissed it. "Back at you, Fee. I always wished for an older sister."

They had been through a lot together, both having experienced tragic losses in their pasts and shared a strong bond due to their Irish backgrounds. When Walter had taken Liam in, he was no more than a feral animal and Fiona's kindness and patience had slowly won him over. Fiona's opinion mattered, so when she said Celia's story sounded legitimate, Liam was silently relieved. He didn't just take anyone in. But the fact that he'd reacted—physical and otherwise—to touching her and holding her in his arms was concerning. It had been a long time since a woman had piqued his interest—and not just physically. Liam closed his eyes, remembering when he had stood in the hallway, holding her close, reveling in the feel of her in his arms. When Celia had touched his shoulder and arm and trailed her fingers through his hair, he'd nearly dropped to his knees. The reaction had been that intense.

For that reason alone, he should consider taking Drew's suggestion that he send Celia to a charity house. He had a long-standing rule never to become involved with the staff, but she would not be a permanent employee. As soon as she had better accommodations, she would leave. Liam's internal struggle was more than evident. It was a constant battle, a war raging within him. He knew what he should do, but his growing feelings for Celia, a woman he had just met and was now responsible for, made it difficult to follow through.

Perhaps it was better that she departed. The last thing Liam wanted was to complicate his life. And a lovely lady in distress could upend his ordered existence—if he let it. However, he could already feel Celia encroaching closer to his heart. And maybe he wanted that more than he was willing to admit.

CHAPTER SIX

CELIA HAD SPENT the afternoon gazing out the window, reading, and napping. She was feeling loads better. The aches were all but gone, and her nose wasn't as stuffy, yet exhaustion lingered. The past month's stressful events had taken their toll, as they would for anyone.

Fiona had brought her volume 4 of *The Encyclopedia of Cookery*, by Theodore Garrett, published in 1891. The book certainly caught her interest. Six pages were devoted to the cucumber alone. Celia had no idea it could be prepared in different styles. All she ever had was cucumber salad or the occasional cucumber sandwich. It made for fascinating reading. The next topic? Curds. These books must belong to Liam. Did he have the entire set?

Where is Liam?

She had barely known the man for more than twenty-four hours and already desired to see him—and knew the reason why. Celia had been lonely for many years. After Carlton became seriously ill, they'd stopped venturing to London and all social activities ended. Living so far north almost meant months of isolation. Being plunked into the middle of a busy restaurant gave Celia an unquestionable thrill. There were actual people to converse with! And there was activity and life inside the restaurant and outside on the busy streets. Best of all, she had a handsome man bringing her meals. It was a dream come true. She couldn't help but feel a growing fondness for Liam, a feeling she hadn't ever experienced before—not like this. A certain warmth enveloped her, making her feel alive and hopeful. She found herself being drawn to him, and not just for his kindness but for how he made her feel.

A knock sounded at the door.

Celia laid aside the book. "Come in."

Liam stood on the threshold. Her bed was against the opposite wall, so she faced him. "How are you?" he asked.

Her heart sped up at the sight of him filling the doorway. He wasn't wearing his winter coat, so she was able to get a good look at him. Those long legs went on forever. The material of his close-fitting trousers hugged his muscular thighs. Celia especially liked that his forearms were visible, as he had rolled up the sleeves of his white shirt. The top button was undone, showing a bit of dark hair on his chest. She had to bite back a moan as her insides fluttered with awareness. This physical reaction was not wise. But then, she'd never been in such proximity to a man so much younger than her late husband—especially one so handsome and vital.

"Even better than this morning," she managed to reply.

"You received a pencil and paper to write your letter?"

"I did, thank you. The letter is here." She pointed to the table by her bed. "It's ready to be mailed, but I haven't got a penny to pay—for the postage, I mean. Quite the predicament."

"I'll see that it's posted. Fiona brought you a meal."

"Yes, the chicken was delicious. I ate everything."

Liam nodded and turned to leave.

"Wait! I mean, can you not visit for a while? I know you're done for the day and are undoubtedly tired, but stay for a moment. Please."

He hesitated, and his response was to sigh resignedly and sit in the chair by her bed.

"Was the restaurant busy today?" she asked brightly.

"Aye. Busy enough."

"Did you serve chicken for the special?"

"No."

Celia blinked. "You made it especially for me?"

Liam shrugged.

She was touched that he had gone to the trouble. How tempted she was to throw her arms around his neck, for she could not recall the last time someone did something special for her. Instead of thanking him again, she asked, "How did you prepare the chicken?"

His eyes widened at her inquiry. "I fried the chicken breast in hot oil to crisp the skin, then roasted it in the oven with sliced mushrooms, potatoes, and carrots. Just before it was ready, I basted it in a white wine sauce."

"Outstanding!" Celia enthused. "You are to be commended. No wonder your establishment is busy."

A smile tugged at the corner of his lips as if he was trying *not* to smile, but she could tell he was pleased by her compliment as his eyes hooded with a sleepy sort of satisfaction.

"I noticed a bathing room adjacent to the water closet. May I take a bath before Doctor Hornsby comes tomorrow?"

"No. I mean, better to wait until after he examines you."

"I will start work the day after tomorrow?" Celia asked, excited at the prospect.

"No. We're closed on Sunday."

Celia was surprised by that. "I would have thought it to be busy, at least in the afternoon."

"Not during the winter. Besides, the staff is tired. It has been a hectic six months. A day of rest is warranted."

"For yourself, too, I imagine," Celia murmured.

"I'll reassess Sunday openings in the spring."

"What are my duties to be?"

Liam crossed his arms, and the muscles bulged. Celia swallowed deeply.

"I discussed it with Fiona, and we plan to expand our afternoon tea offerings. You will look after making sandwiches. It must be done swiftly—on the spot—as you can't make up sandwiches beforehand. The bread dries out, or the fillings make the bread soggy if left a while."

Celia's mouth dropped open; then she swiftly closed it. "I remember my mother making sandwiches for a picnic, wrapping them in parchment paper, and laying damp tea towels over them."

Liam shook his head. "That may be suitable for a family picnic, but not a restaurant. They still wouldn't be as fresh and may become too moist. No, they must be made when the order is placed."

"That is a lot of responsibility for someone you hardly know. I'm not familiar with kitchen work. Well, I can make a sandwich and a cup of tea, but that is the extent of my knowledge."

"Then you're perfect for the job. Weren't you married?"

"My husband employed a cook-housekeeper, so there was no need for me to learn domestic skills. I wish now that I had."

"What did you do, sit in the parlor eating chocolates while reading a book?" The question had a barely discernible mocking tone, but it was there nonetheless.

"No, I was too busy being a nursemaid to my dying husband. It took him close to six years to die, but I was there to clean up after him, wipe his fevered brow, feed him when needed, and sit by his bed, keeping him company. I had no time for leisure activities. The past two days are the first time in ages I have been able to read." Celia held up the large cookery volume.

"Who brought you that?"

"Fiona."

His mouth pulled into a taut line. "I had no business saying what I did."

"We should cease making assumptions about each other. There is always more than meets the eye."

"True enough. I'm sorry."

Celia smiled. "You have done so much, yet I acted petulant, which I assure you is not like me—at all. These past weeks have been a trial. Quite traumatic."

Liam nodded, stood, and then grabbed her letter from the table. "I have to get my supper. Rest."

"First, can you please bring me the 'S' volume? I want to read up on sandwiches. Please, if it is not too much trouble."

"Right-o."

Celia heard his heavy footsteps down the hall to his room. Moments later, he returned and handed her the volume. "Good night," he said.

"Good night, Liam." She smiled warmly.

After he closed the door, Celia flipped through the pages until she found what she was looking for.

It is said that during the last century, the Earl of Sandwich invented the convenient preparations that were afterwards known by his name. The proverbial stale sandwich of the railway refreshment-room, and the slovenly manner in which others are prepared, have brought down upon these convenient modes of taking a snack a torrent of ridicule and abuse. When well and carefully made, sandwiches are very commendable.

Celia grinned. Regardless of her reduced circumstances and questionable future, she would ensure she became the best sandwich producer ever seen.

LATE SATURDAY MORNING, Doctor Hornsby entered the kitchen area and motioned to Liam, pointing toward his office. It was eleven o'clock, and the kitchen was busy preparing for lunch. Usually, on Saturdays, Liam served beef stew, so he had the three boys by the stoves, stirring pots of meat and vegetables. "Tommy, the soda bread is cooled. Start slicing. Remember, not too thick."

"Aye, Liam." The lad hurried to the preparation counter and arranged small baskets in a row.

"Hannah? Stay by this pot until I return." Wiping his hands on his apron, he followed Drew to the office. He closed the door and sat at his desk, giving Drew a questioning look.

"Celia Gillingham is recovering nicely. She will be ready to start work tomorrow for some light duties or training."

"She won't infect the rest of the staff?"

"I do not believe so. Celia Gillingham's illness was borne more from exhaustion and strain than anything. Continued rest and good meals will assist in further recovery." Drew reached into his doctor's bag and brought forth an envelope. "As expected, my father sent his reply by train. I received it last night."

"What does the viscount say?"

"Quite a lot. I will read it to you, forgoing the personal Hornsby aspects. 'Troy Buckingham, Viscount Shinwell, is the only son of William Buckingham, the Earl of Darrington, and his countess, Henrietta—known as Etta—Charles. Etta is the sister of Lady Deborah Charles Gillingham, wife of Sir Anthony Gillingham, baronet."

Liam's mouth dropped open in shock. "Celia is the daughter of a baronet?"

"Late baronet. Celia Gillingham's parents died in a catastrophic boating incident on September 3, 1878. The baronet and his lady wife took a moonlight trip on the SS Princess Alice, where it was struck by another ship on the River Thames. It broke in two and sank in less than four minutes. Over six hundred people lost their lives, including Celia's parents. That's how my father knew of them. The tragedy was all over the papers and the talk of London."

Liam frowned. "Jaysus. That's horrible. Now that you mention it, I remember people speaking of it on the streets."

"Her aunt, the countess, was her only living relative. Celia moved into the earl's home. At some point, she was sent away to school, and at age nineteen, a marriage was arranged."

Liam scoffed. "Of course. Bloody toffs."

"Celia Gillingham married the then fifty-five-year-old Earl of Winterwood about eleven years ago. During the first five years of their marriage, they split their time between London and some remote village by the Scottish border. After that, they rarely came to London. My father says Winterwood hasn't sat in the House of Lords for nearly six years due to ill health. If Winterwood is dead, the news hasn't reached Westminster yet. Then again, there is a recess."

Liam heard a buzzing in his ears. Celia was a—countess? And he was going to put her to work in his kitchen! Liam's eyes narrowed. "She never said a bloody word. And here you are telling me she's ready to go to work. Jaysus. I can't have a countess in my kitchen. Give over."

Drew stuffed the letter in his side coat pocket. "It is patently obvious she has nowhere to go. Women are rarely left money or acknowledged in wills. If there was an heir, he could have kicked her to the cobbles, seeing they were not related. If there was no heir, everything reverts to the crown."

"I don't bloody believe this," Liam growled, growing more annoyed by the moment.

"Lady Celia has suffered a further indignity, being thrown out of her aunt's house by her cruel uncle and cousin. The lady has been through much already. I would advise she contact the solicitor that handled her late husband's estate."

"I posted a letter to the solicitor for her," Liam griped. "Look, I can't have a baronet's daughter and an earl's widow toiling in my kitchen."

Drew stood and placed his hat on his head. "So you have said—more than once. But isn't that up to the lady. We could gather some spare money and place her in a rented room until her aunt returns."

"What if the toff, globe-trotting countess aunt wants nothing to do with her? What then?"

"I do not know, Liam. Do we shame the Darrington earldom into taking action? Write a stern letter of our own to the

Winterwood solicitor? What do you suggest? Women, unfortunately, have no legal leg to stand on when it comes to inheritance."

Liam banged the table. "Of all the restaurants and pubs in London, she had to be tossed into mine."

Drew patted his shoulder. "Try to be patient when you speak to her about this. A little compassion would not go amiss. That is my professional medical opinion. Lady Celia does not need any further trauma. I have a small flat at the rear of my house on Gloucester Square. She can stay there until we contact the aunt or the solicitor. Then, all we need to do is supply food."

Liam crossed his arms. "I assumed Mitchell and Corrine would stay there when they returned from their wedding trip."

"You haven't heard. The new Baron Addington gifted Corrine with her late husband's house in Camden Town. It was not part of the entailment. I imagine they will live there or sell it and find their own residence."

Liam nodded approvingly. "Good for them. A property makes for a good start in life."

Drew picked up his doctor's bag. "That is why my parents gifted me the place on Gloucester Square. Is this place yours? Or is it none of my concern?"

"It's mine, lock, stock, and beer barrels. The previous owner left it to me in his will. I'm lucky it's paid for, but it needs work. The roof needs to be tarred. I want to enclose the outside stairs. I could go on, but I won't."

"Get in touch after you speak to Lady Celia."

"Jaysus," Liam mumbled. *"Lady."*

Drew gave him a wave as he exited the office.

There was no time like the presence to speak to the countess. Liam jumped to his feet and entered the kitchen area. "Enya?"

His head waitress came to stand before him. "Aye?"

"Can you supervise until I return? I need to speak to Celia. I won't be long."

"We've everything under control."

Liam nodded and headed toward the rear door and the out-side stairs. What in the bloody hell was he going to do with a widowed countess? If she was even a widow. Maybe she ran away. Who knew? Aristos could be a flighty lot. Why didn't she tell him she was—or is—married to an earl? He already guessed she was quality, considering her relation to a viscount and her mode of speech. But her uncle and husband were earls? Wasn't that a step or two from being a duke?

Liam took the stairs two at a time and burst into the hall, his exasperation roiling at full throttle. So much for Drew's advice about being compassionate. As for patience? Due to his horrid upbringing, Liam had none, and it fueled his temper above all reason. He pushed the door open to her room, but she wasn't there. Growling, he stamped down the hall and entered the water closet—empty. Then he heard it—someone humming. Liam threw open the connecting door without thinking, and what he saw nearly brought him to his knees. Desire tore through him, heating his blood.

Celia. In the tub, naked.

There were a few bubbles in the water, but not enough to cover those luscious, generous breasts. He stared as a wave of passion tore through him. Liam couldn't move or breathe.

It was the most glorious sight he had ever seen.

CHAPTER SEVEN

CELIA SQUEAKED, SINKING lower in the tub. "How dare you burst in here? Please leave at once!" It was his house and business, but barreling into the room unannounced wasn't polite.

Liam's intense gaze made her heart skip a beat. He didn't move, nor did his regard waver from taking in every inch of her naked state. Celia's cheeks flushed from his heated scrutiny.

He let out a shaky breath. "I'll be back after luncheon. We need to talk," he ground out. Liam's mouth turned downward. "I'll meet you in your room—*Countess*." He spat the last word, drawing out the s-sound. Then he turned on his heel and marched from the room, banging the door so violently, she jumped.

Countess.

He had learned of her identity before they even had a chance to discuss it. Celia had had every intention of informing him of her status—eventually. How had he discovered it? Of course, Doctor Hornsby. Liam Hallahan, for all his sullen ways, had taken her in, offered a warm bed, meals, and time to recover, and this was how she repaid him? Granted, she wasn't well enough the first day to enlighten him, especially after his disparaging remark about peers.

But she'd had ample opportunity since then to broach the subject. Sighing, Celia reached for the pitcher and poured water over her head to rinse out the soap. Then she stood, grabbed the towel from the rack, and dried herself.

A KNOCK SOUNDED at the door more than two and a half hours later. Celia was dressed in the only other wool gown she owned, sitting on the edge of the bed with her hands folded in her lap. After her bath, she washed the clothes she had been wearing for the past week. They hung on a hook near the window.

Clearing her throat, she said, "Come in."

Liam entered, closing the door behind him.

"I apologize for not telling you about my situation in more detail," Celia said contritely. "I intended to do so soon. I reasoned it had no bearing on my present circumstances. What did it matter what title I held? I have no money and no present opportunity except what you offered. I am so grateful you took me in."

Liam grabbed the chair and sat facing her. "I can't have a countess working for me."

"Why not? And I am *not* a countess but a dowager countess, a courtesy title. The new heir is married with children. He is a distant cousin of my late husband. I had no idea he even existed until just before my husband died."

Liam folded his arms. "What's the difference? You're a peer."

"I am a peer only by virtue of marriage, and now my husband is dead. My late father was a baronet, *not* part of the peerage. Dowager means 'to endow' and is related to having a dowry. Guess what? I did not have one. Therefore, I have nothing to live on. My so-called uncle could not be bothered to give Winterwood a dowry, and Winterwood could not be bothered to include me in his will."

Liam shook his head. "That can't be right. You must be entitled to something."

"I have seen the books. The new earl and the solicitor, Mr. Sanderson, were forthright about allowing me to see the accounts. There is very little money. In generations past, peers owned vast properties with numerous tenants paying rent. As a dowager and according to the rules of the primogeniture, I would be entitled to an income from those rents. Alas, most peers no longer have tenants, Winterwood included. No dowry, no rental income from the estate, nothing for me." Celia counted off on her fingers to punctuate each point.

Liam's eyebrows shot skyward. "How did the earl live these past years?"

"He lived frugally. He had a few investments but left them to the heir—not to me. His will was twenty years old. Winterwood never bothered to update it once we married." She shook her head. "Part of this is on me."

"I don't see how."

"I should have demanded that my future was secure."

Liam scoffed. "You were young, far too young to marry an old man. Your family should have protected you. Where was your aunt in all this?"

Celia exhaled. "She and my uncle fought on the exact point you raised. I heard the yelling. Ultimately, Aunt Etta had no say, and neither did I. I did not want to stay in that house. I accused my aunt of taking my uncle's side. We did not part on the best of terms. Only years later did I realize she had no power to stop it— and neither did I. I planned on writing her when we returned from London on the first of December. We have been estranged long enough. But—" Celia shrugged.

"Doctor Hornsby has a few rooms you can stay in, in a small flat at the rear of his house in Gloucester Square. That address would be more fitting for the widow of an earl. You can stay there until your aunt returns from her holiday. Doctor Hornsby and I will see to your meals and the like."

Celia shook her head. "No."

Liam crossed his arms, giving her a dubious look. "No?"

"I thank you both for your generous offer, but it's time I stood on my own two feet. I want to earn money, pay my way, and be independent for once. Surely, you must understand that. I have been handed off to men my entire life—no offense to you and the good doctor. No one here needs to know I'm a dowager countess. It means nothing. Not to me, and it shouldn't mean anything to you. I want you to pay me a wage and take the cost of this room from the salary."

"First, the on-site staff do not pay for the rooms, so neither shall you. Meals are included. Second, we all pitch in, whether handling meal preparation, cleaning the cooking areas, or keeping the living area spotless. It means scrubbing floors and the like."

Celia smiled. "That will not discourage me. I want to do this, Liam. I *need* to do it." Her smile slipped away. "Since my parents died, I have been shunted off to school, married off to an old earl, and then dragged from my aunt's house. Please do not send me to another place I do not want to go. I don't want to be shut away any longer. I want to be free to live my life." Her voice shook with each word spoken. It would be the equivalent of a death sentence if she were cloistered in a few rooms for weeks or months.

Liam looked away, as if her openness made him uncomfortable. "I must be off my head to even consider this. All right, then. I'll pay you thirteen shillings a week."

Celia's heart soared. "Is that a fair wage? I have no way of knowing."

"The wage I pay is better than you would find elsewhere. You will get a small cut of any tips the servers get."

"Why?"

"You prepared the food they're serving, so you will get a percentage. It's only pennies, but it adds up over a week."

"You are really going to hire me?" she whispered.

"Aye. You're hired."

Celia could not hold back her joy. She squealed, leaped to her feet, and threw her arms around Liam's neck. The sudden motion caused him to shift, and Celia tripped over his leg and landed on his lap.

"Goodness. I nearly went head over ears," she commented, still holding on to him for dear life. They stared at each other.

Celia inhaled. Heavens, but this man was stunning. Those cheekbones! Liam's enticing scent—it smelled as if he'd spent time in a forest—made no sense since he toiled in a kitchen. It must be his soap or cologne. However, there were faint aromas of inviting cooked food, like fried onions and bacon. She leaned in, nearly nestling in the strong column of his neck. She turned slightly, squirming in his lap.

"Don't—do not move," he rasped.

Liam was growing aroused. There was no mistaking that hardness, as she could feel it through her gown. A decided thrill tore through her. When had she ever experienced this with Carlton? Never. Sex had been perfunctory; she had never truly encountered this sort of fluttering before. It had to be desire.

Growling like an annoyed bear, he stood so suddenly that Celia almost fell to the floor.

Liam held her arm to keep her upright. "One rule you should know: I don't get involved with the staff. We are employee and employer. Remember that."

"Yes, Chef."

He glared at her, probably to determine if she was mocking him. Celia wasn't—well, maybe a slight teasing. Liam appeared rattled at their intimate proximity. Inwardly, she was pleased. A handsome man found her appealing? When had that ever happened? *Never.*

"Can we meet later tonight to discuss sandwiches and afternoon tea? I have many ideas I want to share with you," she asked cheerily, giving him an eager smile.

"No. I have plans."

The smile slipped away. Of course, he had plans; it was Saturday night. For all her silly daydreaming, she never imagined Liam had a personal life outside his restaurant. That punctured her burgeoning hopes and brought her back to earth. Just because a man became aroused at a woman's nearness, that didn't mean it meant anything it turned out. But it did show her how inexperienced she was around men of her own age.

"Of course. Tomorrow, then."

Liam strode toward the door and gripped the handle. "You're responsible for seeing to your meals. The staff is welcome to any leftovers at luncheon and supper."

"Yes, Liam," Celia whispered.

He departed, closing the door softly behind him.

Celia exhaled. *So much for that.*

LIAM UNLOCKED THE door and entered his mistress's parlor for their weekly tryst. Melanie McElhenny was a grocer's widow who lived above the shop in Stepney. They had been intimately involved for over a year, meeting once a week at first. Lately, not so much. He told Celia that he had never been involved with the staff. His sporadic dalliances were always far from his business.

Celia was the first woman to threaten that self-imposed decree.

Melanie was nine years older than his thirty years and demanding in bed. Liam welcomed it as she became an outlet for his pent-up stress and passions. He matched her fiery desire and then some. But tonight, he'd come here to end it.

"We don't have long," Melanie whispered seductively as she glided toward him wearing a see-through pale blue peignoir. "My son will be home by ten tonight." Bert, her twenty-year-old son and co-owner of the grocery, played in a darts league every Saturday night.

Liam took her hands and held them to prevent her from touching him. "I want to talk to you," he said.

Her perfectly shaped eyebrow arched in question. "When do you ever talk? You hardly say anything."

"Well, tonight is different. Sit." He released her hands and pointed at the sofa.

She did and glared at him questioningly. "Well?"

Liam sat in the chair opposite. "I've enjoyed our time together. But I was upfront with you at the beginning. I wanted nothing serious."

Melanie nodded. "Neither do I, love. We agreed on that."

"It's time to bring this to a close."

Melanie sat back in the chair and crossed her legs. Her mouth turned downward. "You met someone?"

"Maybe. She's caught my attention. If I'm involved with someone else, I can't consider anything with her." Liam couldn't believe he had spoken those words aloud because it was against his core to become involved with an employee, let alone the widow of an earl. But the most surprising aspect? Admitting aloud that Celia attracted him.

"You're throwing me over for who? Some little mousy waitress in your pub?" Her voice raised.

Liam had hoped the conclusion of their involvement would be cordial and respectful. *Wishful thinking.*

"It doesn't matter who it is. This is the first woman I've met in years who's interested me. I want to get to know her better."

"Oh, really?" Melanie snapped.

"Why are you acting like this? What do you care?" Liam was growing annoyed at Melanie's petulance.

"I wanted to be the one to end it," she said, pouting.

"Then go ahead. End it."

Melanie picked up a cushion and threw it at him, clipping him in the head. "Then go. I'm glad we're over. I can't wait to get away from you and your stench of kitchen grease, onions, and chicken fat. Because of that, I have to strip the sheets from the bed after every time you come here. You disgust me."

Liam couldn't muster up enough interest to reply to the vitriolic insult. But he *was* insulted. He had been looked down on his entire life—his poor upbringing with his perpetually sick mother, his living on the streets for two years until Walter took him in. He stood, giving Melanie a pitying look. She was on the verge of tears, and she looked—hurt. Liam had never wanted to hurt her, but it appeared as if he had. She cared more than she had let on, and he should have sensed it. Liam stood. "Goodbye, Melanie. Be well."

He exited the flat and gently closed the door. He stood outside in the hallway, feeling terrible. Then he heard it—loud sniffling. His heart squeezed in compassion. Yes, he had a heart. Sometimes, he wondered if it functioned, as he often kept it closed off and hidden except for his restaurant "family." Even then, he rarely showed any weighty emotions. This affair had not been supposed to end like this.

Liam reentered the flat. Melanie still sat in the chair, wiping a few tears from her cheeks.

"I'm so sorry, Mel. I had no idea," he said softly.

Melanie laughed brokenly. "That I cared for you? Neither did I until you tossed me aside. Don't worry. It's not love, merely an infatuation which will dissipate with time." She exhaled shakily. "I was hurt, and I lashed out. I didn't mean what I said."

A smile tugged at the corner of Liam's mouth. "There's probably truth in the account. Just as an engine machinist probably smells of oil, a cook would emanate food odors." He placed the key on the table. "I forgot to leave this."

"Does she work at the restaurant? This lady that has captured your regard?"

"Temporarily. I've got a rule about fraternizing with the employees. I'll keep my feelings to myself for the time being—not that I even know what feelings are involved."

Melanie gave him a sad smile. "Oh, Liam. When it comes to the heart, rules are made to be broken. The best of luck keeping those emotions to yourself. It's not always easy. Eventually, a woman will know. She'll sense it."

Liam came to stand by her chair, took her hand, and kissed it. "Thank you for making my life less lonely."

"We had a mutual need," she whispered. "So, thank *you*."

Liam released her hand, bowed slightly, and then quit the room without looking back. He slowly descended the stairs and stepped onto the walkway, pulling his peaked cap lower on his forehead and tightening his wool scarf around his neck. It was blasted cold out, but he would go for a walk, regardless. Liam needed to think.

What was at the forefront of his mind?

Celia, the dowager countess. He cared about what might happen to her and wanted to protect her from further harm. Her cheerful disposition despite her downfall, her eagerness to learn new things and become independent—God, he admired that. When she had landed in his lap... Liam nearly moaned aloud, remembering his swift and aching response. There was no way she could have missed his erection, considering the way she wriggled about. How would he resist the temptation, especially after seeing her naked in the tub? All luscious curves... He would never get that breathtaking scene from his mind. It would haunt his fevered dreams for many nights to come.

What Liam wanted most of all was to pull her close and kiss her senseless—until he ceased to breathe. And that temptation might be the hardest to ignore.

CHAPTER EIGHT

SUNDAY CAME, AND Celia felt much better. She was ready to learn about her new duties and look around the place. All was quiet, so she continued to the kitchen. Standing in the doorway, she made an inspection. There were two giant cookers and one smaller one. The surface of the large ones could easily accommodate six or seven stock pots each. Fry pans and copper pots hung from ceiling hooks near the ovens. Two sizeable rectangular preparation tables stood in the center of the room. And along the opposite wall? Pantries with shelves and glass doors containing dishes, platters, glasses, and goblets. Next to the pantries were two wooden ice boxes. In the far corner were two sinks, with another table next to it. The kitchen had piped-in water and gas cookers. She had not expected an East End eatery to have such modern conveniences. Along the opposite wall were several rectangular windows, large enough to allow air to circulate. Numerous gas lights hung from the ceiling, illuminating the large room. The walls had white tiles, ceiling to floor, which added to the brightness. What a magnificent room, with everything laid out for maximum efficiency!

Celia discovered Enya frying eggs with three boys. The youths gave her curious looks.

"Good morning, Celia. My, you look much improved." Enya smiled. "This is Tommy, the redhead is Timmy, and fair-haired Teddy is next to him. They live and work here, and go to school in the afternoons. We're having a spot of breakfast. The Crowing Cock isn't open today—it's the first Sunday we're closed. We're making ham and eggs. Go through the door on the left and take a seat. We'll bring it in."

Celia smiled. "Thank you. Hello boys. I'm Celia Gillingham. So pleased to meet you."

"Cor," Teddy said. "She's got nice manners and all."

Celia entered the room. There was a long rectangular table with mismatched chairs and a sideboard. There wasn't room for much else. She looked around the table—no Liam.

Fiona waved. "Good morning, Celia. I'm glad to see you're feeling better. This is Hannah, and next to her is Morrigan. Morrigan works with me in the pub at night. They both have rooms upstairs."

"Hello. I'm glad to meet you." Celia smiled at the two ladies. "Is this all the people who live here? The boys, you three, Liam and Enya?"

"Yes. The other employees live nearby enough to walk to work," Morrigan replied.

"How many employees are there?" Celia asked as she took her seat opposite from the woman.

"Well, I'm the pub manager and Liam's assistant," Fiona replied. "Morrigan is the head pub waitress. Enya is the restaurant's head waitress; Hannah is her second. The boys are jacks of all trades. Between the day and the evening, we have more than twelve staff. You make thirteen. We are going to need more soon. Ah, here's breakfast."

Enya and the boys quickly filled the plates and placed two toasted Irish soda bread baskets with marmalade pots on the table. Before she even looked up, Celia knew that Liam had entered the room, for every nerve ending pinged with awareness.

Everyone shouted 'Good morning' at Liam, and he responded with a grunt as he sat at the head of the table. No one seemed to mind his non-reply as the toast and jam were passed around along with the teapot, complete with a green knitted cozy with a white shamrock design. Excited chatter broke out as they ate, and Celia cast covert glances at Liam as she cut her ham.

"What do you want us to do today, Liam?" Timmy asked.

"First, we clean. Stem to stern, front to back. Everything must sparkle for the week ahead."

Everyone murmured their agreement.

"There are also some deliveries coming today," Liam continued. "Chicken and eggs from O'Reilly's Poulterers, shrimp and red herring from Billings Fish Market, and pork and bacon from Youngston Butchers. The bread and other bakery items from Mr. and Mrs. Eckley will be here early tomorrow at seven. Tommy, you take charge of that."

"Aye, sir."

"As Fiona and I discussed, starting on Wednesday, we will only offer two choices for the luncheon menu. Instead, we will expand our afternoon tea selections. Our new employee, Celia, will make the sandwiches and take care of the rest. Celia, you stay behind with Fiona after breakfast."

"Yes, Liam," Celia replied.

"Morrigan and Hannah, I want a complete inventory of what food we have on hand, what we're low on, and what we will need for the week. The menu for the next three days is in my office. Lads, the prep work for the noon stew should be done after you're done cleaning. Did anyone show up today?"

"About six people," Enya replied. "I informed them we'd be closed on Sundays for a while."

Celia must have looked puzzled, for Enya said, "We serve free stew before we open to the poor of the neighborhood. It's heartier than a bowl of porridge."

"Do you? I think that is wonderful," Celia replied, her approving gaze landing on Liam. That growing admiration just spiked upward.

"Anyway, I'll see you individually later." At Liam's pronouncement, everyone gathered their empty dishes and quit the room, leaving Fiona, Celia, and Liam.

"So, concerning sandwiches," Celia began.

"I've decided to start serving sandwiches tomorrow instead of Wednesday. Do you both agree?" Liam asked.

"Yes, I am ready to work. I'm feeling much better," Celia responded with a jolly smile.

"Fiona?"

"Aye. Let's do it."

"I liked the recipe for Aberdeen sandwiches—" Celia began.

Liam raised his hand, effectively silencing her. "I know what they are. Too much preparation. No toasted or hot sandwiches, not for teatime."

"Very well," Celia said, disappointed. "Pickle sandwiches, then?"

"We can manage that. We have pickles, and you can use the leftover pork." Liam nodded.

"We should cut the sandwiches finger length, with crusts removed. That is how they are served in upper-crust parlors, or—or so I've heard." Celia's cheeks flushed. She would have to be more careful when in the company of people other than Liam.

"Tommy is an expert at slicing bread. Before he leaves for school, we can have him slice off the crusts as well," Fiona suggested.

"Good," Liam nodded. "Eckley told me he would soon make enough profit to buy a bread slicer, which would cut down on our preparation."

"I saw one of those at the bakery two streets over. Maybe we should get one," Fiona suggested.

"Someday. I'll add it to my never-ending list," Liam replied. "As I told you earlier, Celia, the sandwiches must be made on the spot. Properly prepared bread saves time, but you must make the fillings beforehand. So, the initial offering is pickle sandwiches, shrimp sandwiches, and what else? There should be one more."

"Egg sandwiches with watercress?" Celia suggested. "All we need to do is boil eggs, slice them thin, and serve with watercress, parsley, and a dash of pepper. A dollop of salad cream, too, if you have it. I read that recipe in the cookbook."

"Good. We offer three types of sandwiches. It would save time if you mashed the egg with salad cream and spread it on the bread."

"What a great idea, I'll do that. What about the biscuits, scones, and frosted cakes?" Celia asked.

"We have some delicacies in the icebox, and I hear more is coming tomorrow," Fiona replied. "Some of Liam's acquaintances send along uneaten food from aristocratic kitchens. We get a fair amount of small edibles. You can use the cakes and such for tea."

"What a smart initiative. So much food is wasted in upper-crust homes."

"Celia, you work with Fiona to finalize the tea menu and rework the toff food," Liam said.

"I am very good at decorative writing. I can write the menus to show your customers," Celia suggested eagerly. She enjoyed using her active imagination and talents for a common purpose, being part of a team.

"Fine. I'm going to my office. I've paperwork and bills to pay." Liam poured another mug of tea and stood. "Get everyone working, Fiona. The sooner they're done, the quicker they have the afternoon off." He departed.

Celia watched him leave. It took all her self-control not to sigh at the sight of him.

"Handsome, isn't he?" Fiona grinned. "Almost too handsome, although that's hardly a fault. He acts completely unaware of the reactions he elicits from women of all ages and all walks of life. That's why teatime has become popular. The ladies come to see *him*. They always have, even back when Walter Henning ran things. Liam didn't believe me initially, but I convinced him to do a few walkabouts, asking how everything was and whatnot. Ladies stare at him like he is the main course. Much like you are mooning over him now."

Celia's hands flew to her cheeks. "Oh, no. It's that noticeable?"

"Don't worry. I won't tell anyone. You'd better hide it better, however. Liam doesn't get involved with staff."

Celia reached for her tea and took a sip. "I understand. I do not want any trouble. I want to do my job well and earn some money until I can contact my friends or until my aunt returns, which may be several weeks." Involved? Well, that was a prospect she had not considered. And no wonder, with everything in her life so uncertain. But Celia was eager to move on with her life, and she would not rule anything out at this stage.

Fiona stood. "Then we had best get to work. Bring your tea. We're off to the larder to gather your ingredients and plan for tomorrow."

Celia followed Fiona into the kitchen. Fiona was right. It would be wise in the short-term to show complete indifference to Liam, however difficult that might be, at least around other people.

But when they were alone? Celia was eager to see how things would progress.

LIAM SAT AT his desk with two leather-bound ledgers spread before him. He had a good relationship with his suppliers built on mutual trust and esteem. When one delivery was made, he paid for the previous one. Most took a bank draft on his restaurant account, but he paid Mr. Eckley in cash since the man worked out of his house. He mentioned to Eckley two days ago that he was considering expanding into tea sandwiches, which meant more bread orders. Eckley shook Liam's hand. Because of the extra business, Eckley hired his twenty-one-year-old nephew to sell from the cart, freeing Eckley up for more baking. "Thanks to you," Eckley had enthused. "I'm finally making a good profit. We've found a large second-hand gas stove to add to our existing one."

Liam was glad someone was making money. He stared at the ledgers. The free stew was cutting into his profits, and he didn't like that he relied too much on the bin food from the toffs. Aye, he called it bin food because it was literally rescued from the rubbish. Liam had never learned how to bake. He'd never wanted to. Well, except for a hot crust pastry for meat and vegetable pies, which he didn't serve that often. Expanding his menu meant more food to buy and more staff to hire. Liam was silently relieved when Fiona mentioned temporarily cutting back on the luncheon menu.

Running this place took a lot of work. Besides being perpetually tired, Liam's thoughts were filled with food, menus, profits, and the well-being of his staff. With the bank drafts and cash envelope completed, Liam tucked them and the account books into his small safe, then gathered his wool coat and scarf. He needed to collect the outstanding gaming debts. Other than those debts, the gaming room was doing well enough, especially with the sale of beer and other alcohol. They turned a tidy profit every night. It gave him that extra cushion of security. Anyone looking at his books would be pleased with The Crowing Cock's profit, but to Liam, it was never enough. Living and surviving on the streets would do that to a person—constant money anxiety, even when things were good financially.

He marched through the kitchen, where his staff was scrubbing the counters. "After you're done, go ahead and relax for the rest of the afternoon. Tell the others. Remember, we don't open until tomorrow at two, so there is no rush today. I'll be back soon."

He entered the rear yard, the alley, and onto the street. Taking his leather gloves from his pocket, he waved at an oncoming hansom cab. Once inside, he closed the folding doors and slipped on his gloves. The trap door opened above.

"Yes, sir?"

"Forty-eight Gloucester Square."

CHAPTER NINE

LIAM TRAVELED TOWARD Doctor Drew's residence. He needed to borrow the Hornsby family carriage to bring Celia's trunks to the restaurant. He might as well collect them since he needed to journey to Shinwell's estate to settle the debt. Why wait for the cousin to deliver them as he said he would? Liam did not trust Shinwell to hold up his end in any deal.

Fifteen minutes later, the hansom cab pulled up in front of Drew's residence. Liam had never been here before. The white stucco town house was four stories high and had fancy, wrought-iron fences, trellises, and bay windows with an intricate stained-glass design.

Liam climbed out of the hansom and paid the driver.

He knocked on the door, and a small woman with an apron answered. "Aye? Who is it?"

"I'm here to see Doctor Hornsby. I'm Liam Hallahan."

The woman's eyes narrowed. "And do you have an appointment?"

"Let him in, Mrs. Evans. I know the man." Drew stood in the hallway, waving him in.

He stepped across the threshold. Liam couldn't help but gape at the black and white tile marble floors and the ornate crystal chandelier above.

"You'll be wanting tea, I suppose," Mrs. Evans grumbled.

"Liam?" Drew asked.

"No. Thank you," he replied.

"We will see to ourselves, Mrs. Evans."

Mrs. Evans gave Liam a suspicious glance, then, wiping her hands on her apron, headed toward the rear of the house.

"*That* was Mrs. Evans, my cook-housekeeper and imperial guard. Come to my study."

Liam followed Drew down the hall. "I can't stay long. I hoped to ask a favor."

Drew pointed toward the sofa, and Liam sat, taking in the lushness of the room—shelves of books filled one side of the wall, and a fire crackled in the hearth, making the elegant study cozy. Drew's desk was solid oak with ornate scrollwork. This place reeked of money, inside and out.

As if reading his thoughts, Drew said, "My family has some money. I'm not ashamed of it. But I earn my way, as best as a doctor in free clinics will allow. That is why I am going over this list. I will rent the two stories above at the end of the month, and I have to pick a suitable tenant. One who will pay on time. Can I get you a drink?"

"It's tempting, but I have my collecting duties this afternoon. You mentioned a few weeks ago that you have use of the Hornsby carriage until your family returns in the early spring."

"Yes, I do."

"I must go to Viscount Shinwell's to collect a gaming debt and fetch Celia's trunks. I can't do that with a hansom cab. I know I'm asking a lot. Since we met, it seems all you've done is assist Mitchell or me. I appreciate it."

Drew pushed his spectacles up his nose. "I do not mind. Not at all. I welcome this new twist to my life journey. The fact you are asking for my help tells me you are coming around to accepting the revelation of our blood ties."

"I admit it hit me—hard. I was tempted to tell you and Mitchell to sod off, but in the end, I couldn't do it." It was quite the admission, but also the truth.

"I'm glad of it. Now, as to the carriage. My family has a four-seat Clarence with room at the rear for trunks and other luggage. Unfortunately, it's not here, as I do not have the room to keep it, the horses, and the driver. But we can collect it at my family's residence, which is not far away. Wright would welcome something to do."

"I thought you had the family carriage here. I should have made the hansom wait," Liam stated.

"We can catch another soon enough. They go by here at all hours. Is this part of your duties, collecting gaming debts?" Drew asked as he joined Liam on the sofa.

"No. When I took ownership, I carried over Walter Henning's gaming rules. Most long-time customers pay, but two newer ones are in arrears. I no longer offer credit to those I don't know. Even after doing thorough background checks like I did on these two, some men do not honor their debts promptly."

"I have customers reimburse me with an up-front fee, especially if they are well off. The wealthy have a habit of running up debts and not paying them. It has been that way for decades, even centuries." Drew hesitated. "To change the subject for a moment. When we first met, you said your mother told you who sired you. You never wanted to seek him out, even after your mother passed?"

Liam was not one for rehashing the past. But he supposed if he and Drew—and Mitchell, for that matter—were going to have any acquaintance or friendship, speaking of the past could hardly be avoided. He could growl and refuse to answer, but he had done that already. "No. He never came around but occasionally sent some bully with a handful of coins. It was never enough for us to live on, not long-term." Liam paused, his insides contracting in pain as they often did when thinking of his impoverished childhood.

"I never believed my father was a duke," Liam continued. "I thought it was the muscular, twitching rat bringing the coin. As my mother became sicker, the duke's man offered to take me off her hands—for a price. She kept refusing. When she did pass away, I wasn't sticking around to find out what the rat wanted me for. I did a runner."

"I believe I have an idea," Drew said gravely. "The previous Duke of Chellenham had a scheme where he sold children—his own included—to people needing or wanting them. Apprenticeships, as a son or daughter, or cheap labor. He made a tidy profit over the years, especially when he brought in like-minded men of means wishing to be rid of their—"

"By-blows? Whoresons? Bastards?" Liam offered softly.

"Yes. According to Damon Cranston, the new duke, Chellenham was a cold, cruel man with no honor and no love in his heart. He believed in eugenics. Do you know what that is?"

"I read about it in one of the papers. Procreating for the express purpose of improving the quality of the human population? Why would he do that?"

"Hubris. Arrogance and egocentricity. A belief that his physical attributes were superior and that perfection should be passed on. No wonder my mother moved us constantly and changed our names to hide from him. She was terrified," Drew replied solemnly.

"Jaysus," Liam murmured.

"As far as I can tell, having met you, Mitchell, Damon, and Olivia, none of us have the worst of his personality traits, not deep down where it counts. I have only just met the four young siblings Damon is taking in, and they seem to be well-behaved."

Liam raised an eyebrow. "And they're good-looking, I suppose?"

"Yes. At least outwardly. An older girl at the home was recently reunited with her mother. She had black hair like you. Not all of the progeny are blond. But most seem to be. I hope they are good inside as well. Will you meet the young ones and Damon?"

Liam frowned. "I don't know, at some point. It feels—strange. You say there is a half-sister too, this Olivia you speak of?" Drew nodded. "Let me get used to you and Mitchell first and come to terms with this situation before meeting anyone else."

"Fair enough. Though I welcome it, I am still trying to understand it. My Hornsby family has been very supportive."

"You're lucky to have them."

"I am. The thing of it is, now you have Mitchell and me."

Liam nodded. An odd lump formed in his throat, along with a surge of emotion, which made it difficult for him to reply. He wasn't used to having such a decided emotional response concerning other people. It was bloody confusing and concerning. Celia was also causing him to have emotional reactions. She touched him, more than he cared to admit.

"Now, let's go on your errand. Would you mind if I came? It never hurts to have witnesses when collecting debts," Drew said in a wry tone.

"Not at all. I'd appreciate it."

Drew gathered his coat, hat, and gloves, and they caught a hansom to the Hornsby residence in Mayfair. This peerage home was all brick with wrought iron balconies. As Drew had said, the family had money. This residence looked as if a duke lived there. Liam removed his peaked cap as they entered the front hallway, even more fancy than Drew's.

"Good morning, Taylor. Is Wright about? I need the carriage."

"Good morning, Doctor," the butler replied respectfully. "I will fetch him for you. In his most recent letter, the duke mentioned that if you came by, I should show you some items you may wish for your residence or if you do not want them, you may donate to charity. They are in the study in the far corner."

"Thank you, Taylor. We will find our way."

Liam followed Drew down the hall into the study. "Perhaps you can use some of these items in your various establishments," Drew said. It was a massive room filled with bookcases to the high ceiling and a sliding ladder to reach the top shelves. Dark wood panel walls and gold draperies gave the room an opulent look. Liam had never seen so many books.

"Here we are," Drew said. "A painting of a serene country

lake with a cottage. Do you think Lady Celia would like it for her room?"

"Aye, she would. That table. Is it for ladies?" Liam pointed.

"Yes, a vanity with a stool. It's not very large, but it would fit in the room."

"And those bed tables. If you don't mind, I'd like them for the lads' room."

"Let's take it all. Ah, Wright. There you are. We need your services and the carriage. This is Mr. Hallahan." Mr. Wright, the coachman, touched his forelock in reply. "Fetch some footmen, and we will load all this on or inside the Clarence. Then we need you to take us to a couple of addresses, one to collect two trunks."

"Yes, Doctor. Shall I bring a footman to assist with the trunks?" Wright asked.

"Capital idea. We had best be off."

After the conveyance was packed, they departed. The coach pulled up in front of Elliot Hartright's residence, and Liam exited and pounded on the doorknocker.

"Oh, Hallahan," Hartright exhaled as he opened the door wider. "I can guess why you are here." Hartright worked in a bank, as an officer, or whatever. He was not prosperous, but neither was the man underprivileged. Liam guessed he owed more than he made in a year. Collecting the total amount today was probably not possible.

"I'm here to collect your debt."

"I surmised," Hartright replied contritely. "One hundred fifty pounds, correct?"

"One hundred and seventy-eight, to be exact. And I haven't charged you interest—yet."

"I have 55 pounds to give you. As for the rest—" Hartright rubbed his chin. "I have to go to my father-in-law. That won't be a pleasant prospect, what?" Hartright reached into his trousers' pocket and passed Liam the folded pound notes.

Liam quickly counted the bills and stuffed them in his wool

coat pocket. "One hundred and twenty-three are still owing. Payment is required in one week. I will be sending Bruce to collect. Have you seen Bruce in the pub? He's larger than me, an ex-boxer. You will want to make sure you have the payment."

"I say, there is no need to threaten me," Hartright said aghast.

"This is merely a statement of fact. Until you pay in full, you're banned. If you don't have the full amount next week, I will start charging twenty percent interest. When you pay, you may return, but there will be no more credit. You will have to play within your means." Liam wasn't threatening or aggressive; he just laid the information out straightforwardly. "Understand?"

"Yes, I understand. I will try to have the rest next Sunday."

Liam nodded, returned to the coach, and climbed in.

"Success?" Drew asked.

"Partial payment. It will assist with the free meal program." Liam thumped on the roof, and the carriage moved forward. Wright already had the next address. And Liam was not looking forward to this collection.

"Speaking of your meal program, I recently spoke to Damon and his club, The Rakes of St. Regent's Park. They agreed to offer you a monthly stipend of fifteen pounds. They ask that you set up a separate account for the venture so they can monitor the progress. A daily count of those fed is also required. Any medical supplies I need to treat them every Thursday will also come from that account. A monthly review will be done; if you need more, they can provide it. Do you agree? There is one request: they would like you to present your first month's results. The meeting is on Thursday, February 17th at 7 pm."

Liam frowned. These toffs always had a catch, but he understood the need for accountability. "For fifteen pounds a month, I'll do an Irish jig for them."

Drew chuckled. "That will not be necessary, however entertaining it might be. They have asked that the name you place on the account be 'The Hallahan Initiative' with your name as chief officer and mine as a medical officer. If it all goes well, they can solicit donations on your behalf. More meat and vegetables in the pot means a healthier population. We can expand to provide proper clothes and blankets. Perhaps a few volunteers to free up your staff. But one step at a time."

"You are quite the force of nature," Liam stated, duly impressed.

"I was raised in a family that believed in doing good works. I have seen and experienced how unfortunate people live, and I do what I can to lessen their misery. I also have recently come to understand that I cannot assist everyone. My Uncle Harrison is the Duke of Gransford. While a marquess, he toiled anonymously in an abandoned underground train tunnel in Stepney, offering medical care to the homeless and those who could not afford a doctor. He nearly worked himself into an early grave. That will *not* be me."

Liam's eyes widened. "Doctor Damian was your duke uncle?"

Drew's mouth dropped open. Then he swiftly closed it. "You've heard of him? How astounding."

Liam nodded. "It was too late for my mother. I think we saw him in '80. I was eleven or twelve. My mother barely made it to see him. Doctor Damian kept her for four days, comforted her, and fed her hot soup and tea. When I returned, he took me aside and said I had to be strong, that my mother was very sick and wouldn't recover. He gave me a choice: my mother could die in the workhouse infirmary or at home. We lived in two rooms in a filthy place but kept our living area tidy and comfortable. I chose home." Liam's mouth quirked with amusement. "I think your uncle thought me much older because I was already tall for my age. Anyway, he gave me a packet of willow bark powder, and I cared for Mother for the next two weeks until she passed."

"That would be hard for anyone to deal with. I understand the impact of losing a mother at a young age. That must have been difficult," Drew said empathically.

Drew had no idea—or maybe he did. Liam wasn't going to discuss it now, for he had already revealed more than he'd intended. It was best to change the subject. "It's wise to adopt the 'not going to work yourself to death' theory. It's something I should follow. Ah, here we are."

"Good luck," Drew offered. "Call out if you need me."

Liam climbed down from the conveyance and stared at the house. It was not as majestic as the Hornsby residences but showed a modicum of wealth. He banged the brass knocker, and a man with gray at his temples opened the door.

"The butler, I presume?" Liam questioned.

"I am Baldwin, sir."

"Is Viscount Shinwell about?"

"He is not receiving, sir."

"Of course not. He's still asleep since it's noon. Then, you can assist with another inquiry. I'm here to take Lady Celia's trunks. Shinwell deserted her at my place of business, and the dowager countess wants her belongings. She's about this tall," Liam said, placing his outstretched hand below his shoulder. "With golden brown hair and blue eyes, she has a cheerful disposition, though I don't know why, considering how she's been treated."

Baldwin opened the door wider to allow Liam to step across the threshold, but he held his hand up to stop him from coming further. "I am glad to hear the countess is safe. I will have her trunks brought down immediately." Baldwin snapped his fingers, and two tall footmen appeared seemingly out of thin air. "Fetch the trunks from the attic bedroom."

Attic? What miserable bastards, sticking her up there.

The footmen swiftly ascended the stairs. Liam leaned in and whispered, "Do you know where her Aunt Etta is? An address?"

"No, sir," Baldwin murmured. "But I will venture to discover it."

"Good man." Liam reached into his pocket and held out his card. "My name and the address of my business in Spitalfields. Send word when you can."

"Baldwin!" a slurred voice yelled from the top of the stairs. "Whom are you speaking to?"

Baldwin quickly palmed the card. "Someone to see you, my lord. He is most insistent."

Shinwell descended the stairs and stood before Liam. He wore a dressing gown over his bare chest with matching silk trousers. He looked disheveled and bloated—no doubt from all the imbibing the night before. "You! You have got a nerve. Sod off."

Such class. "I'm here to collect your gaming debt. You owe 240 pounds."

"I paid that, and you know it."

"Do you know how long your countess cousin would have to work to pay off that kind of debt? It would take over five years, not including the interest. I told you when you unceremoniously dumped her at my feet that I would not agree to such a heartless, cruel, and, may I add, illegal scheme."

Baldwin gasped, then quickly arranged his shocked features into a neutral look.

"I will not pay. Get out of my house," Shinwell said dismissively.

"Bruce will be by next Sunday. You've seen him at the pub? He's an ex-boxer. He knows how to collect a debt—if not from you, then from your toff father."

"How dare you threaten me?" Shinwell screeched. Four footmen came down the stairs carrying the trunks. "Put those down immediately!"

Baldwin shook his head, and the footmen continued out the door towards the carriage.

"Where is your father?" Liam questioned.

"He is not here," Shinwell said, sniffing haughtily.

Baldwin slightly inclined his head as if to agree with the statement.

"Tell the earl I wished to see him regarding this debt and his niece. It would be to his benefit to arrange a meeting. I can come by next Sunday." Liam looked to Baldwin. "Will you see he gets that message?"

"I will, sir. I relay all messages to his lordship."

"We will *not* pay," Shinwell shrieked. "Get that through your thick Irish skull. Who cares if it takes five years to work off the debt? My bitch of a cousin has nothing else to do or anywhere to go."

Liam crossed the floor and grabbed a fistful of Shinwell's rumpled dressing gown. "Don't ever call her that. Follow me? Or I'll give you the beating you deserve. It's long overdue, I'll wager." Liam released him and pushed him away. Nodding to the butler, Liam departed. Drew and Wright busily secured the trunks. He could hear Shinwell raging, yelling epithets that would curl a sailor's hair.

As they pulled away from the residence, Liam wondered if he had just made things worse. So much for his plan of not losing his temper. And he had one, enhanced by the injustice he had witnessed every day since he was a child. It took all his well-earned discipline to keep himself in check, for he could not abide anyone being mistreated. When Shinwell called Celia that name, fury tore through him. No one would ever disparage Celia in his presence.

No one.

CHAPTER TEN

ONDAY ARRIVED, AND Celia rose early. Not that she'd
gotten much sleep the night before as she was excited to
start work. How disappointing to find no one was up yet, except
the young apprentices chopping and peeling vegetables in the
kitchen. Frustrated, she climbed the stairs and entered the
hallway just in time to see Liam emerge from the bathing room.

Celia stopped short. He was shirtless, with a towel slung
carelessly over his broad shoulder, and his trousers unbuttoned
partway and riding low on his muscular hips. Her mouth went
dry at the glorious sight of him. Liam stood as tall as a lovingly
carved marble statue of the perfect man, at least in Celia's eyes.
He had just shaved. Running her fingers along his smooth,
flawless skin would be tempting. Liam's hair was disheveled
enough to complete the handsome rogue look.

"Good morning," she said with a smile, keeping her voice
steady. She hadn't seen him since he'd delivered her trunks early
yesterday afternoon.

"I'll meet you downstairs in fifteen minutes." He turned on
his heel and headed toward his rooms.

Watching him walk away was almost as exciting as seeing
him from the front. Liam's back muscles bunched as he gracefully
strode away. His shapely rear end punctuated the perfection
point.

Celia shook her head. *Holy crow, what am I doing?* Desiring a man with her husband barely dead a month? With a deep breath and an exhale, Celia headed toward the stairs and the kitchen below. There had been no love in her marriage, and the sex had merely to beget an heir.

But she imagined sex with Liam would be the exact opposite—passion incarnate. All she could do was imagine; he'd filled her nightly dreams since she met him. Celia smiled knowingly. Now, she had a new vision to fill her heated nocturnal thoughts.

When Celia strode into the kitchen, she put aside all thoughts of the strikingly handsome Liam. "Good morning, lads," she smiled. "Did you have breakfast?"

"Aye, miss," Teddy replied shyly. "There's toast and jam and eggs and bacon on a hot plate in the eating room."

"Thank you." Celia entered the dining area and swiftly filled her plate of food. A pot of tea sat nearby, and she filled her mug with milk and some sugar. By the time she was halfway through her meal, Liam had entered, inclining his head in acknowledgment.

He sat across from her. "I'll get you started on the fillings after we eat. Tommy wants you to show him how thick you want the bread sliced. The good news is that the shrimp is already cooked and deveined. My supplier does it for me. It saves me time."

"How clever," she replied as she sipped her tea.

"Teddy is boiling eggs, and he will assist you in slicing and mashing the pickle. You will have to work fast; if you run out of bread, you must slice it yourself. Have Tommy give you tips. Save the crusts and other bits. We make a bread pudding from it. The lads will assist you when they can in the next few days, but ultimately, you must do the bulk of the work yourself. We can't afford to fall behind. I have the kitchen running like a well-oiled machine. You must learn to move with the flow."

"If I wasn't nervous before, now I am more so. Did you see the menus I crafted? I left them on your desk yesterday afternoon while you were gone."

Liam sliced his ham into bite-sized pieces. "I did. Thank you. We will use them today."

Celia took a piece of bacon and nibbled on it. "About my trunks—"

"You already thanked me."

"Did you see Darrington or Shinwell?"

"Shinwell. He still owes that gaming debt. I went there to collect it. He told me to sod off."

Celia sighed. "Shinwell is a repugnant creature. No wonder he's not married yet. He was always getting into trouble, fights with other boys, stealing, tormenting the staff."

"And you?" Liam asked as he sipped his tea.

"Yes. It started with spitting in my pudding, tripping me, hiding my books. Thank God he was away at Eton part of the time when he wasn't sent home for one infraction of the rules or another. They always took him back, however. When I turned twelve, and he was fifteen, the torment took on a more nefarious angle."

"How so?" Liam asked slowly. His tone of voice showed he had already guessed what.

"He tried to corner me in dark cupboards or pull me into unoccupied rooms. Once, he pinned me against the wall and touched me—all over. I was already developing, you see. He tried to sneak into my room at night on numerous occasions. That was when I was sent away to finishing school. I think Aunt Etta suspected."

"That miserable miscreant. I should've pounded him senseless," Liam growled. "He assaulted you."

Celia nodded. "Yes, he did. I never thought of it in such stark terms, but it's true. I don't know why I told you that. I've never told a living soul before. Be careful when dealing with Shinwell and Darrington—there is something sinister about them. I do not want you harmed. My advice is to wait for my aunt to return. You can collect the debt through her. It would be safer."

"I'll think it over." Liam frowned. "I despise that you were treated that way."

"Women and girls from all walks of life encounter such, I'm sure," Celia murmured.

"Unfortunately." Liam stood. "That doesn't make it right. I'm sorry you were subjected to that. Come, let's get you started. Leave the dishes. The boys will collect them."

He held the door for her, and she entered the kitchen, already a whirlwind of activity. Celia admonished herself for revealing those private and harrowing memories. Perhaps she'd only wanted to prove to him how dangerous her cousin could be. Or maybe, some hidden and dark part of her wished Liam would give Shinwell the pounding he deserved.

CELIA GLANCED AT the clock on the wall—two hours had passed. She couldn't believe it. The restaurant opened in an hour, and she was not nearly finished making the fillings. The stew had been served, the cleanup completed, and everyone was busily preparing the luncheon menu. Today's choices were cream of mushroom and potato soup, already simmering on the stove. Liam had put together a mustard sauce for the baked herring, served with mashed potatoes, boiled carrots, and fried onions. The pork loin was cut into chops and ready for frying. Watching Liam work was like watching a master paint a portrait.

He came over to her station. "You must work faster. Don't chop the shrimp. Use this." He placed a large mortar and pestle in front of her. "Mash everything together in this. Transfer the paste to a bowl, then do it again. This glass bowl should be three-quarters filled. What we don't use today is good for tomorrow." Liam took a handful of shrimp and tossed them in the mortar. Then he took her hand, placed the pestle in it, and guided her. With his hand covering hers, he showed her how to do it. "Like that," he said, whispering in her ear.

"Yes, Chef," Celia whispered so only he could hear. Her insides turned to mush as he hovered near, his hand covering hers. It was challenging to remember to take a breath.

"I like it when you call me that," he whispered huskily in her ear. "Are the pickles prepared?"

"Yes. Tommy's mixing the boiled eggs with salad cream."

Liam took his hand away. "You have to prepare the cakes." He pointed to two large trays sitting on a preparation table. "You have to test those by taking a bite. Are they fresh enough to serve? If a cake frosting is too hard and cracked, scrape it off. But don't toss it. We can freshen it up later. Understand?"

"Yes, Chef," she murmured.

He gave her a brief, dazzling smile before returning to the stoves, and the sight of it caused her heart to skip a beat. The smile made him all the more handsome and shook her resolve to stay detached.

Holy crow, it's hot in the kitchen. Three overlarge gas stoves roiled at full tilt. Celia felt sweat trickling down her back. Everyone rushed about, shouting directions. The waitresses were assisting in the kitchen as well. Hannah lined up ten three-tiered trays for her on one of the prep tables, then ran to the stove to stir the mustard sauce. The frantic activity didn't deter Celia; she soaked it in.

She remained thoroughly engrossed in her tasks for the next hour. Liam came by to check on her progress more than once, and with the fillings prepared, she moved over to the trays of small cakes, biscuits, and loaves. She hurriedly stuffed a piece of currant cake in her mouth. It was still fresh. She cut the pieces smaller, then moved on to the ginger biscuits. They were a little stale. Celia set them aside. Liam mentioned that anything that was not as fresh but still edible was given to the poor.

"Fire time!" Liam yelled. *Whatever that meant.* The servers hurried out front to open the door. The lads had left for school, so Celia would be on her own with preparation. She opened the swinging door partway to see a crowd pour in as the waitresses showed them to the tables and booths.

"Get ready! Service!" Liam yelled. Fiona had joined them in the kitchen ten minutes ago and was preparing plates and bowls.

Kettles of water boiled for tea and coffee percolated in a device Celia had never seen before.

Hannah burst through the door. "Pork chop, table two. Tea tray, table four, soup, table one." She swiftly gathered a teapot and cups and disappeared again. With a pencil in hand, Liam scribbled on a piece of paper, his focus unwavering.

Celia sprang into action. She hastily made three sandwiches with the fillings, remembering how the cookbook said to first spread the thinnest layer of warmed butter on the bread. She cut the sandwiches into finger lengths with a large sharp knife, removed the crusts, and placed them on the bottom tier. Next, she arranged the tea biscuits and currant cake on the second tier and the frosted cakes and tarts on the top tier. What did Liam say to do next—*right*. "Tea tray, table two!" she yelled, perhaps too loudly, as everyone turned to look at her.

Celia started prepping more sandwiches as Enya came into the kitchen next. "Herring, table five! Tea tray tables one and three!"

Pork chops and onions sizzled in iron skillets as Liam pulled a large roaster pan of baked herring from the oven, and new pans were placed inside to replace them. Celia's mouth watered.

"Pick up the pace, Celia!" Liam called out.

How could she go any faster?

It went on like that for the next three hours, with Celia hardly having time to breathe. At last, around four-thirty, things finally settled down. They had used up all the sliced bread. Most of the fillings and the second-hand food was gone. Celia looked down. The front of her apron was covered in egg salad, shrimp, and butter.

Never had she felt more alive.

AT HALF PAST five and with the main dish orders all but over,

Liam headed toward Celia's station. "You did it," he said.

She gave him a wide smile. "I did, didn't I? Is this what it's like every day?"

"More so because the rest of the week we open at twelve, which means our breakfast and the prep work start at seven in the morning."

"What does fire time mean?"

"It means start cooking—the restaurant is open." The three boys entered through the rear doors. "Lads, start the dishes. I'll make your supper." Liam turned to her. "What would you like, the herring or the pork?"

"The pork, if you please."

Enya stuck her head in the door. "Late customer. Tea tray, table two. I'll fetch the tea. And Liam, it's *her* again. She wants to talk to you."

Liam slammed the skillet on the counter. "Fecking hell." He tore off his apron and tossed it on the table. He strode through the swinging door into the dining area.

Celia hurriedly made sandwiches and arranged the tray as Enya gathered a teapot and two teacups from the prep table. "What is that about?"

"Viscountess Hampton. She comes once a week without fail and asks to see Liam. She fawns over him and usually brings a different friend each time to show him off like a prized stallion."

"Oh," Celia replied quietly. She had never heard of the woman, but then, she hadn't met many peers through the years. "Is he involved with her?"

Enya snorted. "Not likely. But that doesn't stop her from trying. I'll be back for the tray."

Enya departed, served the tea, then returned for the tray. Celia followed her to the swinging door and cracked it open wide enough to observe what was going on. Luckily, the nearly empty restaurant made listening in easy.

The viscountess and Liam were facing Celia, and the look of rampant lust on the woman's face was hard to miss.

"Is he not everything I said he would be, Baroness?" the viscountess crooned as she stroked his arm.

The baroness nodded in reply, giving Liam the once-over. How disrespectful.

Liam gently but firmly removed the viscountess's hand, then held out her chair. "Your tea is getting cold, my lady."

She sat, and he pushed the chair in. Liam's mouth was pulled into a taut line of displeasure.

The viscountess grabbed his hand before he could pull it away from the chair. "The offer still stands. Be my personal chef and I will pay you 250 pounds per annum. Or name your price. There would be considerable benefits, as you can imagine."

It appeared men had to endure this kind of behavior as well—being mauled, propositioned, and treated like a piece of prime beef. The viscountess wanted Liam for more than her chef. The sultry tone of her voice made that plain. Celia felt sickened and angry on his behalf. She would do well to remember not to treat Liam as the viscountess was doing. He was more than the outer handsome shell. That was something the viscountess and those of her ilk would never understand.

Liam pulled his hand away. "I thank you for the generous offer, but I'm entirely content here running my own business on my terms. Besides, the staff depends on me."

"Well, bring along your scullery maids!" the viscountess said, dismissively waving her arm. The baroness chuckled.

Liam's face looked like thunder. He bowed stiffly. "Enjoy your tea, my ladies."

He marched toward the door, and Celia hurried to her station. Standing before the stove, Liam grabbed the iron skillet and started cooking. His jaw worked angrily, and Celia thought it best not to say anything. She kept herself busy cleaning up her area, placing her leftovers in the assigned containers, and taking them to the larder and the icebox as Fiona had shown her yesterday.

By the time she returned, Liam held out a plate toward her. "Don't let it get cold."

"What about you?"

"I'm not hungry. Teddy, Tommy, Timmy, get your supper and clean up this mess!" Liam yelled. The boys snapped to attention. "Finish the dishes after you eat, then mop the floors and clean the walls and the stoves."

Liam tore off his apron and exited the rear door, slamming it hard.

"Don't mind him, Miss Celia. He don't—doesn't—mean it," Timmy offered. "It's hard being the boss."

"You're absolutely right," Celia said, smiling as she carried her plate into the dining area. The boys followed, and they joined the other employees at the table. The food, as always, was delicious and perfectly cooked. As Celia was introduced to the nighttime pub employees, she couldn't stop thinking about Liam. Should she check on him later, or would that intrude on his private time?

All she knew was that no one should be treated with such contempt. After finishing her meal, Celia ladled still-hot mushroom soup into a large crockery bowl and grabbed bread, fresh tea, and a spoon to take to Liam. He had to eat. Besides, she was concerned for him and could not relax until she knew he was all right.

Yes, her feelings were growing with each passing day. Celia would have to do her best to keep them hidden. So far, she seemed doomed to fail.

CHAPTER ELEVEN

L IAM SAT AND brooded in his oversized damask armchair. He shouldn't behave in such a manner with the viscountess, but he was bloody well fed up with these aristocratic women making indecent proposals, no matter how veiled. It had happened more than once in his past, even while working for Henning.

Walter always advised him to ignore such flagrant and insulting suggestions, but act politely to keep the customers returning. "If we can use your dark good looks to bring in more ladies, why not? Smile!"

It had worked. At noon, more women came in to order Walter's beef hot pot while Liam served. He received generous tips along with the occasional pinch or lewd suggestion, which gave him a deeper understanding of the harassment women face daily.

Fiona encouraged him to continue making a sporadic appearance in the dining room. She stated that the best chefs came out of the kitchen now and then to receive praise. The concept seemed silly to Liam since he ran a primary dining establishment in Spitalfields. He was *not* the head chef at The Savoy. Still, it turned out that Fiona was correct to expand their afternoon tea offerings. The repast had taken on a life of its own.

A knock sounded at the door. "It's Celia. I have brought you something to eat."

Liam could act like a complete rotter, snarl like a rabid beast, and order her to stay the bloody hell away from him, but he couldn't bring himself to do it.

"Come in."

Celia entered, carrying a tray. "I thought you might be hungry. It's mushroom soup, slices of bread, and some currant cake. There is also a mug of tea. It does wonders after a busy day. I'll just lay it here." She placed it on the table in front of him and then turned to leave.

"Stay. Please." Why he asked, Liam could not begin to fathom. The words escaped from his lips before he could call them back.

Celia sat on the sofa across from him and slipped off her wool coat, laying it beside her.

Liam took a spoonful of soup. "Still warm. Thank you. You saw what happened earlier."

"With the viscountess? Yes. I admit I was curious when I saw your reaction. I *am* sorry you were subjected to such— aggravation."

Liam shrugged as he ate more soup. "It's a difficult situation. I'm positive Lady Hampton spread a positive word about my restaurant. I can't be rude, as I need the business. But I don't understand why she won't take no for an answer."

"Because her ladyship is used to getting what she wants," Celia responded. "Eventually, the viscountess will be more forceful and blunter in voicing her wishes. What will you do, then?"

Liam grunted. "More than she is already? I don't know. Politely refuse and hope she accepts it. In the worst case scenario, she'll start badmouthing my restaurant, and business will dry up. Eating establishments rely on word of mouth."

Celia shook her head. "No wonder you disparage the upper crust."

Liam picked up the mug and sipped his tea. "The viscountess is not the only reason. I'm the bastard son of a duke." What had come over him? The words slipped out. Why *did* he mention it? Because he felt at ease around Celia? As Fiona had said, she *was* pleasant to talk to.

Celia's eyes widened at his revelation. "A duke? When did you discover this?"

"My late mother had always told me I was the son of a duke, but I never believed it. Then, two men showed up at my restaurant about seven weeks ago and claimed we shared a bloodline. One of those men is Doctor Hornsby. The other is Detective Sergeant Simpson. He is away on a honeymoon trip at the moment."

"According to Darrington and Shinwell, my friend is also away on a honeymoon trip. I suppose some couples like marrying during the holiday season."

"Mitchell and Corrine married—"

"Corrine?" Celia cried. "The former Baroness Addington?"

Liam's eyebrows shot skyward. "Addington? Aye. I mean, Corrine."

Celia was shocked, utterly gobsmacked. "You know her? What are the odds? Corrine is one of the friends I'm trying to contact. Is it true the baron was murdered? And when will Corrine return? How is she? I *am* sorry to toss all these questions at you, but this is unbelievable."

"Addington *was* murdered. I don't know all the details. As far as I know, Mitchell and Corrine will return in late February or early March. Both are well. They are staying at a cottage Drew's family offered. I came to know her as she and Mitchell grew closer. She assisted Drew with providing medical care every Thursday to those who came for stew. She said she was a nurse for close to ten years. By the time they were married, Corrine and I were acquainted enough to use first names—at her insistence."

Celia smiled. "That sounds like Corrine. She mentioned nursing in the past. Should I write to her and inform her of my predicament? Perhaps not, as I do not want to disturb her trip. Knowing her as I do, she would drop everything and come to my aid. But I can wait until she returns if you can put up with me that long."

"Stay as long as you like," Liam replied. He didn't want her to leave, which was surprising. He usually preferred to be alone after a hectic day of cooking.

Celia clapped her hands together, her eyes shimmering with emotion. "I am so pleased Corrine found happiness—and with your half-brother!" Celia sobered. "That must have been a shock for you to discover, not only the duke aspect but also that there are others."

"It's worse than you know." Between spoonfuls of soup and sips of tea, Liam told her everything Drew had revealed to him. He had to tell someone, and even though they had only been acquainted for a short time, Liam trusted Celia. That was quite something to admit because Liam seldom let anyone close.

"Eugenics," Celia whispered incredulously. "How despicable. Oh, Liam, that is quite the disclosure."

"It appears we're both dealing with upheavals in our lives," Liam murmured.

"Yes," Celia replied quietly. "And we must make the best of it. Doctor Hornsby is a decent and honorable man. I came to that conclusion swiftly. I'm sure Mitchell Simpson is the same."

"He is."

"Then why not embrace them as friends and brothers? As to the rest, the new Duke of Chellenham and the others can wait until you are ready. Open your heart, Liam. I know you have one. Let them in, as well as the people who work with you. Make them part of your life. You won't regret it. I always longed for siblings. Corrine and Selena were as close as I came. I regret that we grew apart." Celia met his gaze. "I am chattering and should not be making such suggestions. Ignore my misguided advice."

"From anyone else, outside of a couple of people here, I would ignore it. But I appreciate that you—you—"

"Care enough to offer my opinion?" she smiled sweetly.

"Aye. That."

"I do care, Liam. You have all accepted me into your circle. It means the world to me."

His heart skipped a beat at her emotionally charged words. It was best to change the subject before he revealed how much he was growing to care for *her*. "You say your other friend is married to the Duke of Barnsdale?"

"Yes."

"I will escort you as soon as we can arrange it. I'll ask Drew to discover the address, and we'll go from there."

Celia smiled as she stood. "Thank you. I was told the duke was in seclusion with some illness. Selena mentioned she was ready to divorce him because he was cold and harsh. Maybe that is why she's away."

Liam scoffed. "Another miserable peerage marriage. I'm sorry about your friend."

"Me, too. When I saw her in November, she *was* quite miserable. Selena did not want to be touched. She was never like that when we attended school."

Which meant Celia's friend had probably been mistreated mentally and physically. But Liam would keep that to himself, as he did not want to distress Celia further. "Don't tell anyone working here about my family connections. I'll tell them when I'm ready."

"Of course."

Liam rose, took her elbow, and escorted her to the door. "Thank you for listening. You've given me a lot to consider." They were standing close. All Liam had to do was slip his arm about her waist and pull her near, but he resisted. Being her friend was about all he could deal with right now—or so he told himself—because he was also sorely tempted to kiss those luscious lips.

Celia gazed up at him, smiling. God, what he would give to look at her lovely face every morning next to him in bed. He abruptly stepped away. "I'll see you tomorrow morning at seven." Liam wasn't precisely aloof, but neither was his tone as warm as before.

Celia nodded. "Good night."

He stood in the doorway, watching her stride down the hallway. A flood of yearning tore through him, causing his heartbeat to speed up. He ached for her. Absolutely *ached*. When she stopped before her door, he closed his before Celia caught him looking at her longingly.

"Open your heart," she had said.

Easier said than done.

Later that week…

WILLIAM BUCKINGHAM, THE Earl of Darrington, exited his bedroom and slowly descended the stairs. It was already past ten, and he was starving. As his butler, Baldwin, approached him, William snarled, for he had no time to hear complaints about one thing or another. Not when he was famished.

"My pardon, my lord. But a visitor stopped by this past Sunday. You have not been here for me to inform you of the matter."

William had been staying at his Hampstead flat, partaking of the hired pleasures from the nearby brothel. "Make it quick, man. The ham steaks are calling to me."

"Mr. Liam Hallahan came to collect a gaming debt. The viscount refused to pay. Mr. Hallahan asked me to mention it to you as he wants to discuss the 240 pounds owed. He also wishes to discuss the Countess of Winterwood. I have his card, my lord. He says he will be here this coming Sunday afternoon."

Blast it. William had initially thought Troy's debt scheme a lark, but now the chickens had come home to roost. "Very well, I have received the message." William strode away before Baldwin kept him any longer.

William entered the dining room to find his sluggard son eating breakfast at the table. "It's not noon yet. Why are you up? And if you value your life, there better be ham left!"

"I wanted to talk to you," Troy said, his mouth filled with

food. "I did not touch your precious ham."

William lifted the covers from the chafing dishes and began filling his plate with eggs, ham, and sausage. "About Hallahan, I suppose? Baldwin just informed me that he came by. Settle the blasted debt. You have received your monthly stipend. See it done."

"I'm not paying that odious Irishman anything," Troy said, popping another piece of bacon in his mouth. "He can send his bullyboy if he wants, but he'll not get a penny from me."

William rolled his eyes as he sat, and a footman came to his side to pour the tea. "Sean, leave us. We are not to be disturbed." The footman bowed and closed the door behind him.

William cut into his ham, stuffed it in his mouth, and chewed. "I'll not have bill collectors at my door. I have warned you of this. You said you would cease the gambling. How many other debts are there?"

"I *have* quit. I told you," Troy whined. "It's just this debt."

"Then. Pay. It."

Troy crossed his arms. "No. I won't."

William rolled his eyes in exasperation. The boy was thirty-three but still acted like a petulant child in short trousers. "I have reached the end of my rope with your various shenanigans. It's your fault your mother swanned off on a winter holiday. You were at the core of all our arguments through the years. She said I indulged you and allowed your reprehensible behavior, especially when you were fifteen, and caught with a maid *and* the stable boy!"

William slammed his fist on the table. "This devil-may-care lifestyle is at its end. If you do not pick a suitable bride and are not married by the end of the summer, I will make your life a living hell, starting with cutting off your allowance and throwing you to the cobbles. You may inherit the earldom someday, but I will ensure you inherit as little as possible. This townhouse is in your mother's name; I can sell it to keep it out of your hands. As for the investments, they are well hidden. You will never reap the benefits. All you will inherit is the title and the country home. You will have nothing to live on. Mark my words."

Troy's eyes narrowed. "All this over some petty gaming debt?"

"Clean out your ears, boy. It is the final straw. You will accept responsibility and find a wife, or I will select one for you. I need an heir to carry on the title. It's time for you to fulfill your destiny. I never should have allowed you to drag Celia to that Irishman's place of business. I did it in a fit of peevishness. That episode will be one more thing your mother will hold over me."

"You want me to pick a bride? Fine. I pick Celia. She's a tasty dish." Troy gave him a smug look.

"She is your cousin," William thundered.

"Cousins are allowed to marry. It's not illegal."

"Leave it to you to know of that particular legal tidbit. Your obsession with your cousin is unhealthy. Why do you think she was sent away to school? You couldn't keep your blasted hands off her!" William exhaled. "And she's barren. Ten years married to Winterwood and not an heir in sight. Forget her. Select someone else. You know what? Forget it. *I* will pick the lady. I may have to bribe the bride-to-be's father, but there are enough peers mired in considerable debt to sell me their virgin daughter. You will be married by the summer. Once you get her with child and she bears a son, you can live your life as you please."

Troy snarled, clearly agitated.

William cut his sausage and popped a piece into his mouth. "Now that is settled, tell me about Hallahan's visit and what was said."

"He threatened me. First, over the debt, then he had the gall to lay hands on me when I called Celia a bitch. And she is! She sent that muscle-bound Irishman to collect her trunks. That weasel butler allowed the footmen to take them to a waiting carriage. The gig was fancy, too, with a coat of arms on the door."

William stopped in mid-chew. "A peerage carriage?" What

the devil was Hallahan doing with an aristocrat's conveyance? "Was he alone?"

"A fair-haired man with spectacles assisted the footmen in securing the trunks. I had never seen him before. Hallahan said he and his ex-boxer bully would be here next Sunday to collect."

"Did he, indeed?" William murmured as he sipped his tea. "Leave it with me."

"No. Hallahan insulted me. He must be made—"

"Do *not* interfere. You will stay out of this if you want to become more involved in my illegal smuggling businesses." William picked up his knife and waved it at his son. "Agree to the marriage, and I will make you my partner. Then, you can make real money. *Your* money. Forget revenge. It is a useless diversion."

William continued eating while casting glances at his brooding, stubborn son. Troy would not let this go. So William would use this as a test to see if Troy could finally grow up and accept responsibility.

Somehow, William doubted it.

CHAPTER TWELVE

SINCE IT WAS Thursday, Doctor Drew Hornsby arrived to offer medical care to the unfortunates lined up to receive free stew. Celia slipped on her woolen coat, scarf, and fur-lined gloves and hurried toward the doctor with a hot mug of tea. It was cold today, and many people standing in line shivered from the brisk breeze.

"Doctor Hornsby, I've brought you tea and a bag of ginger biscuits to hand out to your patients. Can I assist you for a while? Liam said I could."

"Yes, of course. Thank you." He took the offered mug and took a sip. "Have a seat next to me. It is bitterly cold, and because of it, I will be swift in my assessments today. Hand the patient a piece of paper from the pile before you. It lists the names and locations of the free clinics my family supports. That's if they want the paper—many cannot read. There is also a crate of used winter boots for children. If I point to the box, have a child select a pair. We don't have time for them to try on various pairs. Just judge by the size of their feet. I also have woolen socks for the adults. Give each one a pair."

"Yes, doctor."

"We also need to take a count of everyone we serve. Will you do that?" When Celia nodded, he added, "Use the pencil and paper before you."

Celia was shocked at the state of the individuals in the line:

threadbare clothes, improper footwear for the weather, and a look of weariness borne from ceaseless poverty. Celia silently thanked Providence that Liam had taken her in, or she would have been in this exact predicament. It also made her admire Liam and Drew for doing what they could to aid those who needed it most.

In under an hour, the crowd had dissipated. "Fifty-four patients, doctor."

"Thank you for the assistance, my lady."

"Please, call me Celia. I just discovered the baroness nurse who assisted you is one of the friends I hoped to make contact with."

"Corrine?"

"Yes. Liam explained she was away on her honeymoon. He also told me in confidence of your blood connection with each other and Corrine's new husband."

The doctor pushed his gold spectacles up his nose. "Indeed? Liam told you this? How interesting."

Celia smiled. "Because he does not often reveal personal aspects or let people close?"

Doctor Hornsby's mouth quirked with amusement. "Yes, exactly that."

"Doctor Hornsby, I have another friend. We were together at school with Corrine. Her name is Selena Seaton, and she is married to Lombard Woodhouse, the Duke of Barnsdale. I need to find her, and Liam thought you might be able to help. I was told that Selena is away and the duke is ill, but I do not believe the source. Liam said he would ask you if you know the address."

He stood and gently took her arm. "I haven't seen Liam today. Come, let us head inside where it is warm. And call me Drew." He escorted her through the rear door. "Lads," Drew said to the boys, chopping onions and carrots. "If you could, please place the boots, socks, and other boxes in the shed, lock it, and return the key to me. Thank you." Drew held out a key, and Tommy took it and hurried outside.

"Liam," Drew called out. "May we use your office for a moment?"

Liam turned from the oven where he was basting a large turkey. "Aye. Go on."

Celia loved roast turkey, and the odor of sage, meat, and onion filled the air. Fiona stood at the preparation table, trussing two more turkeys for roasting. This was a wise choice for a main dish, as leftover turkey could make several other dishes, including sandwiches—or so Celia had just learned.

Once inside Liam's small office, Drew and Celia took their seats. Tommy came in with the key and gave it to Drew, and Timmy was right behind him with mugs of tea. Left alone, Drew unwound the wool scarf from around his neck.

"I was called to the Duke of Barnsdale's residence last year. April, I believe it was. The duke stated that his wife had fallen down the stairs. I have been practicing medicine long enough, and have dealt with patients from all walks of life and economic spheres to understand that 'falling down the stairs' is often a euphemism for physical abuse."

Celia gasped, her hand flying to her mouth in shock. "I-I-I wondered. Oh, how awful. I haven't seen my friends since school—well over a decade. We met at your aunt's tea party at the end of this past November. Selena was distant, not like herself at all. Corrine and I knew something was wrong. Corrine came right out and asked if Barnsdale had hurt her. Selena said if he laid his hands on her again, she would shoot him. Here." Celia pointed to her forehead, right between the eyes.

Drew shook his head sadly. "Mistreatment is common, even among the elite of society. I asked the duke if I could contact her doctor. Barnsdale said they didn't have one, which is rare among the peerage. All wealthy families have a physician or two on retainer. To me, it explained more than I cared to know. Abusive men often use different doctors after each episode, so there is no discernable pattern of the beatings. The duchess said it only happened once, and I believed her." Drew sipped his tea.

"Barnsdale was clever; he did not touch her face, but there were a few bruises on her torso. She told me that he kicked her."

"Oh, my God," Celia cried, tears welling. "And there was nothing you could do."

"No. When Barnsdale left us alone, I asked the duchess if she wished me to take her to her family or call the police. She gave me an emphatic no. I slipped her my card, but she never contacted me."

"Selena is estranged from her parents. They'd pushed her to marry Barnsdale even when we were still in finishing school." Celia could not believe this, or maybe she could. How astounding that she and her two friends had terrible marriages, although in dissimilar ways. "What would have transpired if you called in the police?"

"Because Barnsdale is a duke—nothing. Even if he weren't a duke, there are no legal ramifications for any man who beats his wife. However, since '78, a wife can obtain a legal separation from an abusive husband, but it's not easy. There is a bylaw in London saying a man cannot beat his wife between the hours of ten at night and seven in the morning because it keeps the neighbors awake."

"I had no idea the bylaw existed. That is horrendous!"

"Laws are made by, and for, men."

Celia shook her head. "Unfortunately, true. Of all the patients you see, you remembered Selena."

"The duchess is not easy to forget."

Celia gave Drew a sad smile. "She is quite beautiful." She sobered. "How frustrating that nothing can be done about such horrid men. As a doctor, you must witness terrible things."

"I do. The ones I cannot help haunt me. Including the duchess," Drew replied grimly.

"I must go to her. Do you remember the address?"

"I do. You say the duke is ill?"

Celia nodded.

"Allow me to go to the residence first," Drew offered. "Since I was there before in a medical capacity, I might be able to gain entry. I will discover all that I can. I'll return at six and join you and Liam for supper. Is that satisfactory?"

Celia sprang from her seat and threw her arms around Drew's neck, knocking his spectacles askew. "Thank you!" She jumped back. "Oh, I am sorry!"

Drew chuckled as he straightened his eyeglasses. "Quite all right. No harm done." Drew stood and picked up his bag and the mug of tea. "I'll return the cup at supper."

"Wait! I can make you a sandwich to take with you. I have become quite adept at it these past few days." Celia ran from the office before Drew could refuse. She pulled the egg salad container from the icebox, made the sandwich, wrapped it in parchment paper, and returned it to Drew in minutes. "There. Something to eat as you travel. Roast turkey dinner tonight. I will see you at six."

Drew tucked the sandwich into his bag. "I am off to investigate."

Celia followed him through the rear door and onto the walkway. He flagged a hansom cab and waved to Celia before he climbed in. She waved in return and watched the cab disappear around the corner.

⇥⟫⟩⟨⟪⇤

BETWEEN THE RUSH of customers, Celia kept watching the regulator clock in the kitchen, anxious for Drew's return. There wasn't much call for tea items this afternoon, so Celia assisted in filling the plates with food and learning Liam's system of keeping track of what orders belonged to what tables. The orders were completed by half past five, and the doors were locked to transition to the pub and gaming room for the seven o'clock reopening. Everyone had eaten and cleaned the dining area, washed the dishes, prepared the beer barrels, and ensured the few liquors they had available were plentiful. Tonight, they would also offer canapes that arrived this morning from a marquess's dinner party.

Drew strode through the rear entrance, and Liam pointed to the staff dining room door, then handed her two plates. "For yourself and the doctor. I'll be right behind you."

Celia entered the room and placed the full platter before Drew.

"Well, this is quite the meal. Like Christmas dinner." He looked at Celia and smiled. "Thank you."

"It does smell and look wonderful," Celia agreed. "I never celebrated Christmas last month. My husband was too ill. So this is very welcome indeed." With the three of them seated and the door closed to give them privacy, Celia turned to Drew. "I cannot wait. What did you discover?"

"I will endeavor to explain between bites." Drew sliced his turkey. "The residence is on Chapel Street, in Belgravia, with the usual grand terraces and stucco design. The butler, Yarrow, answered the door. Hoping the information you were given was correct, I told Yarrow that the duchess had been in touch and asked me to check in on the duke. I was ready to have the door slammed in my face."

"Did he?" Celia asked.

"No. He looked surprised by my news. 'You heard from the duchess? How is she? When is she coming home?' that sort of thing. I asked, 'When did she leave?' Yarrow claims she disappeared in the middle of the night with a few valises on December 4th. She has not been seen or heard from since. I told Yarrow that I had received a telegraph two days ago. Yarrow asked to see it, and I said I did not keep it as I assumed it came from the Chapel Street address."

Celia looked from Drew to Liam. "Leave? In the middle of the night? I wonder why, besides the obvious reason?"

"I may know the answer," Drew replied solemnly. "When I was called in last year, the duke wanted me to sign papers so he could start the procedure of committing the duchess to an asylum. I refused. We were alone briefly, and I told her of his plan."

Celia's hand flew to her mouth. "Oh, no!"

"Jaysus," Liam muttered. "Can a wife be placed in an asylum at her husband's word?"

"It has been more difficult since a recent law passed. You need more than two doctors' signatures now. I told Barnsdale this. He did not like what I had to say."

"What happened next?" Celia asked, caught up in the narrative.

"Yarrow escorted me to the duke's room. A medical professional can tell when someone is dying. I would say the duke is in the middle stage. He was bedridden, and foul air permeated his room. He had lost weight since I last saw him, and his skin was blotchy. The cough he had in April is considerably worse, as well. I am guessing it's cancer of the lungs. The duke did not acknowledge my presence as he drifted in and out of consciousness."

Drew sighed. "How much time does Barnsdale have left? It differs with each person. Two months. Maybe less, or perhaps a bit more. After my obligatory examination, I instructed Yarrow to hire a live-in nurse to make his last days comfortable. I also left new aspirin powder to assist with any pain and a prescription for laudanum. Will the butler do so? That is up to him. He said the duke and duchess had no children and I did not ask about other family members."

"Bloody hell," Liam muttered. "Rich or poor, chances are you wind up dying alone."

"It happens to some, perhaps more than we know, I am sorry to say," Drew replied."

"I will never find Selena in this populous city," Celia remarked sadly. "If she is even still in London."

"I feel your friend will make herself known once the duke dies. I know that doesn't assist you in the short term," Liam replied. "As I said, you can stay here, however long it takes. You have a purpose here—and a home."

Emotion swelled through Celia. She laid one hand on top of Liam's and one on top of Drew's. "Thank you, both of you. You have saved me from a terrible plight. My dear friends."

Celia meant it. Regardless of their horrid duke sire, these were the two most honorable and generous men she had ever met. In Liam's case, her feelings were growing beyond friendship. She was not sure if Liam reciprocated her growing feelings, but she was content with their current relationship.

She admired Liam's kindness and strength and found herself drawn to him in a way she had never experienced before. He was often hard to read. Could there be something lasting between them? How could she feel such intensity on such a brief acquaintance?

Celia would puzzle it out one way or the other.

CHAPTER THIRTEEN

B Y SIX O'CLOCK Saturday night, Celia looked as tired as Liam felt. It had been her first week of work, and Liam was proud of the job she had done. She managed to keep up with the more experienced workers with only minor missteps. He located her in the staff dining room, scrubbing the table.

"Celia, enough for tonight. We have tomorrow to do the cleaning."

She dropped into the chair and exhaled. "I cannot believe how fast the week went."

"Time goes by swiftly when one is busy." Liam placed a crockery bowl in front of her. "I know you ate supper, but here's some pudding for you to try. It's called flummery. It's milk-soaked bread in Irish workhouses, but I've improved it by adding oats, honey, blackberries, plums, cream, and a drop or two of Irish whiskey."

"That sounds delicious," Celia smiled radiantly. "You used the crusts from the sandwiches?"

Liam would make her flummery every day to bask in her warm regard. "Aye, I did. I'll fetch the tea." Once he brought them mugs of tea, he sat opposite her at the table. Liam watched as she took her first spoonful.

Celia's eyes closed. "Oh, it's warm and delightful." She took another spoonful and then met his gaze. "If I am being too forward, tell me. Is that where you had flummery? In a workhouse?" He must have frowned, for she waved her hand. "Never mind. It's none of my concern. I'm sorry for asking."

"I don't like dredging up the past. I believe it should stay hidden so it will not interfere with the present—or the future, for that matter." Celia appeared disappointed in his firm response. No, she was not disappointed—she was hurt, although she tried to mask it. Since when did he care what anyone thought?

Since I met Celia.

"I'm not saying I'll never discuss it," Liam said softly. "It's just not easy for me. Give me time to warm up to the subject."

"I understand. Honestly, I do. Can you tell me about the restaurant? Enya mentioned it was your idea to change it into a dining room."

Talking about The Crowing Cock, he could handle. "I started learning the business when Walter Henning took me off the streets. He sent me to school in the afternoons."

Celia smiled. "Like you do with the boys."

"Aye. Walter's business was basically a chop house and pub, with a brothel upstairs."

"A brothel? Is that why the place is called The Crowing Cock?"

Liam nearly sprayed his tea across the table. He coughed and took another sip. "No. But I suppose it has a double meaning. There has been a pub on this corner lot since the mid-1700s. Back then, many taverns and coffee houses sold cock ale. The ale was made for medicinal purposes, a nourishing tonic mixed with minced, boiled game cock and spices. It supposedly helped the blood and humors or whatever they believed back then."

Celia sipped her tea. "I had no clue about the ale. When did you close the brothel?"

"Not as soon as I would have liked. I wanted to close it when Walter died, and I inherited the business. But the ladies suggested an arrangement: they would keep it open until renovations could be done."

"Your kitchen is wonderfully bright and cheery. Did you

design it?"

"Aye. I picked up a lot of ideas from books. How to lay out a floor plan for maximum efficiency."

"You are to be commended," Celia enthused.

Liam basked in the praise. "I closed the brothel six months ago. The ladies wanted a say in the business and a small cut of the profits. I agreed to their proposal."

Understanding dawned on Celia's lovely face. "Fiona and Enya?"

"Aye. Hannah, as well. I've known them since Walter took me in at age fourteen."

"You all came together for a common purpose. They mean a lot to you," Celia stated, her voice gentle.

"Aye. They were protective of me, and as I grew taller and more robust, I became protective of them. I did not want to run a low-class chop house or work in an upper-crust place where French dining was the norm. I wanted something in between. I found a cookbook at a second-hand shop called "Soyer's Shilling Cookery for the People," published in '45. The French chef Alexis Soyer was famous for introducing gas cooking and helping craft legislation to help the poor Irish during the potato famine. He even traveled to Ireland to set up a kitchen to feed needy people. He served a thousand people an hour."

"You admired him and emulated him. Cookery for the people, everyday meals, good food, and looking after those less fortunate," Celia observed.

Liam sipped his tea. "Aye, I suppose I did. The basic kitchen design? The chopping boards that slide out of the counter? I got those ideas from Soyer. Also, how to avoid excess food waste and the importance of cleanliness. I could go on."

"How fascinating. What *is* a chop house?"

"It's just what it says. They've been around since the 1690s and usually served chops, steaks, and cutlets with a vegetable or two. Many were not all that clean, and neither were the servers. Wooden tables and benches, sawdust on the floor, tankards of watery ale, usually men only and rowdy. I didn't want that."

Celia smiled. "I admire you for achieving your goal. Building and running a business the way you choose must be immensely satisfying."

Liam nodded. "It wasn't easy, and it still isn't. It's only in the past few months that everything started to gel. For example, Walter allowed a certain criminal element to hang about here. I put a stop to that."

Celia's eyes widened. "Is your business in any danger?"

"No. They were here mainly for the brothel. They've moved on to other establishments. This place became too boring, I suppose."

The door burst open, and Tommy entered the room. "Liam! The shed is on fire!"

Liam ran to the rear entrance with Celia and Tommy right behind him. He flung open the door to find a wall of flame engulfing the storage shed. "Tommy lad, run to the next street for the fire brigade. You know where it is. Hurry now."

Tommy disappeared into the alley. By now, the staff had gathered in the kitchen. Liam pointed at Bruce and his potman, Jack. "There are buckets of sand hanging behind my office. Get them now."

The men located them and handed one of them to Liam. Bruce and Jack carried the other two. Liam stepped outside, and sparks drifted in the slight breeze toward the roof of his restaurant. "Fiona! Find more buckets of anything that can hold water. Start filling them!"

Fiona grabbed Celia and a few others and left the doorway. Liam threw sand on the roiling flames, though it didn't help much. Bruce and Jack did the same. "Bruce, form a line, fill these buckets, and start the relay."

"Aye, Liam." The ex-boxer hurried away, and Liam watched helplessly as the large shed burned with almighty heat. A tall spiral of sparks reached into the night sky. What was in the shed? Fifty-pound bags of potatoes and carrots because the weather was not below freezing, as well as jars of preserves and all of Hornsby's items for the unfortunates, like boots, mittens, and the like. There were also extra pots, dishes, and other kitchen extras. Hundreds of pounds of merchandise and excess inventory. *Gone.*

With the line formed, Liam was handed a bucket of water. He emptied it and passed it along until he was given another. This continued for several minutes as he closely watched the roof overhang. Then he saw it: the corner of the roof of the restaurant was on fire.

The peal of bells clanging and the thunderous clamor of horses' hooves filled the air as two wagons pulled up by the alley. Tommy must have told them the fire was in the rear. *Good lad.* One horse-drawn wagon had an expanding ladder, and Liam pointed to the roof overhang.

The fireman nodded, giving instructions to the others. The men pushed back the crowd that had gathered near the alley entrance. On the rear of the other wagon was a mounted vertical boiler with plumes of steam coming from the top. Liam silently hoped it had a chance to build up enough pressure to allow water to be pumped at high compression.

The station officer ran toward Liam. "Stand back, if you please. We're hooking up the hoses."

"The roof—"

"We'll take care of it, sir. Please take your people to safety."

Liam moved everyone inside, and they watched out the windows. Celia came to him and took his arm, squeezing it. He looked down at her, then patted her hand assuredly since she seemed so worried. Bloody hell, *he* was concerned.

The firefighters, resplendent in their double-breasted serge tunics and brass helmets, worked with precision, extinguishing the fire in twenty minutes. But how had the fire started in the shed? Liam's confidence in the absence of any criminal element in his business was shaken. He resolved to question Fiona about the pub's regular customers and any signs of unlawful activity.

The station officer waved Liam outside, so he pulled on his

wool coat and joined the man near the smoldering wreckage of his shed. The air held a lingering, unpleasant odor of burnt potatoes, carrots, wool, and wood.

"We found this," the officer said, handing Liam a stained rag. "Smell it."

Liam held it to his nose and sniffed. The odor was faint. "Oil of some kind?"

"Exactly. I'm guessing paraffin oil. It's a popular choice as it's odorless except when exposed to high temperatures. That's what you're smelling. It was used as an accelerant. I need to report all suspicious fires to the Metropolitan Police, Mr...?"

The police? Jaysus. "Mr. Liam Hallahan."

"I'm Captain Brannigan. Let's go inside and fill out the paperwork."

"Can I open tonight?"

"There's no need to shut you down; the fire wasn't inside the establishment."

As he led the station officer towards the rear entrance, Liam's frown deepened. The fire was a cause for concern. Maybe it was the work of a criminal element. But why? It was more likely the actions of someone with a grudge against him...like a vengeful viscount settling a gaming debt by hiring thugs to start a fire? The potential danger was palpable.

SUNDAY ARRIVED, AND after breakfast in the staff dining area—where the fire was the main topic of discussion—Liam disappeared. Since it was sunny and not overly chilly, Celia decided to go for a walk and explore. Not many businesses were open on Sunday, as the law stated no one could open until one o'clock in the afternoon, so many shops and restaurants didn't bother. It was probably the reason Liam had decided to close on Sundays during the winter.

Since Celia was not familiar with the neighborhood, she located the boys. Teddy and Timmy were busy chopping vegetables for tomorrow's luncheon. She peeked into the back room where the boys slept. It was rather cramped, with a bunk bed for two and another bed opposite. It was there that she found Tommy reading a cookbook.

"Tommy, I'd like to go for a walk, but I don't know my way around. Will you escort me? I would appreciate the company."

The lad blushed as he scrambled off the bed. "Aye, miss." He grabbed his wool coat and hat off the hook by the door.

They stepped into the alley. Although it was January, the sun held some warmth. "Please call me Celia, Tommy."

"All right," he replied, slipping on a pair of woolen mittens.

"If I may offer some advice. A gentleman should walk on the side closest to the street. That way, if a carriage splashes a puddle onto the walkway, you take the brunt, not the lady."

"Oh, sorry," Tommy replied. He immediately switched sides. "We're on Chicksand Street. There's lots of shops here." He pointed across the street. "A baker, a furrier, a tailor, a drapery shop, a dress shop, some houses, and Mr. Spielman's bookshop. He has loads of used books. Do you like to read?"

"I do. I brought some books with me in my trunks. Is that where you got the cookbook you're reading, or is it one of Liam's?"

"I bought a couple of cookery books at Mr. Spielman's with my first wages," Tommy replied proudly. "The one I'm reading is about baking scones, pies, and such. I want to learn about baking *and* cooking meals. I have other books too, like pirate adventures."

"Good for you," Celia smiled. "When did you come to work at The Crowing Cock?"

"Four months ago."

And that was it. Tommy became as reluctant as his employer to talk about the past.

"Does it hurt to talk about the past, Tommy? It does for me. I lost my parents when I was ten, in a boating accident. I went to live with my aunt, but it wasn't the same. I felt so alone. I was glad when they sent me away to school. I made good friends there, like you did with Timmy and Teddy." Celia's words were empathetic, reaching out to Tommy's painful past.

"I'm sorry your parents died. So did my mum," Tommy replied quietly. "She was sick and put me in the workhouse because she couldn't look after me. Mum said she would send a note to my father, and he would come and get me. She never mentioned my father until that day. That was nearly a year and a half ago. Mum said the man didn't know about me."

"He never came?" Celia asked softly. She motioned toward a small green area at the end of the street with a few park benches. An older lady sat at one, feeding breadcrumbs to the pigeons. She and Tommy sat on the opposite side, far enough away for a private conversation.

Tommy shook his head. "Miss, I mean—Celia, will you keep a secret if I tell you something? I've never told even Timmy or Teddy."

"Yes, of course. I know we haven't known each other long, but I will certainly keep your secret."

Tommy clasped his hands in agitation. "I don't know what to do. Mum gave me his name, the man she claimed was my father. I waited at the workhouse for almost a year. But I didn't know how to find him. The workhouse wasn't a good place, but I met Timmy there, and we looked out for each other. He said we should leg it. They beat us, you see."

Celia gasped. "Oh, no."

"Timmy and me met Teddy on the streets. We did what we could to eat. We were in a bad way, sleeping in abandoned buildings and going through the rubbish for food. I'm younger than them, but they looked to me for protection because I'm taller and bigger."

"How old are you?" Celia asked, riveted by the story.

"I turned twelve on December 5th. Unlike Teddy and Timmy,

I knew my birthday and had some schooling. Mum did what she could; she worked at a dressmaker shop until she got sick. Then everything went wrong. Mum couldn't work anymore."

Holy crow. Judging by his size, Celia thought Tommy was fifteen at least. He'd lived on the streets at age eleven. How heartbreaking. "What was your mum's name?"

"Molly Clahane. My name is Tommy Clahane."

"Did you ever try to find your father after Liam took you in?"

Tommy shook his head. "No. That's the secret, you see. My mum said my father was called—Liam Hallahan. She said she would send him a note to tell him where to find me."

Celia gasped in shock. Liam? "Oh, Tommy. You haven't said anything to Liam in all this time?"

"No. At first, I was scared. He never mentioned being my father, so maybe he wasn't. Maybe the name was a—what's the word?"

"Coincidence?"

"Aye, that. I don't know how he found me, but he did. He said to come with him—that he had a job and a bed for me, but I said I wasn't leaving Timmy and Teddy behind. Liam said, 'Bring them, then.' Just like that."

Celia stared at the lad. She could see the slight resemblance: the raven black hair, clear blue eyes, and a sweet face that would someday be handsome—just like his father's. The height and solidness also spoke to a connection to Liam. If Tommy had just turned twelve, Liam would have been eighteen when he'd sired him. Fiona recently told her Liam was thirty years of age—the same as Celia. How did he find out about Tommy? And how on earth did he find Tommy in this sprawling city?

"So you're wondering if you should mention it? What do you think will happen if you do?" Celia asked, genuinely curious.

Tommy shrugged. "What if he isn't the same Liam Hallahan my mum told me about? There's lots of Irish about. If I reveal it, he might kick us to the cobbles."

Celia took Tommy's hand. "You have to know that Liam

would never do that. Look what he did with me. My dreadful cousin dropped me here without a shilling to my name. I was a stranger, but Liam allowed me to stay. He could have turned me out, but he didn't."

"That's true." Tommy nodded. "I've been coming every Thursday with Timmy and Teddy for stew for over two months. I didn't know Liam owned the place."

"Life is strange," Celia sighed. "Tommy, you should tell Liam—and right away."

"I was wondering if you could tell him. He likes you a lot, I can tell. Liam talked to you more the past two weeks than with anyone outside of Fiona. You can explain it better than me. I'm not afraid of him, not for a long time. He's been good to us. I just don't know what to say. I'm no good at explaining things."

"You explained it well enough to me."

Tommy gave her a shy smile. "You're kind and easy to talk to."

"Thank you. As you said, I've barely been here two weeks. It might not be wise for me to insert myself into something that is none of my business." Celia could hear Liam speak those very words, and he wouldn't be wrong.

"Tell him I asked you to. Please, Celia," Tommy pleaded.

"Why not go to Fiona or one of the others?"

"I like them, but I'd rather you do it."

That was quite the burden the lad placed on her. But Celia understood Tommy's reluctance to speak up, for she'd felt the same when she'd first lived with Aunt Etta and her family. Uncertainty could make a person question their feelings and actions. Assisting with this challenging situation would be one way to repay the generosity she'd been shown since she'd been hastily discarded here. Everyone had accepted her into their little family. No one more so than Liam.

"I'll talk to him tonight. I promise. Now, let's continue with our walk, and when we return, you can show me how to make scones."

Tommy smiled and threw his arms around her neck. This was Liam's son she embraced; she did not doubt it. The adorable gesture caused a lump in her throat. Her conversation with Liam later tonight would be interesting, to say the least.

CHAPTER FOURTEEN

LIAM LOATHED RETURNING to the Earl of Darrington's house, so he decided to collect information on the earl and his slimy son before he did. One acquaintance that Liam, unfortunately, came to know before he took over ownership of the restaurant was Lucian Sharpe. Lucian was a rookery outlaw who'd often gone to The Crowing Cock for a meal and a visit to the brothel upstairs. He was about eight years older than Liam and had lived and survived on the streets since he was nine. He had bragged to Liam once that he had many contacts with aristocrats dabbling in illegal schemes to keep their legacies and titles afloat. Liam wanted to discover if Darrington was one of the toffs in that clandestine underworld league. The earl had a corrupt look in his eye and acted too smug by half. Would Sharpe have started the fire at Darrington or even Shinwell's say so? It was entirely possible if he'd been paid enough. Or maybe the miserable aristos had hired someone else, someone Sharpe might know of. One thing he knew for certain. If Darrington or his son were behind the fire, Sharpe would know about it.

Tracking down Sharpe was a nerve-wracking task, as the man was constantly on the move. Clearances were underway in several slums where the disadvantaged gathered, including Sharpe's usual haunts in Devil's Acre around St. Ann's Lane. The late author Charles Dickens had described this area as 'The most deplorable manifestation of human wretchedness and depravity,' and it was rumored to have inspired Oliver Twist and its infamous characters. The task of finding Sharpe seemed increasingly daunting.

Since the construction of Victoria Street in 1851, which cut through the heart of Devil's Acre, the evicted population has crowded into even less available property and housing. The continued but slow clearances significantly diminished Sharpe's criminal kingdom and influence, transforming the once thriving area into a shadow of its former self.

Liam rode in the hansom cab with Bruce, marveling at the stark contrast between the notorious area of Devil's Acre and the grandeur of Westminster Abbey and the Houses of Parliament. As they turned onto Pye Street, the stench hit him like a slap in the face. This expanse was rampant with marshlands, and he could smell the fetid dampness mixed with odors from the gasworks. Dirty, barefoot children dressed in rags stood on the street corners, staring at him with suspicious eyes. He swallowed hard. Liam had once been one of those children.

Construction was everywhere. Old tenements were being torn down, and new buildings were being erected. It seemed to Liam that Sharpe was king over a pile of rubble. But there were still enough grimy dark alleys, courtyards, and side streets for him to lord over. But for how long? Liam guessed Sharpe had a couple of years—if that. The cab turned onto Duck Lane, and when Finnian's Chop House came into view, Liam pounded on the roof.

"Bruce, stay with the cab. I won't be long." Liam exited and closed the folding doors. Then he stuck his hand in his pocket, keeping it firm on his money folder—not that he carried that much.

He stepped across the threshold into another era, just as he had described to Celia, down to the wooden tables and benches and sawdust on the floor. The lighting comprised of oil lamps, tallow candles, and two gas sconces on the wall. A fire crackled in the ancient hearth in the corner. The dubious odor of frying onions and old meat filled his nostrils.

Scanning the cramped pub, Liam located Lucian Sharpe sitting in the darkened corner near the fire. Sharpe could see the entire tavern from his vantage point, including those who walked through the doors. Sharpe looked like a feral alley cat, ready to pounce on his prey.

A man as wide and solid as an oak tree stepped before him. "And who are you, then?"

"Liam Hallahan. Sharpe knows me."

The man turned and looked at Sharpe, who gave a quick nod. As Liam stepped forward, the bullyboy laid his hand on Liam's chest, effectively stopping him. "I've got to search you, yeah?"

"Then have at it," Liam growled. Still holding his wallet, he raised his arms partway to allow the man to do a pat down. This was an intriguing new layer of security. With the search completed, Liam walked over to stand before Sharpe's table.

"Hallahan. I never expected to see you again since you banished me from your place of business. And you didn't bring me any stew? I'm insulted." Sharpe smiled with a cruel twist to his lips. Lucian Sharpe might be a product of the streets, but he didn't look it. Besides the clean, straight teeth, he wore an expensive suit, though it was garish, with a bold black and tan plaid pattern. His left knuckle had a fresh tattoo, but Liam couldn't distinguish what it was from this distance.

"I'll send a pot tomorrow. It wasn't ready before I left."

"How's Junie?"

Lucian Sharpe had come around The Crowing Cock to see June on numerous occasions, and she'd confided to Liam that Sharpe had tried to convince her to come to live with him.

"June married and left England some months ago."

The only reaction was a slight twitch of his mouth. "Sit there and speak your piece," Sharpe said, pointing to a chair directly in front of him.

Liam took his seat. "There's lots of activity outside. Where will you go once the last remaining streets are cleared?"

"What's it to you? I'll find a place. There's always business to be done."

"True enough. Speaking of business, I came to ask if you do any commerce with the Earl of Darrington or Viscount Shinwell."

Sharpe snorted. "Billy Buck? Aye, plenty of business. Why?"

Billy Buck. Interesting. "His son owes me a gaming debt. I want to know what I'm up against before I stick my nose in to collect."

"Billy Buck is rich enough to pay. Don't let him give you any excuses. He's paid Shinwell's debts for years, some in the thousands of pounds. If old Billy hadn't been born on the right side of the blanket, I swear he'd be one of the most notorious gangsters in London town. Does he keep his word? Mostly, especially if he can profit from it. His son, on the other hand, is a sniveling toad."

Liam nodded. He knew that for a fact. "I had a fire at my place, in the storage shed."

"And? You think Billy Buck is behind it?"

"Or his son. I wondered if you'd heard anything, or know of anyone who'll start fires for a price."

Sharpe shrugged. "I wouldn't put it past Billy Buck or his spawn. But I've heard nothing."

Sharpe probably knew a number of arsonists, but he wasn't about to tell Liam. Criminal types tended to cover for each other.

A man rushed to the table. "Guv, we lost the Golden Angel. She dodged us."

Sharpe banged the table with his fist. "Try again tomorrow. And don't fail!"

The man hurried away.

"I've got a do-gooder lady in my midst," Sharpe announced.

"What's the harm in that? I wish I'd had a do-gooder in my patch when I was growing up."

"Aye, me and all. But it's interfering with my business. Let her do her good works in another rookery."

"'No one is useless in this world who lightens the burdens of another,'" Liam said.

"*Our Mutual Friend*, Charles Dickens," Sharpe replied. "It's actually 'lightens the burden of it for anyone else.' Don't look so bloody shocked. I taught myself to read, same as you."

"Leave her be. What's the angel doing, depleting your prospects of pickpockets and prostitutes?"

Sharpe's eyes narrowed. "It's none of your concern. I'll find her, make no mistake. Anything else?"

Liam stood. "No. Thanks."

"Don't forget that stew. I want it here at this table tomorrow at noon." Sharpe tapped the table. "It's payment for the information."

"I'll send along one of my boys. Let him deliver the stew and leave him be, yeah?" Sharpe was always trying to recruit youngsters for pickpockets and such. Liam had no doubt guessed why Sharpe was annoyed at the charity lady. The worse off people were, the more they were willing to turn to crime to keep bread on the table.

Sharpe nodded, then turned to speak to one of the men sitting next to him, effectively dismissing Liam. Liam departed, and after he gave directions to the driver, he climbed into the cab. During the journey to Darrington's, Liam formulated a plan.

When the hansom arrived at the earl's, Liam paid the driver. "Bruce, stay next to me, but don't speak, yeah?"

"Right, Liam," the hulking ex-boxer replied.

After ringing the bell, the butler stepped aside to allow them to enter. "The earl awaits you in his study. This way."

The room seemed strangely devoid of books, but maybe that was because he'd seen the Hornsbys' studies, which were filled with various tomes. It proved that reading was not on Darrington's or Shinwell's priority lists.

"Mr. Hallahan and friend, my lord," Baldwin announced.

"Sit, or will you stand?" the earl asked. Liam glanced at the leather sofa. Shinwell laid indolently across it, looking bored.

Liam grabbed a padded wooden chair and placed it strategically where he could see both men. Once he sat, Bruce stood beside him, arms folded. "I'm here to make a proposal concerning the 240 pounds owed. I am willing to forego the debt—for a price."

Darrington's bushy gray eyebrows shot skyward. The earl hadn't been expecting that. "A proposal? Of what, exactly?"

"The address of where Countess Darrington is staying. Also, the money he—" Liam pointed at Shinwell, "—stole from Celia and fifty pounds more for the stress caused."

"That is all?"

Liam snorted. "Should I ask for more, my lord?"

"Why would you do this for Celia? Has she bewitched you somehow?" Darrington asked. "She's not *that* beautiful."

Liam snarled. "Do not disparage her again. Not in my presence."

Shinwell laughed mockingly. "By God, he's cunny struck!"

Liam leaped from his chair so fast, it tumbled across the carpet. He punched Shinwell square in the face, catching his eye more than his nose. Shinwell cried out.

"Enough!" Darrington thundered, coming to his feet, which wasn't easy considering his girth. "You!" The earl pointed at Bruce. "Get him under control, or there will be no deal!"

Liam pulled back his arm to punch Shinwell again, but Bruce's massive hand closed over his fist. They locked gazes, and Bruce shook his head and mouthed, 'Stand down.'

Seething, Liam returned to his seat. He had already lost control of the situation. That was on him.

Darrington pointed to his son. "You, keep it shut. There will be no more outbursts."

Shinwell held his hand over his right eye and glowered at Liam. Liam grumbled in response. Bloody hell, he despised this family—especially the son—after Celia had confided about her past living in this house.

"Everyone settle down," Darrington admonished as he sat. "Now, as to your proposal, I will give you the address, the money he stole, and 20 pounds."

"45."

"25," Darrington responded.

"35, and it is done."

"I agree."

"One more thing. My shed was deliberately set ablaze last night. Did you have anything to do with it?"

Darrington looked genuinely surprised. "No. I did not." The earl's gaze slid to Shinwell. "Troy?"

"Burning a shed?" Shinwell scoffed. "I have better things to do on a Saturday night."

Liam's eyes narrowed. "If the address you give me is fake, or anything else untoward happens to my business or the people who work for me, this deal is null and void. The full amount will be due again with interest. And I will collect. Mark my words. *Billy Buck.*"

Darrington smiled slyly. "How crafty of you. We must have mutual acquaintances. I can respect that."

"The fire brigade reported the arson to the Met Police. They asked me for names of suspects." Liam inclined his head toward Shinwell. "I'll give the peelers *his* name if the deal is broken in any way. This is not a threat, just a statement of fact."

The earl pursed his lips. "You have made your point. We can do business." Darrington opened his desk drawer, grabbed his pen, dipped it in the inkwell, and then scribbled something on paper. "My wife's address. I cannot guarantee she will be there now, as she is traveling. But she will return to this address before she comes home. I tell you this to make you understand a reply may not be imminent."

"Fine."

Darrington reached into his bottom desk drawer and brought forth a money box. He opened it and counted out pound notes. "Thirty-five pounds plus the five pounds he took. I rounded up." The earl slid the money and the piece of paper across the desk. "Do I need a receipt drawn up?"

"Aye. Just write out the transaction, and we'll sign it. One copy for me, one for you. My acquaintance said your word on the streets is reliable enough."

"Did he?" Darrington pulled out two pieces of paper and hastily wrote on them. "Come here and sign the papers."

Liam came to stand beside Darrington and bent to write his name.

"Listen closely," Darrington whispered. "I could take the knife from my drawer and pin your hand to the desk. Try stirring a pot of soup with a permanently injured hand. It can't be done. However, I won't—not this time. Do not come near me and mine ever again."

Liam continued to write his name on the second sheet of paper. "And that goes for me," Liam murmured menacingly. "Keep your toad of a son from my property; he's banned. If I see him, I will not be responsible for my actions—or Bruce's. We don't want to take a war to the streets."

Liam stood upright, grabbed the papers and the money, and turned to leave.

"Then we understand each other!" the earl called out.

Liam gave a mocking bow. "Perfectly!" He motioned to Bruce. "Come on. I need a breath of fresh air."

Once outside, Liam smiled. Yes, he did not collect the total amount owed, but in his mind, he came out ahead. He could just imagine Celia's joy at being able to contact her aunt.

And he would do anything for Celia. *Anything.*

"YOU DID IT, the fire?" William roared.

Troy shrugged. "I told the truth. I would never stoop to start a fire. On the other hand, did I hire a couple of dodgy lads to do it? Now *that* is the question."

William scrubbed his hand down his face in exasperation.

What in hell was he going to do with this boy? "I have made a deal, one to my advantage monetarily speaking, and I don't want it spiked. Hallahan has connections on the street and within the aristocracy. I discovered that the fair-haired spectacled bloke with him last week is the nephew of the Duke of Gransford and son to Viscount Hawkestone. Gransford is a powerful man, the family is close to the queen, and Hawkestone runs an influential progressive group within the House of Lords. I do not need that kind of scrutiny."

"So what?"

"By God, you're thick. No one can know of my double life, which could ruin me financially and in society. And with Hallahan's connections on the streets, the last thing I need is a war between rookery bosses. Stay away from Hallahan, his business, and your cousin!"

"And I am allowed to let this stand? He hit me!" Troy whined.

"To hell with waiting until summer to arrange a marriage for you. You will be wedded by next month. I will find a strong-willed young lady to keep you in line. Your days and nights of running the streets are over. Grow up." William had just the lady in mind—the daughter of an acquaintance. Mr. Silas Foster was an American steel magnate, and was in London on business. William had heard that the daughter had traveled with him, and was looking for a husband. He would contact Foster right away and broach the subject.

"And if you jeopardize this deal, I will cut you off," William continued. "Your mother will be livid when she hears what you did, dragging Celia to that pub owner. I should have discovered where in Spitalfields you took her and brought her back here the next day. What a blasted mess."

Troy scoffed. "But you did *not* bring her back, not that she would have come. You were glad to be rid of her, admit it. And you won't toss me out. You need me to produce an heir. Keep pushing me, Father, and I will make sure there is never an heir to carry on the title. Remember that. You may force me to wed, but the wife? I will never bed her. Push me too far, and I will ensure there are no children. None at all."

William glared at Troy with a mixture of admiration and revulsion. The boy possessed a backbone when the moment called for it, but William loathed being threatened—first by Hallahan and now by his only son.

"Stay away from Spitalfields."

"No, I will not make such a promise. I will continue to do as I please. Now, I am going to the kitchen to locate a slab of meat for my eye. Then I will return, and we will discuss prospective brides." Troy stood and exited the room.

William slumped in his chair. Troy would exact some form of revenge, and he could not stop it. He should never have let it be known that he yearned for an heir—that shifted the power to his son. Perhaps he was getting too old for this game. Should he warn Hallahan?

No. He'd let the chips fall where they might.

CHAPTER FIFTEEN

L IAM ARRIVED HOME shortly after four in the afternoon. Celia had waited all day for his return. Thankfully, making the scones had taken up part of the time, and they'd turned out lovely. When she learned Liam had gone to his rooms, she swiftly prepared a tray with tea and scones and took them up to him. As she entered the hall, she again pondered how to broach the sensitive subject of Tommy.

Celia knocked on the door, and Liam flung it open.

"Hello. I hope you don't mind. I have brought scones and tea. Tommy and I made them."

He stood aside. "Come in."

Celia entered and placed the tray on the table. After removing her coat, she poured the tea, passed him the mug, and then poured a cup for herself and sat on the sofa across from his chair. "I think they taste fine for a first attempt. We added currants and cinnamon."

"I have something for you," Liam said as he sipped his tea. He pointed to an envelope on the table. "That is yours. It's the five pounds your cousin stole from you plus thirty-five more for your trouble."

Celia's heart sank like a stone tossed into a lake. Liam wanted to be rid of her. All her nightly dreams and imaginings that something profound had grown between them... Had it just been her overwrought imagination? She'd believed that sparks danced all around them when they touched. But then, what did she expect? They had only known each other for two weeks. This was not some grand romance. "Darrington paid Shinwell's debt?"

"No, not exactly."

Celia's eyebrows furrowed. "I do not understand."

"I made a deal with Darrington. I would forgo the gaming debt owed me in exchange for payment for what your cousin stole and the negotiated thirty-five pounds. I also got your aunt's address in Italy."

Celia blinked rapidly, trying to take in what he said. "You did that for me? Why? You left close to two hundred pounds on the table."

"You deserved justice. This was the best way to see it done."

"Is that the only reason?" Celia whispered.

"No. You're a fine lady—a dowager countess—and should not be toiling in a kitchen for a few shillings a week."

"What if I told you I felt more alive these past two weeks than I have in the past several years? Before I arrived here, I had been shunted around and made to feel invisible from the moment my parents died. And my marriage to Winterwood was a barren expanse of nothingness. The age difference between us negated any reflective conversation or shared amusements. Oh, we formed a polite friendship, I suppose. But as far as intimate relations? Perfunctory and swift, for the possible making of an heir—"

Liam held up his hand. "You don't have to tell me any of this."

Celia knew she was prattling, but she had to get this out. "I must. For five years, I tolerated his weekly visits to my bed. It was—I do not know how to explain it. If that is my total understanding of what intimacy exists between a man and a woman, then I never want to experience it again. It left me feeling more alone than ever. Is it always like that?" The words poured out of her. Celia couldn't stop them.

Liam shook his head. "No. It's not like that, not with the right partner. It can be mutually enjoyable."

"That is your experience?"

"Yes, for the most part. I hear it's even more intense when love plays a role. I wouldn't know about that. I'm sorry you did not take any pleasure or were given any. No young woman of nineteen should be married off to a doddering fifty-five-year-old."

"No, she should not. But it happens far too often, especially in the aristocracy. I tell you this to show how much I enjoy being here on *my* terms and how it has given *me* purpose. Thank you for the money, but I will not move to Drew's empty flat. Unless you want me to go."

Liam looked down at his hands, and Celia's heart sank deeper as she waited for his reply. If he asked her to leave, that would be the end of it. With forty pounds, she could find a suitable place to rent a room until she located her friends or her aunt returned. She would mail a letter as soon as possible and inform Aunt Etta of everything that had transpired. Celia would never return to the Darrington residence, not even for her aunt, but it was past time she and her aunt reconciled.

Liam exhaled, then looked up and caught her gaze. His eyes darkened with emotional intensity. "I don't want you to go. I've never felt like this before. I can't even explain what I feel. Everything is jumbled inside of me. I'm revealing too much, but I don't want to lie—not to you. All I know is I want *you* to be happy."

Celia's eyes shimmered, and her heart thundered with powerful emotions. "Thank you for being truthful. I will also speak the truth. I am happy *here*. It already feels like home. Why would I want to leave? I have not had a home or people who care for me since my parents died. And I have never felt like this before, either."

He gave her a sad half-smile. "We must be practical. There can be nothing permanent between us. You're a countess, a daughter of a baronet, and not of my class."

"I do not accept that. Corrine and her police detective have made it work," Celia said firmly.

"Mitchell was raised by loving parents and given a good home in a middle-class neighborhood. Drew was raised in the aristocracy. You don't want to know of my past and what I did to survive," Liam growled.

"I *do* want to know."

Liam sighed and looked toward the window. Light snow flurries tumbled from the sky. "I was raised in grinding poverty. My mother and I moved constantly from one dingy room to another. From ages six to eight, I was a pickpocket. From the age of eight until I was eleven, I worked as a house thief. Dodgy blokes often use youngsters because they are small and can climb through windows. Often in the early morning, servants open windows to air rooms out. I grabbed anything I could get my hands on, such as silver spoons, snuff boxes, or whatever could fit in my pockets."

"Oh, Liam," Celia whispered. "That must have been frightening."

He nodded, then met her gaze again. Celia could see the recollections caused pain. "I was good at it until I started growing. Then I moved into attic thievery. I'd wait until the family and servants were having dinner below stairs, climb in, then make my way to the family bedrooms, grabbing jewelry and the like. My cut from these jobs kept my mother and me in a couple of rooms. We were able to eat meat at least once a week."

"Then your mother got sick."

Liam nodded. "I didn't stick around to have the duke's rat locate me."

"Who was the duke's rat?" Celia asked softly.

"He was Chellenham's man. He came a few times and gave my mother coins for my upkeep. For a while, I wondered if that muscle-bound bloke was my father. Then he offered to buy me. After that, my mother and I left the Seven Dials and crossed the Thames into Spitalfields. I found out from Drew that Chellenham sold children, his own included, for profit. Anyway, after my mother died, I spent the next two years doing what I could survive: pickpocketing, robbery, and digging through rubbish to find edible food. That is where Walter Henning found me, nibbling on a piece of stale bread beside his shed."

Her heart throbbed with empathy for him. "Mere words cannot express the depth of my sorrow for what you have endured. I would never hold your past against you. The strength you've shown in surviving surpasses all. Where did you receive your schooling?"

"I went to a ragged school in the Seven Dials until we left. Once Walter took me in, he sent me to school in the afternoons. I learned how to do the books and math problems related to cooking. I also read a lot, not just about cuisine."

"I became an even more voracious reader once I married. There wasn't much else to do in Northern England. Mr. Henning made you an apprentice. Did you like him?"

"Yes," Liam murmured. "I cared about him, faults and all. He became the father I never had. Or what I imagined a father could be."

"And he loved *you*. He left you the business." She took a deep breath, then let it out slowly. "Now that you have shared your past with me, please enlighten me on why you believe it will hinder us from being—more."

LIAM'S EYELIDS FLUTTERED shut. He felt a raw vulnerability, his dark soul laid bare. He instantly regretted revealing his past. He hadn't even shared the full story with Walter. But there were some aspects he didn't dare tell Celia. She didn't need to know how he was bullied, or how the criminals had tried to coerce him into selling himself for extra coins. He'd also been the one to insist that he and his mother escape the Seven Dials; staying there had become intolerable, especially with the duke's rat sniffing around.

Could there be more between him and Celia?

At night, when he was alone, Liam indulged in fanciful dreams of Celia working alongside him in the coming years, sharing everything, as partners and lovers. But there was an even more secret aspect of his life, and he did not know how to broach the subject.

He opened his eyes and met her gaze. "Be serious. You would give up a life in the upper class to toil sun-up to sundown in an East End kitchen?"

Celia leaned forward. "If not, where do you think I will live? Even if I reconcile with my aunt, I will never live with Darrington and Shinwell. I cannot stay with my friends longterm. So, I live on forty pounds a year, renting a cheap room in the West End. How is that any better? At least here, there are people I care about. I'd have a purpose in life, and pride in a job well done."

Liam stood and headed toward the window. The sun was setting, casting red streaks across the cloudy sky. "It's only been a couple of weeks. You will soon tire of it—and me."

Celia ran to his side, grasped his arm, and pulled him to face her. "How dare you make pronouncements about what I feel! I—"

Liam leaned down and kissed her deeply, effectively cutting off her sentence. He cupped her face, laying soft kisses at the corner of her mouth, only to dive in and retake complete possession. Celia moaned and met every thrust of his tongue as she threw her arms about his neck. She tasted glorious, like a sweet dessert, which made him crave her even more. He slipped his arms to encircle her waist and pulled her close so that she could feel exactly how she moved him. Bloody hell, he ached, utterly *yearned* for her. This emotion he could name: lust, passion, desire. Liam felt it all. It was the deeper, more complicated feelings he was having difficulty with.

Celia ground against him, causing his erection to harden further. In a deft move, he swung her about until her back rested against the wall. His hands slid over the curve of her hip until he grabbed her arse and lifted her far enough from the floor to rest against his leg. She gasped, then smiled and kissed him fiercely. The room spun. The heat they created rivaled the kitchen cookers roiling at full tilt. Liam cupped her breast, his thumb brushing against her erect nipple. He trailed feverish kisses down her neck only to retake possession of her luscious mouth.

Easy, lad.

That annoying voice inside his head brought Liam back down to earth. He was moments away from losing control. This was not the time or the place. Shuddering from unspent passion, he gently lowered Celia to the floor until the toes of her boots rested on the floor. Taking a shaky step in reverse, he met her wide-eyed gaze.

Her hair was mussed, her lips swollen and well-kissed. It took all his inner strength not to kiss her senseless again, tunnelling his hand under her wool skirt until he found wetness at her feminine core. And he knew instinctively she was wet for him. Oh, how he wanted to make her come apart in his arms. Over and over again. The depth and breadth of his desire stunned him.

"Why did you stop?" Celia rasped.

"I wish I knew, lass."

Celia cleared her throat. "It's overwhelming, isn't it?"

He leaned in, took a stray tendril of her golden-brown hair, and tucked it behind her ear. "Aye. That's the truth."

She clasped his hand, and the contact sent his heart racing. Celia kissed each knuckle tenderly. "You think we should not rush into anything," she murmured sensually.

Liam was ready to sweep her into his arms and take her to his bed. Instead, he stood stock-still, frozen. That had never happened before in his life, which proved this was beyond his experience. "Aye," he croaked.

Celia took his hand and laced her fingers with his, then looked up and caught his gaze. "Then we will not hurry. Not tonight. Come and sit on the sofa with me. I came to speak to you about something else entirely."

Could he bloody well sit? He was painfully aroused. However, he allowed Celia to pull him toward his sofa, and they sat on it.

"I have come to talk about Tommy," Celia said matter-of-factly as she turned slightly to face him.

That dampened his passion and sent his senses on full alert. "What about the lad?"

"We went for a walk this afternoon, and he confided something very personal to me. He asked me to speak to you as he wasn't sure how to approach you about such a sensitive subject. Can you guess what it is?"

Liam closed his eyes. "Aye. I believe I can. What did he tell you?"

"He says you are his father."

Liam's eyes popped open as he met her steady gaze. "What else did he say?"

Celia relayed everything Tommy had told her. His insides churned at hearing the details, and his heart ached to hear everything Tommy had gone through.

"Did you know?" Celia asked softly.

Liam shook his head. "At first? I had no idea. Molly and I were involved for less than two months. I was eighteen; what did I know about the consequences? Walter took me aside and asked if I was seeing a lass since I went out some nights and didn't come back until late. He also asked if I used protection." Liam snorted. "I hadn't. He gave me a shake and told me to grow up. If I was going to rut with the lass, I had to be a man and take responsibility. I used protection after that. You'd think I would know better, considering the way I was conceived. It showed how stupid and thoughtless I was then. Ultimately, I realized I wasn't ready for anything serious, so I ended it with Molly."

"And she never contacted you after discovering she was pregnant."

Liam shook his head. "Molly knew where I lived and worked. She never came near. And I never sought her out again, either.

Jaysus, I *am* as bad as that despicable duke who sired me."

Celia touched his arm. "Never. You were eighteen, still a lad in many ways. Walter should have spoken to you about the consequences a few years earlier. When did you find out about Tommy?"

"A woman contacted me a few months ago. She was Molly's landlady. Some of Molly's things were still there, and the landlady was cleaning them out when she found an unfinished letter tucked in an envelope. It was addressed to me. In it, Molly stated she was dying, and that she had placed Tommy in the Strand Union Workhouse. By the time I got this letter, more than a year had passed."

"Oh, no. Molly never sent the letter. How tragic," Celia murmured. "That explains why Tommy waited so long in the workhouse before he ran away."

"I journeyed to the workhouse as soon as possible. I was told Tommy left with another lad, Timmy Cagney. How would I ever find him in this city?"

Celia was utterly caught up in the narrative. "How on earth *did* you find him?"

"I tried checking various rookeries in the East End where the homeless tend to congregate. But I didn't have much luck. Then, one day, I saw three lads in the line waiting for stew. I heard the names Tommy and Timmy. It couldn't be them, I reasoned. But I followed them to an abandoned house in Bethnal Green. The building was about to be pulled down. When I came face-to-face with them, it was obvious which of the lads was Tommy. He agreed to come and work for me if he could bring the other two."

"And you've said nothing these last months?" Celia said incredulously.

Liam trailed his fingers through his hair. "I didn't know *what* to say. I wanted him to become comfortable here, to feel safe before I broached the subject."

Celia shook her head. "He's certainly your son, for he didn't know what to say, either. I'll go fetch him."

"What? No."

Celia stood and placed her hands on her hips. "Liam, Tommy knows I'm here speaking with you. He will ask me questions. Isn't it better to get this all out in the open?"

Liam's emotions were whirling—first, he'd almost lost himself in a passionate encounter with Celia and now, he had to decide how to deal with Tommy.

"Aye. Fetch him."

There was no time like the present.

CHAPTER SIXTEEN

AFTER SLIPPING ON her wool coat, Celia hurried down the rear stairs. Once inside, she peeked into the boys' room, but Tommy wasn't there. She entered the kitchen and found Tommy slicing pickles.

"What are you doing, Tommy?"

He smiled. "I thought I would get a head start on the sandwich fillings for tomorrow. I already cut up some chicken."

Celia smiled and playfully tousled his hair. "You are a fine lad. Thank you."

Tommy laid the knife on the cutting board. "Did you talk to Liam?"

"Yes, I did. Tommy, do you want a father?" Celia would not push them together if there was any chance Tommy would reject Liam outright. Both man and boy were vulnerable. She could sense it. Although, if confronted with the notion, neither would admit it.

"I think so. I never had one. Sometimes, when I felt low at the workhouse, I wondered if my mother lied about my father coming to fetch me. Maybe she didn't want me to see her die. But my mum had never lied to me before. And she wouldn't fib about something important."

"That is correct. Your mum would not tell falsehoods about this," Celia replied firmly.

"Will Liam ask—do I take his name?" Tommy asked tentatively.

"There is no rush. I'm sure the choice will be up to you. Maybe you could keep your mum's name, too."

"Oh. Like Thomas Clahane Hallahan?"

Celia smiled. "That has a nice ring to it. Get your coat, and I will take you upstairs to Liam, where you can discuss it. Do not hold anything back, Tommy. Tell Liam everything you are feeling."

"What about the pickles?"

"You can put them away later." Celia grabbed the roll of parchment paper, tore off a piece, and placed it over the food.

Tommy nodded, wiped his hands on the tea towel, then collected his coat and scarf. Once they entered the upstairs hall, Celia waved to Liam, standing before the door. They walked toward him.

"I'll leave you two to talk in peace." As she turned to go, Liam took her hand. The warmth of his touch caused her heart to speed up, as it did every time he came near.

"Please stay. Is it all right with you, Tommy?" Liam asked.

"Aye. Please, Celia?"

How could she refuse? "If you wish."

They headed into Liam's sitting room and removed their coats. Liam sat in his chair, and Celia and Tommy sat on the sofa opposite him.

"I swear, lad, I knew nothing about you. Not in all these years. Your old landlady found an unfinished letter addressed to me. By the time I received it, a year had already passed since your mum died. I went to the workhouse immediately, but they said you'd run off with a boy called Timmy Cagney."

"Oh," Tommy said softly. "That's why you didn't come. You never got the letter."

"No. According to the landlady, your mum died a few days after she placed you. Mrs. Tingley moved your mother's remaining possessions to the cellar."

"To sell them?"

Liam nodded. "Aye. For the rent owed, she said. Mrs. Tingley was going through the last of the clothing when she found the letter tucked in a pocket. Why did you run from the workhouse?"

Tommy shrugged. "I didn't like it there. There was never enough food, and a lot of hard work. And they beat us. Timmy said he was escaping, so I went with him. I was soon sorry I followed him. Living on the streets was worse."

"Aye," Liam whispered. "It is at that."

"How did you find me?"

"Fate, I suppose. Or pure luck. I looked in a few places in the East End. Then, one day, I saw three lads in the line for the free stew. I heard the names Timmy and Tommy. I followed you to Bethnal Green. When I saw you—I knew your mum was correct."

"How long did you know my mum?"

"Not long," Liam replied. "I was eighteen and unwise, but that's no excuse."

"Why didn't she tell you? About me?"

"Molly Clahane was a good woman. She must have had her reasons. Maybe she assumed I wasn't ready to be a father. And I wasn't. I still had growing up to do."

Tommy's brows furrowed. "But she could have told you later. And told me when I got older. Mum never said anything about you until she placed me at the workhouse."

"That was your mum's decision, and we must respect it, yeah?"

"Aye. I suppose you're right. Did you have a father?"

Liam shook his head. "I had an upbringing much like yours, only worse. I'll tell you about it someday. I only just found out who my father was."

"Oh," Tommy whispered. "You're a bastard like me."

"Lad, don't use that word. It's society's way of shaming those of us who came from unfortunate backgrounds."

"They called us that at the workhouse," Tommy whispered. "Whether we were or not."

"I'm sorry. Forget it, lad. You don't want to dwell on it."

"Mum told the dressmaker shop she was a widow."

"She did it so you both could have a roof over your head and food on the table. Your mother would never have been given the job at the shop if they had discovered she was unmarried with a child. Such is society's harsh and unfair judgment. Maybe someday, the government will acknowledge children born outside marriage as equals. Until then, we look out for each other."

"What happens now?" Tommy asked.

The frank discussion fascinated Celia.

"There is a room upstairs," Liam ventured. "You can move in there. It's larger than the one you're in now."

"What about Teddy and Timmy?"

"They're apprentices and will stay in the room behind the kitchen."

Tommy frowned. "Timmy looked after me in the workhouse, and when we left and met up with Teddy, Teddy protected us from the coppers, crooks, and other bad ones on the street. He found us food and places to sleep." Tommy's voice raised with each sentence. "I'll not leave them below stairs. No!"

Tommy's emotional outburst obviously surprised Liam, judging by his reaction.

"We don't have to decide on living arrangements right now," Celia offered gently. "Why not talk to Timmy and Teddy first and see what they say? Explain about Liam being your—being—"

"My father?" Tommy offered softly.

"Yes. Take your time, both of you, to adjust to this new situation." Celia blushed. "Sorry. I should not be offering my opinion."

"I don't mind," Liam replied.

"Me neither," Tommy added, quickly over his burst of anger. He swung his gaze to Liam. "Why didn't you tell me who you were in Bethnal Green when you found me?"

"Well, you were tired and sickly, and I wanted to give you time to recover and feel safe in your new surroundings. Why didn't you mention it to me, then?"

"I wasn't sure I could trust you. I wanted to see if the job you offered was real," Tommy replied quietly.

"Very wise."

"So, when can we tell everyone else?" Tommy asked.

"Whatever you want, lad," Liam said. "Talk to Timmy and Teddy first."

Tommy jumped to his feet and grabbed his coat and scarf. "I'll go tell them right away!" Then he ran from the room, slamming the door behind him.

Liam exhaled deeply, and his shoulders slumped, emotionally drained.

"You did well," Celia offered.

"Except about the room. Thank you for smoothing that over."

"It will get better. You and Tommy will become better acquainted, and in doing so, you will move your relationship from employer and apprentice to father and son. That will take time and patience. I know you can do it. And so can Tommy. He is a fine boy, you know. A credit to his mother's upbringing."

"Aye, he is. Molly did a fine job. I wish she had contacted me."

"I know." Celia stood and headed toward the door. As she turned the handle, Liam came up behind her and nuzzled her neck. "Thank you for listening. Thank you for being—a good friend," he whispered, his voice husky. Celia's insides turned to custard at the sound of his deep voice as his lips brushed across the exposed area of her neck. "And I thank Providence that you are—here."

"Y-y-you're welcome."

Celia opened the door far enough to slip through. It was best she departed, or she would be tempted to stay all night. Already, her insides fluttered like mad. She rushed down the hall and stopped at her door, peeking over her shoulder to see Liam leaning against the doorframe, arms folded, watching her intently. The man was darkly handsome, enticing beyond words. With a sigh, she reluctantly entered her room and closed the door.

LIAM DID NOT sleep much last night.

I have a son.

How many times did he repeat that statement while he tossed and turned? Granted, Tommy had been at The Crowing Cock for close to four months, but he'd never truly accepted the familial bond until last night. Not that he doubted Molly Clahane's word, far from it. All he had to do was face the lad, and he could see the resemblance. Liam could have claimed him in Bethnal Green then and there. But he remembered the stress and horror of living on the streets. As he said, he wanted to give Tommy time to adjust to his new surroundings and situation. Maybe Liam needed time to accept this change as well.

Tommy had taken to restaurant life like a duck to water, proving their blood connection, at least in Liam's mind. As the weeks ticked by, Liam remained unsure of how to broach the subject. The specter of rejection hung over him like a storm cloud, exacerbating his deep-seated vulnerabilities. Yes, he possessed them. That had become apparent in his dealings with Celia.

But he had no time to wallow in doubt. Liam strode about the kitchen, giving orders. The kitchen was where he felt in control—and in command. He offered a light menu since it was Monday and the restaurant had shortened opening hours. Three large stockpots simmered on the stove, with Hannah and Timmy stirring them constantly to prevent the creamy seafood chowder from burning. Liam made the chowder with chopped potato, grated carrot, scallops, salmon, shrimp, onion, and celery. He took a spoon, dipped it in the pot, and tasted it. It had turned out rather well.

"Tommy! Is the soda bread sliced and the butter whipped?"

"Aye, Liam."

"Line up the bowls and the trays of soup spoons and knives on the prep table."

Enya stuck her head in the door. "There is quite a crowd outside, Liam."

"Get ready!" Liam called out. "Celia, sandwiches!"

"Yes, Liam. Chicken salad, Cheese and pickle, and cucumber."

"Is there any more chicken?"

"Chopped and ready in the larder," Celia replied as she hurriedly sliced the cucumber into thin slices.

"Then go and fetch it as we will need it."

Celia hurried away.

"Teddy. Come here, lad."

The boy finished the last of the dishes from the free stew served earlier. "When you're done with the dishes, I want you to deliver this pot of stew to someone for me." Liam pointed to the nearby counter. "You must take a hansom cab to Duck Lane in Westminster."

A shadow passed over Teddy's expression.

"You know of the place?" Liam questioned.

"Aye. Devil's Acre. My mum and me lived there a while back. I ain't—haven't—been there for a few years."

When Teddy arrived at the restaurant with Tommy and Timmy, he'd been the one in the roughest shape. Undernourished, pale, and wearing rags, he'd had to stay in bed for two weeks because of his lingering cough and overall weakness. The change in him over the past four months had been nothing short of amazing. He'd grown two inches and filled out, his face glowing with vibrant health. The power of proper eating. And he'd made great strides in learning to read and write.

"The delivery goes to Finnian's Chop House, to Lucian Sharpe. Have you heard of him?"

"Aye. Everyone from Devil's Acre has heard of Sharpe. But I

don't know him. I heard he's a bad 'un." Teddy slipped and used street slang, which had Liam wondering if Teddy was apprehensive about returning to the area.

"You don't have to do this. I will ask Timmy to deliver it."

Teddy grabbed the wooden handle of the small, covered iron pot. "I can do it."

"All right, if you're sure. Here are some coins. Just drop off the pot to Sharpe and leave right away. Have the cab take you right to school." He handed the money to Teddy. The boys were already late for school today, but it couldn't be helped.

"Aye, Liam." Teddy left to gather his coat, gloves, and scarf and gave Liam a brief wave as he exited the rear door.

Liam glanced at the clock. "Fire time!" he yelled. Everyone snapped to attention, and the wait staff hurried to the front doors and opened them. Then, the deluge began.

"Chowder, table two; tea tray, tables four and five; two chowder, table three!" The waitresses' voices echoed with urgency, setting the pace for the bustling kitchen.

One large stockpot and part of the second were gone in less than an hour. Liam's heart raced as he realized he was going to run out. The boys had left for school, so no one could assist him. But he would not panic. He glanced at Celia's workstation. She was working furiously making the sandwiches.

"Pick up the pace, Celia!"

"Right away!" she called out.

He ran over to her. "Are you getting low?"

"I can mix up more chicken salad, but I'm running short of the cheese and pickle," she replied breathlessly.

"Go to the larder and find the tins of salmon. Mash it with a fork and add salad cream and fresh dill."

"Good idea." Celia rushed away as he turned his attention to the stove. It was apparent he would have to hire one or two more workers for the day shift and the pub. But he couldn't think about that now. Another hour passed, and he only had half a pot left. There was no time to make anything else.

Enya entered the kitchen, grabbed a cup and saucer, and placed them on her tray. "Doctor Hornsby is here. He's at table eight. I'm getting him tea and chowder. He said there was no rush; come see him when things slow down."

Early this morning, Liam had had Timmy deliver a note to Drew informing him of the shed fire and the loss of goods. He was no doubt here to discover more about the incident. "Give him a full pot of tea. I may be a while." Liam ladled chowder into a bowl and slid it along the counter toward Enya without spilling a drop.

Thirty minutes later, the pot was empty, and Liam turned off the gas. He removed his apron and unrolled his shirt sleeves, buttoning the cuffs as he headed toward Celia. "How are you doing?"

Celia wiped her forehead with a tea towel. "All I have is the salmon left."

"Go to the icebox and bring out the rest of the toff food. We'll serve tea and cakes until closing—nothing else. Can you manage the kettles for boiling water?"

Celia gave him a warm smile. "Leave it with me."

Liam caressed her cheek, then tucked a tendril of her lovely hair behind her ear. "You did well today. Grace under pressure. Amazing work."

Celia blushed prettily. "Thank you. It *was* busy today."

"I may have to rethink Monday's hours."

"With the cold weather, people look for warmth in the food and the surroundings. I read that in one of the cookbooks."

"Aye. You're right. I'm going to speak to Drew. Call out if you need me. I'll tell the waitresses about the food."

"Yes, Chef," she whispered.

Liam chuckled as he grabbed an empty mug and exited the swinging door. The restaurant was still two-thirds full, but everyone had been served, and they were chatting and eating. He located Enya and took her aside. "The chowder's gone. Tea, cakes, and biscuits until closing. There are a few salmon sandwiches available." Liam started to step away, but he leaned in and whispered, "Well done today. Please pass on my words to Hannah and the rest."

Enya smiled and winked as she moved away to attend to a customer.

Liam sat across from Drew. "Any tea left in the pot?"

"Good afternoon. Yes, and it's still warm. I have been sitting here marveling at your kitchen and wait staff's efficiency. Impressive. And the chowder was delicious."

"Thank you. Today was uncommonly busy. I should serve more stews and chowders during the rest of the winter." Liam poured tea into his mug and added milk from the pitcher. "You got my note?"

"Yes, the fire. How unfortunate. What occurred, exactly?"

Liam relayed the events of Saturday night, along with his visit to the earl and his slimy viscount son the next day.

"Do you believe Darrington was involved?" Drew asked.

"He acted surprised at my declaration. But Shinwell did not. I think Shinwell was involved, but I have no way to prove it. I *am* sorry for the loss of goods, yours and mine."

"That is distressing. It appears we will be using the fifteen pounds we received from The Rakes to build a new shed and replenish the food and supplies."

"Bruce collected the rest of the gaming debt from Hartright yesterday. We can use some of those funds. I know of someone who can build—"

Tommy and Timmy burst through the swinging door, running up to Liam. "Teddy never showed up at school!" Timmy's voice was filled with worry, his eyes wide.

"Is he in trouble?" Tommy asked worriedly.

"Leave it with me, lads. Go help Celia in the kitchen." The boys scampered away, and Liam pounded his fist on the table, causing the teapot lid to rattle.

"Is the boy in danger?" Drew asked, showing concern.

"I will soon find out. Come with me to Devil's Acre. I'll explain the particulars on the way."

Liam and Drew entered the kitchen. Liam grabbed his wool coat from the hook by the rear door, then turned toward Celia as he wrapped his scarf around his neck. "I'm going to fetch Teddy. Can you handle things here?"

"Yes. Fiona's here, too. She's in the larder gathering ingredients. Since there's no chowder left, I'm making sandwiches for the staff."

Liam smiled. "Good. Thank you."

As Drew and Liam stepped onto the walkway to look for a hansom cab, Drew said, "I take it things are progressing well with you and Lady Celia?"

Lady. Right.

Sometimes, he forgot Celia's aristocratic ties. How that would bode for the future remained to be seen, although Celia had expressed a desire to stay here, and a desire for him. That filled him with hope. For now, he had to locate Teddy. He never should have sent him to Lucian Sharpe. Liam should have listened to his gut. *Too late now.*

"Progressed with Celia? You can tell?" Liam asked.

"I may not have much experience with women as my medical practice has hampered my social interactions. However, I can recognize yearning looks when I see them."

This meant others may have noticed as well. Liam had always been cautious with his emotions, packing them away deep within. Not with Celia, it seemed. "Aye, but how wise is it? That's another conversation altogether." Liam waved down an oncoming cab. Wise or not, there was no denying his growing feelings, and knowing Celia felt the same had his heart beating double time.

As they climbed in and gave the address, Liam felt a growing dread. Lucian Sharpe was not to be crossed. They shared a begrudging and wary respect and even had brief conversations several times in the past.

Liam preferred to keep his distance from the man.

But now, there was no choice.

None at all.

CHAPTER SEVENTEEN

INNIAN'S CHOP HOUSE had seen better days, a carryover from another century. In the last fifteen or twenty years, a new breed of chop houses had opened, serving stews, puddings, rump steaks, mutton chops, and pork chops in a more modern and hygienic setting to the growing working class.

Unlike any other place, Finnian's seemed frozen in time, its decor and atmosphere a direct portal to the 1790s. Drew couldn't help but wrinkle his nose at the distinct scent as they settled the cab fare. The sun had set, and the street lamps cast an unnerving glow over the proceedings.

"That's the stench of dubious meat, probably mere hours from being rotten," Liam explained. "It's what makes this pub a haven for those seeking a cheap meal. And it's also what draws a particular crowd."

"Like thieves?" Drew murmured.

"And the working poor. I'm unsure we will find Sharpe here. He has taken his meals here for years, though I don't know why."

They stepped inside the dimly lit tavern. The smoke from pipes, cigars, and cigarettes hung in the air like a dense fog. The tobacco smell, mixed with the dodgy food and the odors from the working men, made for a toxic mix. Liam often wished he could run a smoke-free eating establishment, as the smoke clung to everything and coated the walls. Keeping the ashtrays empty was enough of a challenge. But placing no-smoking rules would lose him two-thirds of his customers.

"Look, in the corner. I can see his beady eyes from here," Liam whispered, his voice barely audible.

As before, a muscular bullyboy halted them. "Liam Hallahan and Doctor Drew Hornsby to see Lucian Sharpe," Liam stated loudly.

Sharpe gave a brisk nod, and the bullyboy quickly checked them before waving them forward.

"Come to collect your pot?" Sharpe stated emotionlessly. Today, he wore another garish suit of blue and green plaid. A black derby hat sat on the table before him. Sharpe wore several gold rings, one with an enormous onyx. With his golden hair and chiseled looks, Lucian—with the appropriate evening wear— could pass for quality at any society occasion. He remained remarkably unscathed for a man from the streets—no visible scars or tattoos (except one on each index finger) to mark him as a rookery boss, and the aforementioned dead eyes, which bespoke of a soulless bastard with no morals.

The more Liam studied him, the more a shocking revelation took root: tall, blond hair, blue eyes—*bloody hell*. Sharpe couldn't be the old Duke of Chellenham's son and another possible half-brother, could he? Most of Chellenham's offspring had those same features. Liam shook his head, dismissing the disturbing thought, for he didn't care to discover the truth. Apparently, he would suspect every man and woman with those general golden physical attributes for the foreseeable future. At least the 'soulless bastard with no morals' fit the late duke. *Back to the matter at hand.*

"Keep the pot. I've come for Teddy Chisholm, the lad who delivered the stew. Where is he?" Liam asked, looking around the dim tavern. There was no sense beating about the bush. The sooner they were out of here, the better.

Sharpe's fingers drummed on the table. Next to him was a plate of half-eaten, gristle-filled steak, and boiled potatoes attracting flies. "The boyo is staying with me," he declared, his tone challenging.

Liam's heart sank. Then, a fury rose within him. "I told you to leave him alone. He works for *me*."

"Not anymore." Sharpe's astute gaze landed on Drew. "Why did you bring a sawbones here? Will you need a doctor? Planning to start a fight, yeah?"

Sharpe's men chuckled. The man sitting beside Sharpe turned sideways, hauling his trousers down partway. "Hey, Doc. I've got this carbuncle on me arse, oozing pus and the like. Can you look at it?"

Sharpe's men laughed boisterously, and Sharpe even smiled slightly.

Drew nodded, showing he understood the joke, as he had no doubt heard it before—many times. "I can lance the boil. All I need is a sharp knife, although I must place the blade into the fire to get it nice and hot first." Drew pointed to the knife on the table. "That one will do nicely."

The man grumbled as he hoisted his trousers, and the laughter continued. Sharpe banged the table with his fist, and the men were silenced immediately.

"I want to talk to Teddy. Now," Liam demanded.

"He's mine," Sharpe hissed through clenched teeth. "I've staked a claim, and no one will gainsay me."

Liam ignored the threat. "Any number of boyos living on the streets would gladly work for you. You don't need this one. Teddy is doing well in school and has recovered his health after his recent stint of living on the streets. He was in a bad way."

"You've looked after him; I'll give you that. He speaks highly of you. It's the only reason you're still standing here." Sharpe gave a high-pitched whistle.

Teddy came out of the kitchen wearing an apron, giving Liam a sheepish look.

"Teddy, you don't have to stay here with him. You have a place with me. Timmy and Tommy want you to come home. So do I," Liam said firmly. "I mean it. You're a part of the restaurant family."

"Sharpe's my father," Teddy said softly, "Tommy told me you're his da. I decided I wanted one, too. Time to stop running and denying my past—and *my* family."

Liam was utterly shocked. That revelation added a new layer of complexity to the situation.

"It's true," Sharpe interjected. "I said he's mine, and he is. His mother, Meggie Chisholm, told me so years ago. The boyo scarpered off. I've been trying to find him these last months."

"Aye, I'll bet you were," Liam snapped. He turned his attention back to Teddy. "He's lying to you, Teddy. Sharpe will tell you anything you want to hear to keep you here and turn you into one of his pickpockets or worse." Liam said, effectively ignoring Sharpe.

"Watch your mouth, Hallahan," Sharpe said menacingly. "Don't cross me."

"He's not lying, sir," Teddy said. "My mum told me who my da was years back. I tried to deny it. But I figure having a father is better than *not* having one. Tommy said so, and I agree." Teddy inclined his head toward Lucian Sharpe. "Besides, he's the only family I've got left."

"What really happened to your mum, Teddy?" Liam asked.

Teddy looked down at the straw-covered floor. "Prison," he whispered. "I know I told you she died. I didn't mean to lie. But I was ashamed."

Liam took a step closer. "I understand. But you don't want to be part of Sharpe's life. He will pull you into his criminal world, like he no doubt did with your mother."

"Enough of this shite. I had nothing to do with Meggie's troubles; she brought that on herself, and the lad knows it. Teddy's staying here," Sharpe said firmly. "Where he belongs. With his *real* family."

"What about school?" Liam asked Teddy, ignoring Sharpe again.

"Lucian said I can keep going. There's a school not far from here. I'm sixteen, Liam. I can make up my own mind."

Teddy's courage and determination shone through, and Liam couldn't help but feel a surge of pride. *But sixteen years old?* Teddy seemed much younger, a stark reminder of the toll poverty took on children's growth due to prolonged malnourishment.

Drew whispered, "He's of an age to make his own decisions."

Drew was correct. There was nothing else to say. Liam looked directly at Sharpe. "Teddy is a good lad. Eager to learn and intelligent. When I took him in, his health had deteriorated to such a state that he was bedridden for weeks. He's grown taller and filled out since. If Teddy is honestly your son, take responsibility and look out for him. Allow him to thrive."

Sharpe snarled but then gave Liam a brisk nod. Those cruel eyes briefly flashed a rare show of emotion, and Liam understood what it meant. It was an acknowledgment of what Liam said, and a promise to do right by the lad—as much as Sharpe was capable. To Liam, it was as good as he could have hoped.

Teddy stepped forward and held out his hand. Liam shook it. "Thanks, Liam, for everything. Tell Tommy and Timmy I'll see them soon. Lucian owns this tavern. I told him I could make it better. I'll use what you taught me at your restaurant. I'll be all right."

"You always have a place with me," Liam replied kindly, his words carrying the warmth of his support. "Remember that. I'll send along your clothes and books."

Teddy turned and waved, then disappeared into the kitchen.

"You got your answer, so sod off." Sharpe dismissed him with a wave of his hand. His sycophants chuckled. Liam understood that most of Sharpe's arrogant behavior was theatrical. All street gangsters acted the same. Regardless, it incensed Liam. For someone who kept his emotions in check, he was having trouble containing them lately.

Liam lurched forward, but Drew grabbed his arm. "Don't," he murmured. Drew understood Liam was about to threaten Sharpe, but it would not be wise. Liam turned to leave.

"Send along his stuff, yeah?" Sharpe called out. "And don't

come back here again unless I say so."

No worries there.

Drew held Liam's arm firmly. "Keep walking, ignore him. He is trying to bait you."

Liam knew that, and he admonished himself for allowing Sharpe to get under his skin. They stepped out on the walkway, and Liam took a deep breath of cleansing air and then exhaled. "Thanks. I would have threatened him. It could have turned ugly."

"We were certainly outnumbered and—" Drew reeled about. Then took numerous steps toward an alley across the way. Liam swung his gaze in that direction, catching sight of a long wool cape disappearing around the corner.

"Did you see her?" Drew questioned eagerly as he faced Liam.

"No. Just part of a gray cape."

Drew sprinted toward the alley, and Liam followed him. But the alley was empty and led to a maze of courtyards. "Blast it. She is gone. It could *not* have been her. In this notorious section of London?"

"Who?" Liam questioned.

Drew lifted his spectacles and rubbed his eyes. "I thought I saw the missing Duchess of Barnsdale, Celia's friend."

"Right. You said you treated her last April."

"I only caught a fleeting glimpse. It may not be her, though. I am more exhausted than I thought."

"Then let's get you home. We will have to walk a bit to find a hansom cab. Then I must explain Teddy's situation to everyone."

"That will not be easy. And pardon for asking, what did the lad mean when he said you are Tommy's father?"

Liam exhaled. "That, my friend, is another recent disclosure. I'll explain on the way."

CELIA SAT AT the dining table with the daytime wait staff and the evening pub staff. Everyone was talking animatedly, passing around platters of sandwiches and pouring tea. She had long yearned to be a part of such a scenario, surrounded by family and friends, but it had never come to pass. Her dreams had been cut short by her parents' tragic and untimely deaths.

Although she had experienced comforting camaraderie at the finishing school with Selena and Corrine, they had all grown apart as friends often did. Granted, their unstable lives did not translate to writing letters and visits. Could she be opening herself up for more rejection from Liam or the people seated here at the table? Yes, she had moments of doubt. But closing herself off emotionally was not an option.

"We should do this every day," Celia announced.

Everyone quieted and stared at her. "Do what, ducks?" Fiona asked.

"Gather together for a staff meal—all of us. Let us call it—a family meal. Right at this time and place, when the restaurant closes and before the pub opens." Celia felt her face grow hot. Did she long for a family so much that she revealed her innermost longing to people she had only known for a few weeks? She had gone too far. Embarrassment covered her from head to toe.

Fiona gently patted her hand. "A *family* meal. I like that. We are a sort of family, yeah?"

Everyone agreed, which eliminated much of her mortification. Warming to the subject, Celia continued. "We can eat leftovers, or for menu purposes try out new recipes or make suggestions for different types of food from our backgrounds."

"I have a suggestion!" Tommy cried. "Let me go get my book!"

Tommy was back in a flash and handed a book to Celia. The cover was well-worn. "*The Cook's Oracle,* by William Kitchiner." Celia opened the cover. "Published in 1817? My, that's going back a few years."

"I marked the page there." Tommy pointed to a piece of

paper between the pages.

Celia turned to the section. "Fried potato shavings?"

"That's it," Tommy said proudly.

"'Peel large potatoes, cut a quarter of an inch thick or in shavings, dry thoroughly, then fry in lard or drippings.' That sounds interesting. What would we serve them with?"

Tommy rubbed his chin, deep in thought. "Well, they would go with hot sandwiches on the side of the plate, like when Liam serves toasted cheese and bacon. Or we can serve them in the pub! It only takes a few minutes to cook them. We always have potato skins and shavings left. Why not use them? Maybe we can salt them and put some malt vinegar on them!"

Fiona clapped, and the rest joined in. "Well done, Tommy!"

It was that boisterous scene Liam walked into. His face looked like thunder, which immediately silenced everyone. "What's this, a bloody tea party? Fiona, the pub opens in thirty minutes. Let's get a move on, chop, chop. This isn't a countess's parlor. Tommy and Timmy, clear these dishes and start the stew prep for tomorrow. Hannah and Enya? Start cleaning the kitchen and readying glasses and mugs. Teddy isn't returning. He's staying with his father. Don't ask me any bloody questions about it now. Get to work!"

The staff scattered, but Celia remained seated. *A countess's parlor?* Was that sarcasm directed at her? Celia fumed. "No orders for me?" she asked mockingly. "Scrub the floors, clean out the chowder pots?"

Liam plopped in the chair opposite and unwound his scarf, tossing it on the table. His angry look changed to one of weariness.

With that, Celia's irritation dissolved. "What happened with Teddy?" she asked gently.

"I sent him into the lion's den," Liam murmured. "Lucian Sharpe is an acquaintance I've known for years. He came to The Crowing Cock for Walter's hot pot and the doings upstairs. He's a rookery boss at Devil's Acre, a slum area in Westminster. Long story short, I used Teddy to deliver something to him, not knowing they had a shared past."

Celia waited for him to continue. Liam grabbed a wedge of sandwich from the platter and devoured it. "My gut told me not to send him, but I did. So that's on me," Liam continued gruffly. "Get this, Teddy is Sharpe's son. Or so they say. He wants to stay with his father because Tommy now has a father—or some such reason. What a bloody mess."

"Is he Sharpe's son? *Could* it be possible?" Celia asked, stunned by the turn of events.

Liam shrugged. "He knew Teddy's mother. Intimately. So, it's possible."

"Sometimes, the pull of family can be hard to ignore. From what you've told me, Teddy had a rough time. Perhaps he wished for familial contact and stability."

"He had that here!" Liam barked. "I gave him a home, schooling, clothes, and more besides."

"He was an apprentice, Liam. You only took him in because Tommy insisted. I am not denying you were kind to him because you were. But you are *not* his father. Perhaps he wants more from life than what you offered."

Liam snatched another sandwich wedge and chewed thoughtfully. "Teddy is sixteen, can you believe it? I thought he was no more than twelve. He says he will take Sharpe's derelict chop house and turn it around. I believe he will do it, as the lad seemed determined. What an unbelievable turn of events."

"You gave Teddy a purpose in the four months he stayed here. You taught him life and work skills he will put to good use. He was ready to leave, Liam, and took the opportunity of running his own eating establishment. He just used his possible father as an excuse. Do not blame yourself. However, you should have a serious discussion with Timmy and see what goals he wishes to achieve. How old is he?"

"I have no bloody idea."

Celia shook her head and tsked. "Do you want some advice?"

"Aye, go on."

"You must take more of an interest in your staff, day and night."

Liam's eyes narrowed, giving her such a look of desire that her heart skipped a beat. "I've taken an interest in *you*."

"That is not the same, although I welcome it. I proposed something to the staff: We share a family meal every night between the restaurant closing and the pub opening."

Liam's eyebrows shot upward. "Family?"

Celia shifted uncomfortably in her seat. She had no right to suggest radical recommendations about how Liam ran his business. "I-I-I—blast. I thought the people who work—especially those who live here—would appreciate feeling valued and part of the bigger picture. For some of them, this group of people will be the only family they have. It is like a manor house where the family lives upstairs, and the family of servants lives downstairs. But what I propose is better. Everyone is part of the same group, sharing goals and ambitions and giving support."

Liam shook his head. "I'm not sure—"

"Let me finish. You should join them, open up, and welcome them into your heart. I know I told you that before, but it's still true. Sit at the head of the table and get to know them better. Share a laugh and praise them for a job well done where warranted. Talk about food and possible improvements. Do not go to your room immediately after your day is done or come down to breakfast after everyone has eaten. Sit and talk and share a meal with your employees. Your *family*. Please say you will try it."

"I eat breakfast with them," Liam grumbled stubbornly.

"But not every day."

"I'm not one for conversation."

"I understand. But you won't know how it will go unless you try," Celia urged.

Liam exhaled. "Fine. I'll give it a go. What in the bloody hell do I talk about?"

"As I said, food. The restaurant. You enjoy those subjects. You can try out new recipes and allow the staff to make suggestions. Tommy already came up with a wonderful idea. We were talking about it when you came in." Celia stood, brought over the old cookbook, and handed it to Liam. "On the left-hand side, middle of the page."

"Fried potato shavings?" Liam read the directions. "Interesting," he murmured.

"Tommy said we could serve them with a hot sandwich for lunch or the pub at night!" Celia enthused excitedly. "Perhaps sprinkle a little vinegar and salt on them. I will bet they would taste good with fried meat or fish."

"Hmm. Splashing vinegar on them would make them soggy. We could place a dish or bottle of vinegar on the side. In Alexis Soyer's cookbook, he has a recipe for fried fish that is dipped into flour and water and then submerged in oil and fried until crispy. A few fish and chip shops have opened in the East End, actual sit-down restaurants that serve the fish dish with bread and mashed peas. You can also buy it from costermongers on the street who wrap the fish and potatoes in a newspaper. It's a cheap, hot dish and very popular."

"What is a chip?"

"I don't suppose you came across it in your aristocratic house."

Celia placed her hands on her hips, exasperated. "Right. And what was that aside about a countess's parlor, you said earlier? A slam at me?"

Liam gave her a contrite look. "I *am* sorry. Why I said countess, I have no idea. It was not meant as a slam, as you call it. Not at all. I was cross because of Teddy's situation and took it out on everyone."

"I accept your apology. It wouldn't hurt to say you're sorry to the staff. I know talented chefs can be temperamental, or so I've read in books. That does not have to be *you*. You are better than that. I know you are."

Liam nodded, his expression reflective, as if he took in all she had said and considered it.

"Now, I ask again. What is a chip?" Celia questioned.

Liam gave her a quirky smile. He looked so adorable when he did that. "It's long, thick strips of potato fried in oil. I considered adding it to the menu, but working with hot oil or fat didn't appeal to me. I believed the dish should be left to the street vendors. I want to serve food a step or two up from the street."

"I can see that. But if it is catching on beyond street food, perhaps you should consider it," Celia suggested.

"It would mean someone would have to operate the stove for the frying. A pot full of oil or drippings can be dangerous—and messy. It can catch fire like that." Liam snapped his fingers.

"You said you were going to hire more people anyway. You can also train someone to fry the thin potato pieces safely and properly. Less waste, too. I imagine they would take a minute or two to cook. Here is a thought: make the fish and chip dish part of the pub's offerings. Not every night, but occasionally. Or not."

"I welcome your interest in the business. But fish and chips should not be part of my menu, at least for now. I like the idea of the shavings, though."

"You know best." Celia turned to return to her seat, but Liam grasped her hand and brought her toward him so swiftly that she lost her balance and wound up on his lap.

"I like you sitting right here," he whispered as he nuzzled her neck. "Why *are* you so concerned about my restaurant?"

Celia leaned back and stared at him. "Because it is part of you. Because I have watched you preparing meals and can plainly see how much you love it. Never have I seen you more alive than when cooking food."

Liam wrapped a loose tendril of her hair around his finger. Celia's hair always came loose when working in the kitchen. He gently pushed it behind her ear, then caressed her cheek tenderly. "Never have I felt more alive than now, with you close like this."

Celia's heart swelled. "I must admit I feel the same. Also,

regarding the business."

"You like working in the restaurant?" Liam asked incredulously. "Truly?"

"Yes, Chef."

Liam chuckled. "Put your arms around me."

Celia did, never breaking contact with his intense and sultry look.

"Now, kiss me."

Celia blinked. "Kiss you? Here?"

"Yes, in this room." He placed the tip of his finger against his lips. "Right here."

"Someone could walk in," Celia said worriedly as she glanced about.

"That, love, makes it more exciting."

Liam was correct. A thrill of exhilaration skittered along her spine. Celia cupped his face, studying every aspect, every sharp cut of cheekbone to the dark whiskers already showing through. "You have such beautiful eyes." She tenderly kissed that enticing mole at the corner of his right eye. "So clear and blue, like a summer or winter sky, depending on your mood." Celia trailed kisses along his whiskered chin, teasing him. Then, she captured his lips, kissing him ardently. She tangled her fingers through his thick, wavy hair, so silky and longer than most men wore. It suited him.

Liam responded with something like a cross between a moan and a growl. Their tongues clashed as he trailed his hand over her hip, grabbing a fistful of her wool skirt, lifting far enough that he could caress her leg. As their kiss deepened, his hand traveled higher until he reached her upper thigh. She could feel his erection under her. That was exciting, too.

Celia moaned and instinctively spread her legs. The feel of his hand against her bare skin made her grow wet at her feminine core. "Touch me," she urged between the passionate kisses. His fingers reached her drawers when the door flew open and banged against the wall.

"Liam! Oh, bloody hell. Excuse me."

Celia sprang from Liam's lap, blushing furiously as she smoothed her skirt.

It was Fiona, and she looked worried. "Liam, a fight broke out in the pub. The blokes have knives."

CHAPTER EIGHTEEN

L IAM JUMPED TO his feet and swiftly buttoned his wool coat. "Celia, fetch Tommy and Timmy. Have them go for the coppers. They know where the station is. Then I want you to go upstairs to your room and lock the door."

Celia nodded. "I'll gather weapons first in case you need them. Knives, rolling pins, and the like." Lifting her skirt partway, she ran toward the kitchen before Liam could reply.

"How many men are involved?" Liam asked.

"At least four," Fiona replied breathlessly. "They came in fifteen minutes ago. Even after Bruce warned them, they continued to cause a stir."

Liam strode to the larder and grabbed two axe handles, which he kept hidden for just such an emergency. Fiona followed close behind. He swung open the door to find Bruce had one of the men in a headlock. Two other men stood nearby, and one of them brandished a knife, and so did the bald man that Bruce restrained. Without hesitation, Liam ran up to the ginger-haired man with the knife and bashed his knees with the axe handle. Ginger cried out and fell to the floor, dropping his knife, which Liam hurriedly snatched.

Wait. Fiona said four men. Where's the other one?

Liam tossed an axe handle to Bruce, who caught it with his free hand. The second man, still standing, took reverse steps and fell into one of the tables. It upended, scattering playing cards, betting chips, and money across the floor. The customers shouted, trying to gather up the money. Liam held the handle aloft, ready to attack. The man toppled another table, and the pub erupted into complete chaos. The customers panicked, racing toward the front exit, and in doing so, caused other tables to tumble over. Food and drink littered the floor.

Then, a menacing voice cut through the pandemonium. "Here! Bossman!"

Liam whirled about as the pub fell silent. Everyone froze. The missing fourth man had his arm around Celia's neck with his blade pointed against her throat.

Liam's blood ran cold. The thought of Celia in harm's way—he could not bear it. His insides tumbled with fear for her safety. "Let her go," Liam said with soft menace. "Leave here now before the police come, and do not harm her."

"Oh, aye? She means something to you, eh? Maybe we'll take her along for a bit o' fun."

"I will break every bone in your body," Liam growled through clenched teeth. "Harm her, and I will hunt you down—all of you—and pick you off one by one. And I will. Find. You."

"Fair enough. We'll get gone. Get your beast to release him," the man holding Celia indicated with a nod toward Bruce.

Liam's heart ached to see Celia so frightened. "Bruce, let him go."

"Out the rear door, boyos," the man holding Celia instructed.

Just as Bruce loosened his hold on his captive, distant shrill police whistles filled the air. In a few seconds, Bald Man snarled and gave a glancing slice across Bruce's lower arm. Fiona cried out. Bald Man and the bloke who had knocked over the tables swiftly gathered up Ginger and ran toward the back exit. With the man restraining Celia sufficiently distracted, she picked that moment to sink her teeth into her captor's arm. He yelled, loosening his grip, but not before he sliced downward on Celia's side.

Liam saw nothing and no one else. He dropped the axe handle and rushed to Celia. The miserable bastard who'd cut her ran off after his companions. Liam didn't care.

Celia looked dazed. She brushed her hand against her hip, and blood droplets gathered on her fingers. "It is all right," she murmured, "Only a scratch." Then her eyes rolled over, and Liam caught her before she hit the floor.

The police entered the pub area, and Bruce and Fiona ran toward them, shouting and pointing at the rear door. Two of the four police officers gave chase.

"Who's the owner?" one of the coppers asked.

Liam lifted an unconscious Celia into his arms. Timmy and Tommy stood by the door, shocked at the chaotic scene. "Tommy, get money from my office drawer for a cab. Go for Doctor Drew. You know where he lives."

Tommy nodded and disappeared, with Timmy hot on his heels.

The police sergeant halted Liam from leaving the room. "I said, are you the owner?"

"Aye. Liam Hallahan. Speak to my manager, Fiona. This woman is injured, as is my employee, Bruce. He and Fiona can give you the details."

"No one is to leave until we get this sorted!" the copper shouted.

"My money is on the floor!" one customer cried.

"We'll get it sorted, sir. Take a seat." The policeman nodded toward Liam. "Where are you taking her?"

"Upstairs, the boys are fetching the doctor." Liam glanced toward Fiona. She looked worried and wrapped a cloth around Bruce's lower arm.

"Right. Go ahead. We will talk later," the copper replied.

Liam raced outside and climbed the wrought iron stairs, holding Celia close as if she were precious cargo.

And she was most precious, indeed.

⇥⇤

WHEN THE COLD air hit Celia's lungs, she jumped awake and exhaled sharply. "Holy crow. Did I faint?"

"Aye, love. You did."

Snowflakes rested on her eyelashes as she tightened her grip around Liam's neck. It took a moment for her to realize she was being carried. They entered the upstairs area, and Liam kicked the door shut with his boot.

"I like it when you call me that," Celia sighed as Liam hurried past her room. "Where are you taking me?" she asked.

"To my rooms. You need looking after."

"It's only a scratch."

"So you said. We'll let Drew determine that. He's on his way."

Celia felt lightheaded, as if in a dream-like state. "It's so far for him to come."

Liam opened the door to his flat, which wasn't easy since he still held her in his arms. "I could take you to a hospital but the only one in the vicinity is a workhouse infirmary, and I am *not* taking you there. Besides, I trust Drew far more to see to your care than some stranger." He laid her gently on a bed. "Where are the buttons on your skirt?"

Celia closed her eyes. All she wanted to do was sleep.

"Celia! Stay awake!"

"I am awake," she murmured. "How can I not be with your yelling? You must stop that, you know." Her eyes flew open at the sound of fabric tearing. "What are you doing?"

"That miserable cur cut your skirt. I'm just removing it."

How mortifying. Her undergarments and petticoats were not in the best condition. Liam pulled them below her waist.

"Jaysus," Liam whistled.

"Is it bad?" she asked worriedly.

"It doesn't look deep, but it's a long gash." Liam opened his dresser drawers as if frantically searching for something. "Your multiple layers protected you from a worse injury." Then he grabbed a white shirt and bundled it up.

"Oh, don't use one of your shirts!" Celia cried.

He placed it firmly against her wound, and she winced in pain. "I have dozens. Why didn't you go to your room as I said? Do you know what it did to me to see you being held by that bloody barbarian?"

Celia touched his arm gently. "Do not be cross."

"I'm not," Liam replied in a calmer voice. "I'm frightened more than anything."

"After gathering weapons, I was about to go to my room as you suggested, but—I could not leave you. You were in danger. I *am* sorry, and I know it was against your expressed wishes. I do have a mind of my own."

"I know you do. And a fine mind it is." Liam pulled back the shirt and looked at the wound, his thick brows furrowed with worry.

"Is it bad?"

"I've seen worse."

"You have witnessed someone being injured by a knife?"

"Aye. Other lads. And myself." Liam stood, removed his wool coat, and unbuttoned his shirt partway, pulling it aside to show a scar on his left shoulder.

"When you lived on the streets?" Celia asked softly.

Liam sat on the edge of the bed and continued with the compressions on her injured side. "Aye. It was horrible. A time in my life I would rather forget."

"Walter Henning saved your life—as you did mine," Celia whispered. She groaned as pain shot through her side.

"Celia!" Liam exclaimed.

"Just a slight jolt, nothing more. It's true what I said, you saved me. I cannot tell you how wonderful it is to have someone look after you as you do now."

"Always. I—" A sharp rap on the door interrupted his sentence.

"It's Fiona. Sergeant Morrisey wants a quick word. I've seen his I.D. card."

Jaysus. Couldn't the world leave him and Celia alone for more than a few minutes? "Come in."

A man in a long wool coat and a derby hat entered the room with Fiona directly behind him.

"Detective Sergeant Morrisey of H Division, 1st District." The older man removed his hat and patted it against his thigh to remove the snow. "Mr. Hallahan. I'm sorry to intrude, but the investigation will not wait. How are you, miss?"

"This is the Dowager Countess of Winterwood," Liam introduced, his tone firm.

Fiona inhaled sharply, casting a glance at Celia. Well, her true identity was public knowledge now.

"My pardon, my lady," Morrisey bowed slightly.

"I am awaiting the doctor's arrival," she replied.

"Then I will be swift in my inquiries, my lady." The detective placed his hat on the bed, then pulled a notebook and pencil from his side coat pocket. "Where were you when the man took you as a hostage?"

Hostage? Holy crow. That shook her up a little. She'd had no time until this minute to realize just how much danger everyone had been in, herself included. "I was gathering weapons," Celia said steadily despite her lingering fear.

The sergeant's eyebrows shot skyward.

"I located items in the kitchen that could be used, such as rolling pins, cast iron frying pans, knives, and the like," she continued. "I had them laid out on the counter, but alas, I could not grab one to use before that loathsome man grabbed me from behind."

"Did he say anything, my lady?"

"It all happened so fast." Celia concentrated and tried to recall the sequence of events. "He said, 'Ain't you a tasty dish. Just like he said.'" Celia frowned.

"He?" the Sergeant questioned. "Do you know who 'he' might be, my lady?"

"I have only recently arrived in London. The only men I know work here. Except—" *No.* Not her so-called uncle and cousin? What other 'he' could it be but one of them? She knew of no one else. And a tasty dish? Her cousin had called her that before in the past. It could be a coincidence... It was too terrible to contemplate. By the growing rage showing on Liam's face, he must have reached the same conclusion. "I am recently widowed, impoverished, and came to stay with my aunt, my only remaining blood relative, only I discovered she is wintering in Italy. My uncle, The Earl of Darrington, and my cousin, Viscount Shinwell, were *not* very welcoming." *A decided understatement.*

Liam snorted. "Shinwell dropped her here to work off his gaming debt. The countess had nowhere else to go, so I offered her a room until she could locate her aunt and friends."

The detective wrote notes furiously. "An earl and a viscount," he murmured.

"Is there a problem, Sergeant?" Liam asked. "Are toffs too high and mighty for police inquiries? That must be the case because they're never brought to justice. Aristocrats get away with all sorts."

"Steady on, Hallahan," Morrisey replied gruffly. "I'll not have that kind of talk. I follow an investigation wherever it leads. My duty is to uncover the truth, regardless of the social status of the individuals involved."

Tommy burst into the room. "Here's Doctor Hornsby!"

"I will be fine. Talk to Sergeant Morrisey outside. Tell him everything, including the shed fire, which I believe was *not* an accident."

He kissed her hand before releasing it. "Fiona, come sit by Celia. And keep it to yourself about her being an earl's widow. For now, at any rate."

"Aye, Liam."

Celia watched as Liam, Tommy, and the sergeant departed.

Drew placed his doctor's case on the table by the bed. "Well, Celia. You have been through a lot."

She nodded in response. Unshed tears shimmered in her eyes, for Celia wasn't sure how much more she could take. Drew lifted the shirt away from her side. and examined her closely.

"Not deep at all. I wager that you will need a few stitches, but otherwise, all will be well, I promise. I would suggest you stay abed tomorrow and allow for healing. But you must be careful and not exert yourself or lift anything heavy for at least two weeks."

"Oh, but I cannot stay in bed. The sandwiches—"

"Leave it with me, ducks," Fiona soothed. "I'll cover for you tomorrow."

Celia gave Fiona a trembling smile. She was correct; these people were family. In every way that counted. If only the arrangement could be permanent.

CHAPTER NINETEEN

Liam walked into complete bedlam. Customers yelled, pointing at the floor at the coins and pound notes covered with spilled drinks and smeared food. Bruce and the remaining two uniformed policemen tried their best to control the situation.

Sergeant Morrisey walked toward one of the officers and held out his hand. "Your whistle, Murray." The copper handed it over, and the detective blew it, the shrill noise cutting through the loud din. A tense silence settled over the room. The detective inclined his head toward the crowd, indicating Liam to speak.

"I do apologize for the uproar and inconvenience. We have never had this happen before. I assume the pub will be closed the rest of the night?" Liam looked toward Morrisey.

"I am afraid I must insist," the detective replied.

"Only three tables were upended. I suggest those whose tables are still upright gather their money and any other belongings and depart—unless you wish to speak to them, Sergeant."

"Murray, did you collect names and addresses?"

The policeman nodded. "I got everyone's."

"Then those men can leave," Morrisey stated.

"If you return tomorrow night, there will be a free round of drinks on the house," Liam stated. "I assure you, something like this will never happen again."

The men groused as they collected their possessions, some muttering under their breath, and Liam felt he had just lost some steady customers. *Blast it.*

"As to the money on the floor, there is no way to know who had what amount," Liam continued. "I suggest we gather, count, and divide the money evenly. It's the fair way to go about it."

"Look here, Hallahan, I know exactly how much I had on the table!" one man yelled, his face red with anger. Some of his customers started complaining, some nodding in agreement, others shaking their heads in disbelief.

Morrisey blew the whistle again. "If you gentlemen prefer, I can take *all* the money back to the station as evidence, and God knows when or if you will ever see it again. What the owner proposes is just. I suggest you follow his direction in the matter."

"Bruce," Liam waved the ex-boxer over. "Are you well?"

"Aye, Liam. Fiona wrapped my arm. The doctor said he would come and tend to me soon. He had a glance and said I'll be fine."

"Good man. Gather up the money, sit at this table, and count it. Let me know when you have an amount." Liam turned toward Morrisey. "Can one of the officers assist him?"

"Of course. Northrup, help the man."

Morrisey took Liam's arm and led him away. "I am curious. How do you make money on this gaming?"

"I collect a flat fee as they come in and another when they leave. It's how the previous owner did things. I also make money on liquor and beer sales and serving food."

"Where do you keep this money?" Morrisey asked as he wrote in his notebook.

"There's a safe in my office."

"This episode does not sound random. In talking to your patrons and the staff, they claim these men entered the pub to cause trouble, not to rob it. They made lewd comments to the waitresses, grabbed someone's pint of bitter, threw it around, and upended the trays the staff carried. When your man approached them, that's when the knives came out. They never mentioned or moved toward the money lying on the tables or demanded that anyone open your safe. They were there to cause trouble and harm your business. Why?"

Liam hesitated. He recalled his promise to Darrington that if he were interfered with, he would give their names to the coppers. *No time like the present.* "Shinwell owes me two hundred and forty pounds from cards. That's the reason he brought his cousin here, to work off the debt. I refused and, in turn, could not bring myself to turn the countess onto the streets. I went to their residence to collect, but the viscount declined. So, instead, I made a deal with the earl."

"What kind of deal?"

"In exchange for the money owed, the earl would furnish his wife's address in Italy and 35 pounds for the stress the countess endured. You see, Shinwell stole her remaining few pounds before he unceremoniously dumped her here."

Morrisey whistled low in his throat. "What's this about a shed fire?"

Liam explained the particulars and how the fire brigade found oil-soaked rags. "The station officer, I think his name is Brannigan."

"I know him," Morrisey murmured as he continued to write in his notebook. "And I have the address of the earl's residence. But I want to offer a word of advice. Allow the police to investigate, and do not enflame this situation further. Do you understand? I won't have you acting as a vigilante. I will keep you informed every step of the way."

Liam frowned. "And how will you prove Darrington and his smarmy son are involved? It will be next to impossible." Liam wondered if he should mention the earl's alter ego—Billy Buck— and his criminal doings. He hadn't told Celia about it as yet, and figured it would be best to keep that information to himself for now. If Liam had learned anything from living on the streets, he knew not to reveal all his weapons at once.

The two police officers who had given chase to the men entered the room.

"Did you catch them?" Morrisey asked.

"No, Sergeant. But under the street lights, I got a good look at two of them and recognized the injured one with the red hair."

Morrisey turned to Liam. "See? We have a lead."

"We've counted the money," Northrup stated. "We each tallied it twice: four hundred forty-seven pounds, 10 shillings, and sixpence."

"Bruce, go to the till and get enough money to bring it to 450, then divide it eight ways. The amount will be 57 pounds each."

The same man who complained before stepped forward. "I had more than 57 pounds. And everyone at my table knows it."

"Oh, shut it, Williams. You can afford to take the loss," one of the men said with a sneer.

Williams took the money offered, then grabbed his coat. "Well, I won't be returning here. It's located in a bloody slum, anyway. I will ensure others know what a cheap, grifting card palace you run, Hallahan." The man exited, slamming the door behind him.

The man who had spoken against Williams took his money and shoved it in his coat pocket. "It's just as well Williams stays clear; we think he cheated, though there was no way to prove it." The man touched his forelock. "I'll be back tomorrow night for that free drink."

After the rest of the patrons collected the money and departed, Liam exhaled.

"We should be going as well," Morrisey said, tucking his notebook away. "As I said, I will keep you informed regarding the investigation. Allow the police to do their job. Please stay away from the earl and his son. Agreed?"

Grudgingly, Liam nodded. "Aye. Agreed."

Drew came up to stand beside Liam. "The detective speaks sense, Liam."

Liam turned to face Drew. "How is Celia?"

"It is just a scratch; regardless, she must heal. I stitched part of the wound and wrapped plasters and gauze around the gash. I suggest she stay abed for tomorrow, and after that, light duties, no heavy lifting. She must take care moving about until the injury heals, I would say two weeks at most, probably ten days. There is no sign of infection, and we certainly do not want any complications. I will come by in two days to check."

"Drew, as always, thank you," Liam said sincerely.

"Now, I believe I have another patient. Bruce, is it? Come and let me inspect your injury."

The pub staff stared at Liam, looking for direction. For Liam's part, he swung his gaze about the room, taking in the damage—broken chairs, glasses, dishes, food, and drink everywhere. Tonight was a complete loss. He glanced at the regulator clock on the wall—a quarter past nine.

"Unfortunately," Liam said, "what happened here tonight occurs often in pubs and taverns, especially in the East End. But that is no excuse. I want you all to feel safe, and tonight, I've failed in that basic premise. There will be changes; Fiona and I discussed them before this disturbance occurred. I will hire more men for the pub, and any ladies who wish to move to the day staff, please let me know."

Morrigan, his head pub waitress, raised her hand. "I'd like to move to the day staff."

"All right, let's meet in my office tomorrow night at half past six to discuss it."

Morrigan nodded. Liam looked at the other three waitresses. "Anyone else?"

Two shook their heads; the third said, "Can I think about it?"

"Aye, Sally. You can. Now, we must do a clean-up for the rest of the shift. I'll fetch the boys to assist."

"We're here, Liam."

Liam turned to find Tommy, Timmy, Enya, and Hannah. "We heard the commotion, and the boys told us what happened," Hannah said. "And we've come to help."

Despite the upheaval, Liam was touched. Maybe Celia was right. They *were* a family. And it was time he started acting as if he were part of it.

CELIA AND FIONA were left alone. Awkwardness lingered about the room like a spectral apparition.

Fiona sat on the chair by the bed, facing Celia. "So then, *Lady Celia.*"

Celia sighed. "I'm sorry I did not inform Liam right away that I am the widow of an earl. I suppose I was afraid he would toss me to the cobbles, for he made his disdain for the upper classes plain. I told the truth in everything else."

"A lie of omission, then," Fiona replied.

"Yes. I like being part of the group and having you all treat me as an equal. As a countess, I lived in a cottage near the Scottish border. There were no fancy balls or other social events in my life, not for a long time. I spent the past six years tending to my ill, much older husband. Liam and Drew offered me Drew's rear flat until I could contact my aunt and friends, but I wanted to stay here with all of you."

"And with Liam," Fiona interjected softly.

"It is that obvious, then?"

"Aye, it was when I first mentioned it, and it's more so now. On both sides, it seems. The look of horror on Liam's face when that loud-mouthed git cut you. It spoke volumes."

Celia's heart hitched. "It spoke of what?"

"Ducks, I walked in on you sitting on Liam's lap with his hand up your skirt. That proves desire. But it's more than mere lust. I saw the concern on his face when you were injured. I've also seen you and he cast longing glances toward each other when you thought no one was looking, including yourselves." Fiona chuckled. "It's the talk of the staff."

Celia groaned. "Oh, no. I so wished to avoid that."

Fiona's eyes narrowed. "What happens when you contact your aunt or friends? Will you rejoin the upper crust? Find another elderly aristocrat to hitch your wagon to? Swan off to some country estate to live a life of leisure and privilege?" Fiona's words cut, as if she were purposely trying to taunt her.

At first, Celia felt hurt by the assessment. Then, she grew annoyed, but she would not take the bait. "I am not some pampered countess," Celia declared evenly.

"Is that so?"

"I was forced into that marriage at age nineteen when I had nothing and no one. Not even my aunt spoke up for me. Well, she tried. Regardless, it's the reason we are estranged. My parents died in a boating accident when I was ten, and I had no choice but to move in with my aunt and her family." She kept her voice as steady as possible.

"What happened to your parents' money?"

"My father was a baronet, not part of the peerage. We lived comfortably, but we were not wealthy. The residence and belongings were sold to settle the mortgage and other debts. There was nothing left when it was all said and done." Celia caught Fiona's gaze. "Why am I explaining all this to you? What business is it of yours?" Her voice raised with each sentence; so much for keeping emotion out of it.

"Liam *is* my business," Fiona replied, her voice fraught with feeling. "He's family, and we look out for one another. I don't want to see him hurt. You should have seen him when Walter took him in. He acted like an untamed animal, too thin and sickly by half. Already, he kept his feelings well hidden. It took months for Liam to show even a smidgen of trust. To this day, he keeps a part of himself removed from everyone. Until you arrived here." Her concern for Liam was palpable in every word she spoke. Celia could not fault her for it.

"Me?" Celia gasped.

"Liam's had plenty of lady friends through the years, some relatively recent. But he never brought them around here for us to meet. He keeps you close even when the opportunity arises to hand you off to the doctor. He wants you at his side. And that has me worried. This life is not for everyone. It's hard, grinding work from dawn to dusk and beyond. Do you honestly believe you can live and work at Liam's side for the foreseeable future? Have you ever given any thought to it? Because I can guess Liam has when he's alone with his thoughts." Fiona paused. "He's in love with you."

Love? The thought filled her heart to near bursting. "Has he said so?"

Fiona shook her head. "I don't think he's quite aware of it yet, or at least he can't put a name to his feelings. As I said, Liam keeps his emotions well concealed. He's never talked of his past much, but I assume it had something to do with him being—"

"Aloof? Withdrawn? Distant? Reserved?"

"Aye. To a point. More often than not. It also speaks to his vulnerabilities, and aye, he has them."

"Don't we all? He talked about his past with me," Celia declared. "Some of it, at least."

Fiona's eyebrows shot skyward. "Well. That gives further proof."

Celia held out her hand, and Fiona leaned forward and took it. "I do not want to hurt Liam. I'd rather cut out my liver."

Fiona chuckled. "You heard Bruce say that more than once."

"Yes. I like the expression as it conveys how I feel. My feelings for Liam are private; when I voice them, it will be to him and no one else. For once in my life, I have choices before me, and I am going to do what is right for me and my happiness. We all deserve it."

Fiona squeezed Celia's hand and nodded, her eyes shimmering with emotion. "Aye, ducks. Contentment. Love. We all deserve it. Even me. Bruce has said he wants us to be together, permanent like."

"You and Bruce? I think that is wonderful!"

Fiona scoffed. "He's twenty-eight to my forty-one! It's complete bollocks." Fiona pulled her hand away to wipe away tears gathered at the corner of her eyes.

"Never!" Celia exclaimed. "Who cares if you are older?"

"What about children?"

"I do not hold to the notion that the only reason a man and woman should come together is to have children. There is so much more to a loving partnership than that. I did not have it with Winterwood, but I genuinely believe in it. My late parents had it." Celia paused, then sighed wistfully. "I had no children with the earl, and maybe I cannot have them. While that possibility saddens me, it will not rule my life. So you should not let that be a deterrent to future joy." Celia smiled. "Take love with both hands and welcome it. I intend to do the same—when and if the time comes."

"Thank you. And you're right. Everything you said."

"Fiona, what are friends for?"

Fiona smiled and patted her hand. "Aye, ducks. We are that."

"Maybe you could help me to my room," Celia suggested.

"Liam brought you to his private place. Let him care for you."

The outer door opened, and Celia recognized Liam's heavy tread.

"Speak of the handsome devil," Fiona whispered.

Liam entered the bedroom. "Fiona, cleanup has started. Can you supervise? I'll be down soon."

"Aye. I'm on it."

Liam gently grasped her arm. "Please say nothing about Celia's dowager countess status. Not yet."

"No worries, love." Fiona patted Liam's hand, then departed.

"How are you?" Liam asked worriedly.

"I'm a little tired. With some rest, I will be as right as rain in a day, two at most. I'm ready to tackle sandwich making once again."

Liam picked up the quilt folded at the end of his bed and gently laid it over her. "Then sleep. I must help downstairs."

"Yes, Chef."

Liam chuckled softly.

"I will be fine, I promise," Celia added.

"Aye, love. I know you will." Liam caressed her cheek, then turned down the gas light on the wall. After he left, Celia pulled the quilt up to her nose. It smelled of Liam, his shaving soap, a faint odor of enticing food scents, and a masculine scent all his own.

Feeling comforted and protected, Celia smiled as she drifted off to sleep.

CHAPTER TWENTY

THE NEXT TIME Liam glanced at the clock, it read one in the morning. Finally, they had finished the scrubbing. Timmy swept the last of the broken glass from the floor, and the staff stood in a semi-circle, staring at Liam.

Right. He should say—something. Celia's words entered his tired mind.

Open up, and welcome them into your heart. Sit at the head of the table and get to know them better. Share a laugh and praise them for a job well done where warranted.

"I want to thank you for all your hard work. I also want to apologize for my rude behavior earlier tonight. I was angry over Teddy's situation and took it out on you. I'm sorry. As far as Teddy is concerned, I sent him on an errand, but little did I know that the man in question would claim to be Teddy's father. Teddy elected to stay with him."

Gasps and murmurs moved through the staff, and their expressions showed shock and worry. Liam couldn't blame them; the entire incident sounded fantastical—as did many other incidents and revelations over the past several months.

"Teddy is sixteen, old enough to make up his mind," Liam continued. "His father owns a chop house, and Teddy wants to work there, make improvements, and the like. Timmy and Tommy, he says he will be in contact soon. Meanwhile, we're to pack up his things. It's nothing against you, lads, or anyone else here; Teddy was ready to move on. If you have any questions about this, ask me tomorrow, yeah?"

Everyone nodded, but Tommy looked genuinely hurt, and that made Liam's heart tighten. "One more thing, Celia mentioned about the staff sharing a family meal. I think it's a brilliant idea. Starting tomorrow, we'll close the restaurant at half past five, instead of six. Gather for the meal, day and night staff, then continue our duties afterward. I figure about forty-five minutes will be enough. Tommy, your suggestion of the potato shavings is brilliant, lad. Well done."

Tommy flushed with pleasure.

"It's late. Let's call it a night. A little extra will be in your pay packets for tonight's hard work. I appreciate every one of you. Thank you."

The staff moved toward the exit. Some touched their forelocks, and some smiled. Liam heard one of the night staff whisper to another, "Cor, I ain't never heard him speak that much."

"Tommy, come here, lad."

Tommy came to stand before Liam. "Aye, Liam?"

"Are you upset about Teddy?"

"A little. I thought he liked it here."

Liam smoothed Tommy's thick, black hair. "He did. But Teddy is older than we thought and ready to strike out alone. He saw an opportunity and he took it. His father is a criminal type in Devil's Acre, where Teddy lived with his mother for a while. Is he this man's son? They claim the connection."

"Like we do?" Tommy whispered.

"Aye. Your mother says so, just like Teddy's mother says so. That's all the proof we or anyone needs."

"Timmy says I should move upstairs since you're my father. He said he would stay in the room behind the kitchen."

"Whatever you decide."

"I want to think about it," Tommy murmured.

"Aye. You and I will talk with Timmy soon to see what he

wants to do. He can continue being an apprentice here, working his way up, or finding a job elsewhere when the time comes. Do you know how old he is?"

"He thinks he's thirteen, maybe twelve, like me. He has no family."

"He does now, here with us. Timmy has plenty of time to consider his future." Liam hesitated a moment. "I'd like to mention to everyone tomorrow at the meal that you're my son. Is that all right with you?"

Tommy nodded and gave him a wide smile.

"Good. Go to bed, lad."

Tommy nodded, then scampered toward the door. But he stopped, turned, and ran toward Liam, throwing his arms about his waist. Liam was so shocked by the embrace that he momentarily froze. Then he hugged him, patting him on the back.

"There, lad. It will all work out. We move forward together," Liam said tenderly.

Tommy looked up at Liam, smiled again, and then ran toward the door.

Liam stood alone and glanced around the eating and gaming area. This was *his* place, and he had worked hard to bring it along as far as it had. At age twenty-one, he'd been offered a *commis* or junior chef job at one of The Savoy Hotel's restaurants, but that had not appealed to him. Being his own boss meant much more. If Liam had accepted the Savoy job, he would have gained a reputation over time and moved up the hierarchy that existed in elite and expensive restaurant kitchens, like in ten years, making it to chef *de partie* or *sous* chef.

Besides, he had no interest in learning French or gourmet cooking—not that there was anything wrong with such fare. Liam wanted to bring flavorful, everyday meals to the masses. Alexis Soyer's cookbook had become an instruction manual for his life—the one he'd wanted most to live. He'd studied the famous chef and all aspects of his life and career. Alexis Soyer was French and started his career in the best Paris kitchens. However, the chef had grown up in poverty and understood what it was like to be hungry. Soyer believed that hearty eating and good cooking should not be only available to the wealthy. Liam believed that, as well.

Once the famous chef moved to London, Soyer became renowned for his extravagant banquets for any aristocrat who hired him. But it was Soyer's work beyond cooking for the elite, like assisting in feeding those caught in the Irish potato famine or tirelessly assisting Florence Nightingale during the Crimea War, that caught Liam's attention. Many soldiers had been ill from malnutrition, and Soyer had shown the army how to run a well-organized kitchen and create healthy meals, which slashed mortality rates.

While Liam could never aspire to the late Soyer's multi-layered achievements, he could affect change in his little corner of Spitalfields. His customers consisted of the underprivileged, the working class, the middle class, and every now and then a few toffs even wandered in. That was when he'd been offered the position at The Savoy. Someone in upper hotel management had liked his meal and wanted to speak to the chef. It so happened that Liam had cooked it. What dish had he prepared that day? Probably grilled steak, onion puree, and grilled mushrooms. It had been—and still was—one of his most popular dishes.

Did he have any regrets? Liam may have been young, but he wasn't without some intelligence. He took the man's card and spoke to Walter about it. Walter touched his shoulder and told him, "Go if you want, but know that I'm leaving this place to you. I'll put you in charge of the menus this very day, but I must agree to the meals. Nothing too fancy, eh? I'll make up a will and show it to you. Stay, Liam, and become the carriage driver of your future. Once I'm gone, you can do what you want with the place. Until then, we're partners, eh?"

Was that what Liam wanted with his son? His *son*. It was still hard to grasp. *We move forward together.*

Liam had no past regrets regarding his choice of occupation.

His commercial plan came to fruition, and everything clicked into place—until the shed fire and the disturbance last night. Bad word of mouth could put him out of business, which might be what the person or persons behind this mischief wanted. Liam yawned. *Enough of this.* After collecting his wool coat and scarf, he turned the gas lights off and headed through the rear exit, locking the door behind him.

The bracing cold wind slammed him hard when he stepped outside to climb the stairs. The snow fell gently, collecting on his coat and in his hair. Hopefully, it would not accumulate, which might affect his customer traffic tomorrow.

Liam tapped his snow-covered boots against the stairs and then entered. Someone had lit the coal stove, which cast a rolling warmth along the long, wide hallway. He silently entered his room. Had Celia returned to her bed? God, he hoped not. He tore off his coat and scarf, tossed them to the sofa, and entered. He listened and then heard her quiet breathing. One panel of the draperies was open, casting muted moonlight across the floor. She was lying on her side and looked beautiful, her long golden-brown hair spread across his pillow. Removing his shirt and boots, he crawled in next to her. He was too bloody exhausted to wash up.

Celia stirred. "What time is it?" she whispered.

"It's past one in the morning." Liam hesitated. "Do you want me to carry you to your room?"

"No. I want to stay here. If you do not mind."

Mind? What would he give to have this lovely lady waiting for him every night, warm in his bed? "Aye. Stay." He curled in next to her, careful not to lay his arm across her injury. Celia sighed contentedly and pulled his arm under her breasts. Tired or not, he grew hard. "Ignore that; it happens whenever you're near."

"I don't mind." Celia yawned. "Good night, Liam."

He kissed her cheek and drifted into a deep sleep. It turned out to be one of the most restful nights of his life.

⫸⫷

"MY LORD!"

William snapped awake. Baldwin stood over him, looking worried. "What is it? Is the house on fire?" William roared.

"No, my lord. Detective Sergeant Morrisey from H Division wishes to see you as soon as possible. He says it is of the utmost importance."

Damn, and blast it! "Did he ask for Shinwell?"

"No, my lord. Just you."

"Hand me my dressing gown." William had a sinking feeling that this copper visit had to do with his reckless son. Troy had been acting cagey the past few days. William tied his gown as he stepped into his slippers. "Where is this copper?"

"In your study, my lord. Shall I bring tea?"

"Yes, along with toast and cheese. I am ravenous." William slowly descended the stairs and found himself breathless when he reached the ground floor. That boded ill. One usually became winded when ascending. William shook away the worrying thought and lumbered toward his study. He entered, and the detective stood.

"What do you want, Morrisey? And how dare you call at such an early hour! Coppers have no manners," William grumbled as he sat behind his desk.

"It's half past eight, my lord, the beginning of my work day. Regardless, here is my card." Morrisey laid it on the desk and then sat in the chair opposite him.

William ignored the card. "Well, speak your piece."

"Is your son, Viscount Shinwell, available? He should be included in this interview."

"He is not at home. I assume he stayed at a friend's residence." The slugabed was likely upstairs, sleeping off a drunken revel from the night before.

Morrisey removed a notepad and pencil from his side coat

195

pocket. "No matter. We will address that later. Last night, four hoodlums entered The Crowing Cock at approximately half past seven and caused a disturbance, even grabbing one of the female employees and holding a knife to her neck."

William's blood began to simmer. He fought to keep his expression neutral. "What is that to me?"

"The man threatened bodily harm and said to the woman hostage, and I quote, "Ain't you a tasty dish. Just like *he* said." The woman is Countess Winterwood, your niece. You are aware she is at The Crowing Cock in Spitalfields?"

"I am aware," William ground out. "And she is a dowager countess." William had no idea why he added that. It made him sound petulant, like Troy. As Etta had told him on many occasions, Troy had had to learn that abhorrent behavior somewhere. *Tasty dish. God above!* Troy had just used that phrase to describe Celia the other day.

"Some weeks ago, she was dragged there by your son, Viscount Shinwell, to pay off a debt of some 240 pounds, correct?"

"I met with Hallahan, and we came to an agreement as to the debt. Celia is welcome to return here any time she chooses. It was an ill-advised prank on my son's part, and I reprimanded him severely." *Not severely enough, it appears.*

Morrisey wrote in his notebook, not reacting to William's reply. "Your recently widowed and impoverished niece came to you, with no other place to stay. Since Lady Celia only recently arrived in London after living away for years, not many men in her acquaintance could be this mysterious 'he,' correct, my lord?"

"I could not say," William growled between clenched teeth.

Morrisey looked up and gave William a curt smile. "I can say, my lord. There is Hallahan and his employees, Bruce Shepherd and Jack Davies. Beyond that, there is only you and your son."

Damn Troy's blasted hide! All the threats and warnings had come to naught.

"There was also the arson incident at the property," the detective continued. "A shed and all its contents were destroyed. I spoke to the brigade captain early this morning, and he said the fire had been deliberately set. He has the proof."

"Hallahan mentioned the fire at our meeting. It has nothing to do with me," William stated emphatically.

"Well, we will see where the investigation leads me. And we do have a lead. So, my lord, you state that you have no knowledge of the assault, property damage, or the arson?"

"That is correct," William replied icily.

Morrisey snapped his notebook closed. "I shall return in three days at the same time. Have your son available for an interview, or I shall send out uniformed officers to forcibly take him into custody. I can do that, for he is a suspect. Top of my list, as a matter of fact." Morrisey fetched his hat from the nearby table and touched his forelock. "Good day, my lord."

Baldwin stepped into the room to escort the detective to the door, returned with the tea tray, and sat it before William. "My lord, a note arrived. It is from Mr. Hallahan." He held out the folded note toward William. He snatched it from the butler and opened it.

Billy Buck. I told you that if anything happened to me, my employees, or my business, I would give your slimy son's name to the peelers. After last night's doings at my pub, you have left me no choice but to do so. You also owe me the original debt of 240 pounds, as our agreement is now null and void. I'll accept a bank draft. If the payment does not arrive by six o'clock the evening after next, I will have no choice but to tell Morrisey about your secret identity. I have witnesses to back up the claim. If you do pay, the police will hear nothing further from me. You have my word.

Hallahan

William crumbled the note in his fist. It was rank extortion, but William had no choice. Hallahan would keep the money for himself or give to Celia. Either way, he'd have to pay. He must protect his criminal identity as it was his only means of income. It also meant he would have to accelerate his plans for his idiot son.

"Listen to me," William hissed menacingly to Baldwin. "Do *not* tell the viscount of the copper's visit. Instruct the staff as well." He splashed tea into his cup. "Also, no one is to know of this note. You are to go to Brown's Hotel and ask to see Mr. Silas Foster. He is American. Tell him I am ready to close the deal, and he is to meet me at my place in Hamstead at one this afternoon. The man has the address. Got that? I want *you* to deliver the message, no one else. See me when you return."

Baldwin bowed slightly. "Yes, my lord."

"Tell my valet to have my afternoon suit pressed and ready. Tell the cook to hold breakfast. I will eat at my flat." William frequently had food delivered from a nearby tavern. A tasty fried steak with all the trimmings and a pint of bitter would be just what he needed to calm his anger.

"Yes, my lord." Baldwin turned and exited, closing the door behind him.

William stuffed a wedge of cheese and toast into his mouth and chewed furiously. There was nothing else to be done. He had warned his son more than once. Now, he was in trouble with the law. A competent solicitor could see that Troy served little or no prison time, if his stupid son's involvement was proven. Regardless, the family name would be tarnished, and Etta would never forgive him. His distant wife would blame him—and rightly so— for allowing Troy to run amuck. And Troy in Newgate Prison? That pampered pillock would not handle one night there, let alone several weeks or months.

Foster's heiress daughter yearned to marry into the British aristocracy. Foster showed William a mini-portrait of the girl— what was her name, Louise? Lynda? Who cared? The girl looked presentable enough.

With this latest development, he had no choice but to act swiftly. He had thought a few weeks of courting would not go amiss, but that plan had gone by the wayside. If he had to, he would throw Troy on a ship bound for America with Foster and his daughter himself. Foster had agreed to put Troy to work in the man's Pennsylvania steel factory, learning the trade from the bottom up. His son would have to stay in America for several years until this nasty business calmed down. Or until William cocked up his toes, whichever came first.

There *had to* be an heir. The earldom had to live on, Troy was his only hope. He would get Troy's assurance on the matter, one way or the other.

No son of his would ever be arrested. Not while William drew a ragged, wheezing breath.

CHAPTER TWENTY-ONE

CELIA AWOKE, AND it took a moment for her to realize where she was. The curtains were drawn, and not much light peeked through. She was curled up in Liam's arms, and one of his hands was grasping her breast. He breathed deeply, obviously sound asleep. Did she dare move?

"Liam," she whispered.

He groaned sleepily and brushed his thumb across her breast, causing her nipple to harden. The sensual sensation that tore through her made her gasp, then moan. Just that slight movement caused sparks to skitter along her nerve endings, and she felt wetness between her legs.

Celia had never experienced this with Carlton—not at all. But then, her husband never touched or kissed her. Once Carlton had caught his breath from their brief encounter, he'd returned to his room, often without speaking. Because of her husband's swiftness, she'd never had the luxury of any enjoyment in the act—not even a twinge.

But Liam? Celia closed her eyes. Just looking at him caused her to tremble all over. Kissing? What a revelation. Celia wanted more. She wanted that hardness she felt whenever he pulled her into his arms deep inside her. The carnal thought was more than she could bear.

However, as much as she yearned to become intimate with Liam, Celia realized there was much to settle first. Communication was paramount. Despite her loveless marriage—and outside the marriage bed—she and Carlton had always spoken to one another if an urgent item had cropped up. She'd also let him know if she was concerned about something. Because of this back and forth, they'd formed a sort of friendship even though they did not have much in common. Then Carlton had become ill, and most conversations had ceased.

If Celia was to have any future with Liam, they had to be honest with one another. She grabbed his upper arm and gave it a vigorous shake. "Liam!" she said more loudly.

"Jaysus! What?" He came awake with a start and sat up partway, blinking rapidly. "What's amiss?"

"I am sorry to wake you so abruptly. Nothing's happened."

Liam sighed and lay prone.

"Did you get up sometime during the night, or did I dream that?" Celia asked.

"At the crack of dawn or close to it," he replied. "I wrote a note to Darrington and delivered it to his butler."

"Oh. Was that wise?" Celia murmured.

"Probably not."

Celia listened as he relayed the contents of the letter. "My uncle will not react well to that."

"It wasn't a threat, but a promise I made when last we met and agreed to the terms. Shinwell broke that contract with the doings last night. We both know your cousin is the 'he' in that statement. I imagine Morrisey will pay a visit to Darrington this morning."

"Yes. I believe Shinwell is the 'he', as well. The man who grabbed me used the same phrase Shinwell used to say to me before I was sent away to school. I should have told the sergeant, but my mind was spinning."

"I heard him say it the day he brought you to me, and I let Morrisey know that. Your cousin is a degenerate fool."

"I know."

Liam glanced at the clock. "It's close to nine. I should be up already."

"I want to talk to you first," Celia said in a lower voice. "I am so sorry."

"For what?" Liam murmured.

"For a few things. I have been saving them up. First, I apologize for not telling you I was a dowager countess when Shinwell brought me here." Celia rested on her side, staring at the opposite wall. "There is no excuse for keeping that from you. Initially, I was scared that you would toss me into the street. As Fiona succinctly told me, I lied by omission."

"You had your reasons. I understand why you didn't, and I don't judge you. I know about survival. Don't worry about it."

"Still, I want us to be honest and open with each other. I also apologize for bringing all this upheaval to your door. M-m-my uncle and cousin." Her voice trembled. Blast it; this was harder than she thought. "It's because of me that they are threatening your livelihood with their criminal acts," she whispered miserably.

"It's interesting that you say criminal. I recently discovered that your uncle is known on the streets as Billy Buck. Lucian Sharpe told me. It seems that the earl is leading a double life. What he's involved in, I've no idea."

Celia gasped. "Why did you not tell me this before? Oh, no. The note will certainly anger him!"

"As I said, I only just learned it, but aye, I should have told you right away. I wanted to protect you. I wanted to conclude business with the man and have nothing more to do with him. And he agreed. I believe Shinwell caused this latest mischief without your uncle's knowledge. Darrington will be livid, and perhaps he will finally harness in his son."

"This is what I mean about telling each other important information," Celia said matter-of-factly. "It does not change the fact that I brought them into this."

Liam gently turned her onto her back. He then laid on his side, resting on his elbow. He smoothed the tendrils of hair that had come loose from her pins. "Love, all of this would have happened anyway. Shinwell owed the money before you arrived in London. I never should have given the viscount any credit to begin with. That failure of judgment is on me."

"But because of *me*, you left most of that debt on the table to secure my aunt's address and a small settlement."

"I will get it back when your uncle pays what is owed—something he will have to do now that Shinwell broke our agreement. Besides, I would do anything to assist you. Love, I'll do anything to keep you safe and keep that cheerful smile in place."

Celia touched his cheek. "What is happening between us? Do you know?"

He took her hand and kissed it. "I still don't know. I can't put it into words."

"Fiona said you have had plenty of lady friends. I am not disparaging your character, far from it. All—or most—men have a past. It's expected."

"Expected? Maybe with the upper crust. Fiona is speculating. I've not had 'plenty of lady friends.' My restaurant kept me too busy for most interactions with women. Many Saturday nights, I went for a walk or to a pub to observe what the competition was doing. Recently, I visited a widow once a week," Liam murmured. "I broke the connection."

"When?"

"Two days after I met you."

A lump of emotion settled in Celia's throat. She had no idea what to say. Could it be? Had he felt something toward her that quickly?

"Since we're being candid," Liam ventured, "I want to tell you that I not only mailed your letters to the new Earl of Winterwood and your aunt, but also sent telegraphs."

"You did? That must have cost you a pretty penny. Why?"

"It cost a few shillings, but I could afford it. I suppose I wanted you to receive the help you deserved. Letters take too long, although I was told the telegraph to Italy would take longer than the one to Northern England. I also considered sending a telegraph to Mitchell and Corrine, but you said to let them enjoy their honeymoon, and I think you're right." Liam sighed. "It doesn't sit well with me that you are laboring in my kitchen, cleaning counters, making sandwiches, taking orders—"

Celia laced her fingers through his. "I do not mind taking orders from *you*. Now, I want you to listen closely. I *want* to work here and assist you. Believe me; I would have told you upfront had I not liked it. I am not some delicate flower that needs to be coddled. If I were, I would have taken Drew up on his generous offer. But I've had enough of that life. I do not *want* that life, now or in the future."

"The future?"

It was hard to see in the dimness of the room, which made Celia bold. "We can have one. Together. Because I have never felt like this. I adore you, Liam Hallahan. I cannot imagine a better life than being at your side. There is nothing we cannot accomplish—as long as we do it as partners."

The room became still, and the growing silence became awkward. Liam never moved; Celia couldn't even hear him breathing. Had she shocked him into a frozen, uncommunicative state? Had she gone too far?

"Liam?" she whispered. *No reply.* Celia reviewed the recent conversation. He said he wanted her to be happy. But perhaps he only meant in the present. Liam sent telegraphs—to be rid of her? No, it couldn't be. "Speak to me. Do not withdraw from me." She grasped his shoulder and shook it. Just how deep did his wounds from the past go? Blast it. She *had* gone too far, too fast. Liam had started—in increments—to come out of his shell, but her declaration of affection might have set things back. Celia had never witnessed anyone shut down emotionally like this before.

"I will take you to your room," he replied, his voice detached.

Celia's heart sank. But she would not become angry and shrewish. It was not her way, no matter how infuriating this man acted. "Liam, if you do not feel the same toward me, say so now, and I will depart."

Again, silence.

"It's all right if your feelings petrify you. It is also new and strange to me," Celia continued. "But it's also exhilarating."

He pulled his hand away, but Celia grasped it again. "Please do not hide within yourself. You have come so far, not only with me but with your staff—your *family*. You must be completely honest with them. Tell them of your recently discovered son and your duke-father background. Acknowledge Drew and Mitchell as your brothers—publicly. Allow them into your heart. Only then will you be able to accept your feelings toward me."

"Celia," Liam croaked.

She carefully pulled herself upright and swung her legs around. Gingerly, she stood. "I know I'm asking a great deal. I also know that you care for me, more than simply concern for my safety and comfort. I will leave you to think about what I said. I can go to my room on my own. The injury is not that serious."

Celia headed toward the door, then halted. She had come this far—she might as well dive into the deep end of the bathing pool. "I more than adore you, Liam. I am falling in love with you. There. I said it—the dreaded 'L' word. The time has come for you to decide what you desire for your remaining years. Your choice. I know you have it in you to stop hiding. Come and find me when you do."

Holding her head high, she exited the flat. Liam did not follow.

Celia might have to walk out of his life if he could not accept his feelings.

And that horrible prospect nearly cleaved her in two.

LIAM STUMBLED DOWNSTAIRS thirty minutes later. He'd barely

slept, not only because of the message delivery but also because Celia's brave and emotional plea had played repeatedly in his head. There was nothing else for it. He was a complete prat. An emotionally damaged, hollowed-out husk of a man. How could one's past cast such a shadow over the present and the future? Living on the streets had hardened his heart, no mistake. Even these past years of having a steady job and a roof over his head had done nothing to eliminate the feeling that it could all end with a snap of his fingers. Even when he'd inherited the business, he'd lamented over every burnt sauce and every outstanding invoice to such a point that Fiona had slapped his face when they'd been alone in the kitchen, telling him to get a grip.

Fiona should give him another whack across the chops to beat some sense into him now. He had managed to rein in his overwrought anxiety concerning the business, but when it came to showing his emotions regarding people, that aspect still alluded him.

A beautiful woman had just told him that she was falling *in love* with him, and he'd became immobilized, unable to think or speak. Any rational man would have gathered her into his arms and been damned grateful, opening his heart and telling her how he felt. But not him. He'd stood as still as a granite statue covered in bird shite.

"Liam, we have breakfast laid out. Come join us." Enya smiled as he entered the kitchen. He inhaled, and the enticing aroma of bacon hung in the air. He nodded and followed Enya into the staff eating area. His staff was efficient and well-trained, just as Drew had observed. A few people cheerily said, "Good morning," and Liam acknowledged them with a brisk nod as he strode to the sideboard. He heaped his plate with fried eggs, bacon, and cheese. There was an empty chair at the head of the table.

Sit at the head of the table and get to know them better. Share a laugh and praise them for a job well done.

Celia was right about that and so much else. This was as good a place as any to start. "Good morning, all," Liam said with a smile as he sat. "Who cooked breakfast?"

"Timmy and me," Tommy said proudly. "Enya took a tray to Celia already."

Liam cut into the fried egg and took a bite. "Perfect. The edges are crispy."

"Just as you taught me," Tommy replied.

"Enya, when Fiona awakens, I want you two to ensure all the staff is here at half past five for a meal and a meeting."

She nodded. "I will. Fiona said she's making sandwiches for Celia today. There's grilled chicken, cucumber and watercress, cheese and onion. After the lads start the stew, they will assist Fiona with the sandwiches. There are also lobster puffs from the toff trays."

"Good. Now, what's on the menu for today?"

A knock sounded at the rear door. "That's Mr. Eckley with the bread order," Tommy stated.

"His money envelope for yesterday's bill is on my desk, lad. Go fetch it and pay the man."

"Aye," Tommy replied. I asked Mr. Eckley for four dozen ginger biscuits and five dozen treacle tarts. I meant to tell you yesterday, but with everything—"

"That's fine, Tommy. Well done. Eckley said he was branching out with his second cooker purchase. Ask him for a full menu when he has it, as we will purchase more baked goods."

"Yes, Liam!" Tommy ran from the room.

Liam spread blackberry jam on his toast. "Enya, see that Fiona uses Eckley's items today with the tea trays. Now, the menu?"

"Shrimp and haddock chowder served with Mr. Eckley's fresh bread," Hannah replied. "I've already chopped the shrimp and the haddock fine, as you showed me. I'll do the potatoes and onions after breakfast. There are also cod and shrimp cakes served with boiled potatoes, carrots, and peas with chive sauce. That's your dish."

Liam had decided to serve it for tonight's family-staff meal. He knew the staff would be dedicated to their tasks, including boiling eggs and chopping potatoes and onions for the seafood cakes. Billings Fish Market gave him a good deal on the fish, most of it pickled since it was winter. He didn't serve oysters or eels because they could be had at a cheap price at any street corner or merchant's cart. Eel shops had opened in the East End, becoming as popular as the fish and chip places. Liam would stay with his plan of serving food that was a notch or two above the street. "Timmy, you will work with me today. We will put on extra potatoes and will need more onions chopped. Several eggs need to be boiled hard for the cod and shrimp cakes."

"Yes, Liam," Timmy replied as he popped a piece of bacon into his mouth.

Tommy entered the room and laid a plate of treacle tarts on the table. "Mr. Eckley said these are for us to try, no cost. He also said he will have a complete menu for you tomorrow. Mrs. Eckley has her niece assisting, so there will be more offerings."

Liam bit into the tart. *Delicious.* He would gladly give Eckley more business. "If any of you know trustworthy people who want to work here, let me know. I'll be looking for night staff, a waitress, and another barman-waiter. Morrigan will be moving to the day staff later this week. I'll also need someone to replace Teddy."

After the breakfast dishes were cleared and washed, the staff simmered the stew on the stove as they prepared the fish chowder and cod and shrimp cakes. Once the free stew concluded, the kitchen staff had their assignments and got to work. Fiona joined them at ten o'clock and started preparing the sandwich fillings. The staff's adaptability and resilience in the face of these challenges were genuinely commendable.

The kitchen smelled like a fish market, but that was to be expected. Even though it was chilly outside, the kitchen windows were open halfway to allow airflow and some relief from the hot gas cookers roiling at full tilt. Liam had also installed vents in the walls and extra windows so some air could circulate. It was during this mad dash to opening time that Morrigan entered the kitchen.

"Blimey. A man at the front entrance is asking to see Celia. I told him we weren't open. But he said it was important."

Blast it. "What's his name?"

"He said he is the Earl of Winterwood."

CHAPTER TWENTY-TWO

CELIA SAT UPRIGHT in bed, wearing her wool skirt and a simple white blouse. Acting as a patient did not appeal, and she only stayed in her room today because Drew insisted. Browsing through "Shilling Cookery for the People" by Alexis Soyer, the book that gave Liam's life a decided purpose, she stopped at the front of the book and read:

> *Therefore you will perceive that nothing more disposes the heart to amicable feeling and friendly transactions, than a dinner well-conceived and artistically prepared.*

Was this how Liam had found his joy? Could cooking be the only thing that touched his heart? It was a rather depressing thought. Celia always believed that if someone had a passion for a particular hobby, career, or object, surely that would translate to life itself and the people in one's life. What did she know about passions since she lived such a sheltered life, with hardly any interaction with anyone besides Carlton and a few servants?

A sharp knock at the door tore her from her troubled thoughts. "Come in."

Liam entered. The wind had tousled his hair, and he wore an apron under his coat. "There is someone to see you. The Earl of Winterwood."

Celia blinked rapidly, completely shocked. "Here?"

"Aye. I'll send him up. Use my parlor. I must return to the

kitchen. We open in twenty minutes. I can't spare anyone to serve tea, but I'll ask Timmy to bring a few sandwiches. The water closet behind my bedroom has a cupboard with dishes. You'll have to serve water."

Celia had no idea Liam had his own WC in his flat. "Yes, I will do that. Thank you."

Liam turned to leave, then stopped. "The family meal is at half past five. Can you attend?"

"I will be there," she replied softly.

Liam disappeared into the hall.

Celia set the cookbook aside and stood. Taking her time, she made her way to Liam's flat and stood in the doorway. A few minutes later, Franklin Gardiner, brushing snow from his shoulders, entered the hallway.

"Good day, my lord. Let us meet in here." Celia stepped aside.

Winterwood removed his hat and bowed. "Thank you for receiving me, my lady." The new earl followed her into Liam's flat.

"You can hang your coat on the hook, my lord."

"If you don't mind, I will keep it on, my lady."

After they sat across from each other, Celia asked, "What brings you here, my lord?"

"A telegram, my lady. From Mr. Hallahan. But it was more than that. I sent a cablegram to my wife soon after you departed, giving her the condensed details of what I had discovered of the late earl's estate. She sent back a scathing rebuke of my behavior towards you, and I have come to make amends."

Timmy knocked on the door, entered, and brought the platter into the parlor. "Thank you, Timmy. Please place it on the table." He did and hurried away, closing the door behind him.

Celia stood slowly, holding her side.

"Are you injured, my lady?" the earl asked worriedly.

"Not severely; I will heal. I cannot offer you tea or coffee as there are no facilities here to prepare it, and everyone downstairs is hard at work serving the luncheon crowd. I can offer water."

"That is satisfactory, my lady."

Celia located the cupboard Liam had spoken of and grabbed two small plates, mugs, and paper napkins. She also found a tray. After filling the mugs with water, she strode into the parlor, taking small, careful steps.

Franklin Gardiner jumped to his feet and hurried toward her. "Allow me to take the tray."

Celia gladly gave it up. Once seated, his lordship took the small plate and placed the sandwich wedges on it.

"You mentioned amends, my lord?"

"Yes. Allow me to apologize. I followed Mr. Sanderson's suggestions because he assured me that was how peerage estates were settled. He promised me your family would look after you and that this was how it's done. What do I know about such things, being from Canada? We are a commonwealth country but do not follow such strict rules of society."

"Not to agree with Mr. Sanderson, but as a solicitor to the earldom, he followed the letter of the law, such as it is. His primary concern was keeping the earldom intact for you as the new earl. A dowager countess with no dowry or mention in the will is not deemed important."

Winterwood tsked. "That is not just. I had no idea. As my dear wife said, ignorance is no excuse." He chewed his sandwich thoughtfully. "Mr. Hallahan said your uncle left you on Mr. Hallahan's doorstep. I was horrified to hear that, my lady."

"It was my cousin, Viscount Shinwell, but my uncle did nothing to stop it. My aunt, my only blood relation, is away wintering in Italy. I am thankful Mr. Hallahan allowed me to stay and work here. Otherwise, I would have had nowhere else to go."

The earl's eyes bulged in shock. "You are working at this restaurant? Oh, that is not to be borne. As my wife stated, you are a Countess of Winterwood and should be afforded all assistance and respect. I could not agree more. 'Make it right,' her ladyship demanded, and I follow her edict in all things."

Celia could not believe this. She could scream and cry and reprimand the earl for not 'making it right' in the first place. Then again, what would be the point? He had only followed the solicitor's advice. The entire peerage primogeniture system needed massive reform. "My lord, how do you intend to do that if there is not much money in the estate? I've seen the books. You have a family to look after and an earldom to keep afloat."

"I do at that, my lady. However, there may be a silver lining for my family—and for you." The earl sipped his water. "Mr. Sanderson put the cottage up for sale as soon as you departed. I am unsure *why* it is referred to as a cottage, as it seems more of a large-sized residence. Well, a Scottish lord expressed an interest. Or is it laird?" Winterwood scratched his chin thoughtfully. "Yes, it's laird. Nonetheless, he wants it for a hunting retreat, or so he said. Mr. Sanderson, wily as he is, discovered the laird is also interested in the timber on the property. It is worth quite a lot. There were negotiations back and forth, and the laird has put forth an offer. Twenty-five thousand pounds, can you imagine? Most of that amount is for the timber."

Celia was stunned. She'd never dreamed the property was worth that much. Several thousand acres were included with the actual residence. "I cannot imagine," she murmured.

"Mr. Sanderson said I could keep the property and work the timber myself, but that would be a costly outlay for men and equipment, let alone building a lumber mill. It's money that I do not have, not even with my late cousin's modest investments."

"Why are you telling me all this, my lord?"

"Because I wish to share the proceeds with you, my dear lady."

Celia's mouth dropped open, but she swiftly closed it. "How?" she whispered.

"Mr. Sanderson has worked a deal with Roderick MacAdam, the aforementioned Scottish laird. The earldom will receive a yearly stipend of six percent of the profits from MacAdam's lumber business. I wish to split it down the middle: the cost of the cottage, timber, and three percent of the lumber. That will be twelve thousand five hundred pounds to you."

That much? Plus three percent on the lumber? Holy crow! "Does Mr. Sanderson know you are here, my lord?"

"He does, my lady, although he tried to talk me out of it."

She could well imagine. "Your offer is generous and much appreciated. I have a counteroffer."

The earl's eyes bulged again.

"I will accept nine thousand pounds and nothing more. That should have been my dowry or the settlement Carlton should have left me in his will or at least the two combined. Besides, my lord, you have an heir, a family, and the manor house, which is in a shocking state of disrepair. The yearly profits for the lumber should remain with the Winterwood earldom."

"Are you certain, my lady? The lumber venture could prove to be lucrative."

Celia could live quite comfortably on the interest of nine thousand pounds. "I am sure. And please, call me Celia."

The earl gave her a beaming smile. "Then you must call me Franklin. What shall we do next?"

"Will you be in London for long, Franklin?"

"I came to gander at rentals here in the city besides visiting you. I do not think I wish to rent an entire town house, however. I have seen a few already. I find them too ostentatious. My lady wife will concur." Franklin sighed, his vulnerability showing. "I am not cut out to be an aristocrat. And attending Parliament in the House of Lords? The prospect has me quivering with fear."

"I will do all I can to assist you. My dear friend, Doctor Drew Hornsby, has a viscount father and a duke uncle in the House of Lords. I am sure they would be glad to show you the ropes, as it were." Celia smiled. "Drew also has a flat for rent in Gloucester Square; if that is not available or suitable, we can find you another."

"I *am* glad I came to see you," Franklin smiled. "I do hope we can keep this acquaintance."

"We shall be good friends. Wait and see."

"I am exceedingly pleased. Now, you must hire a solicitor and have him contact Mr. Sanderson with the details."

Solicitor? Again, she would have to confer with Drew. "I will do that as soon as possible. Why not stay for a meal, Franklin? Mr. Hallahan is quite talented. I believe shrimp and haddock dishes are on the luncheon menu."

Franklin clapped his hands together. "I adore haddock! Being from Nova Scotia, seafood makes up a great part of my meals. Will you join me?"

Should she? Why not, indeed?

HANNAH HURRIED INTO the kitchen. "Two fish cakes, table four!"

Liam wrote on his floor map and turned toward the stove.

Hannah leaned in and whispered, "It's for that earl. Celia's with him."

Celia, sitting down and breaking bread with Winterwood? Why? Liam shook his head and flipped over the shrimp and haddock cakes sizzling in the cast iron frypan. She had too kind a heart. Liam turned toward the nearby prep table, slid the cakes onto two plates, and then served the vegetables, drizzling them with warm dill sauce.

"Table four!"

Hannah grabbed the plates and exited the kitchen. Liam had no time to contemplate what was happening, for the servers called out more orders.

He glanced at Fiona, busily making sandwiches. "How are the fillings holding up?"

"So far, we're fine. At least for the next hour."

Someone pounded at the rear entrance door. Liam definitely needed more help in the kitchen. "Fiona, see who that is. Please."

She returned with a man carrying a large box. "It's toff food!"

"And I've got another box this big out in me cart," the man stated.

Bloody hell. What was he going to do with all this? Usually, only a tray or two were sent maybe twice a week, not boxes filled with food. "Set them on the table there. Where did it come from?"

"The Duke of Chellenham. He said it was from a banquet that was canceled. It's from some aristo acquaintance or some such."

The Duke of Chellenham, Damon Cranston, the half-brother he had yet to meet—or accept.

Drew and Mitchell had told him that Chellenham was a decent sort despite his aristocratic manner. Liam should make it a point to meet the man before the February meeting where he was to discuss The Hallahan Initiative and the funding of it. What a pretentious name for a charity venture. Regardless, he would mention arranging an introduction with Chellenham the next time he saw Drew. "Thank the duke for me."

The delivery man touched his forelock and left the kitchen to bring in the other box.

"Fiona," Liam said after the delivery man departed, "In between your sandwich orders, see what's inside the boxes."

"I don't have any now. I'll check." Taking a small paring knife, she slit the tape on the box and open the flaps. "Cor, blimey. It's a feast for a queen. There's a saddle of mutton here! Battenburg cake, that's what they call that checkered cake, aye?"

"Aye. Slice off a piece. Is it fresh?"

Fiona tore off the corner and ate it. "Oh, that's lovely, that is."

She then approached him, holding out a small piece. He opened his mouth, and Fiona popped it in. It melted on his tongue. It was absolutely delicious. "Slice some of that for the tea trays," she said.

"There are also what look like almond cakes, Bakewell tarts, and savory crackers. We should serve some of this tonight for the family meal."

"See if Enya can come in here for a moment. I've got to place the meat in the iceboxes or larder."

"Right-o." Fiona hurried out into the restaurant and located Enya.

With Enya tending the stove, Liam got to work emptying the boxes: roast pork, duchess potatoes, dinner rolls, mustard pickles, baked trout with a sauce, mince pies, and more.

Right. He'd have to offer some of this on today's menu because there was too much food to fit into cold storage.

"Enya, are all the orders up to date?"

"For the moment."

"Go and fetch the servers. We will switch some of the items on this afternoon's menu." Enya departed.

Hannah stuck her head in. "Two chowder, table five!"

Liam waved her into the kitchen. "Is that it for the orders?"

"Aye, but more people are coming in."

Liam served up the chowder. "Come right back. There's a quick meeting."

Liam wrapped the uncooked fishcakes in parchment paper and placed them in the icebox. Enya, Hannah, Daisy, and Fiona were waiting for him when he returned.

"The cod and shrimp fishcakes are off the menu. Tell any new customers there is baked trout in a—" Liam opened the sauce container, dipped a spoon in, and tasted it. "—lobster sauce with duchess potatoes and the carrots we already cooked. Charge one shilling for it."

Fiona whistled. "That's pricey. Are you sure?"

"The food is above what we usually serve, so I'm charging top prices. Fiona, use the tarts, mince pies, cake, and whatever else you find for the tea trays. I need you to unpack everything and, in between orders, make an inventory of what we have left. Back to work!"

The women scattered, and for the next two hours, Liam and his wait staff were run off their feet. After the trout was gone, he heated a few portions of the roast pork. Finally, as the clock approached half past five, Liam turned off the stoves.

Fiona handed him two foolscap papers. He scanned the list. The amount of food the upper crust provided for a banquet for maybe a dozen or so people was obscene. What would have happened to this food? Perhaps the servants would have some, but the rest? In the bin. Aristocrats did not eat leftovers—God forbid.

His icebox was stuffed to the gills. He could not place another crumb in there if he tried. "Looks like mutton is on the menu tomorrow. Fiona, fetch the cod and shrimp cakes from the icebox. I'll cook that for the staff meal."

Timmy and Tommy came through the back door. "Glad you're here, lads. We've had a busy day. Start washing the dishes, yeah? Then bring clean plates and mugs into the staff dining area."

By quarter to six, the entire staff, day and night, sat around the table. Liam placed the food on platters or in serving bowls. Celia entered the room, and Liam rushed to her side, taking her coat and hanging it on the wall.

"How are you feeling?" he asked.

"Better, thank you."

It was not exactly a warm reply, but he could not blame Celia, considering his actions—or lack thereof—this morning. Liam pulled out a chair next to him, and she sat.

The platters were passed around, and friendly conversation broke out.

"Oh, I almost forgot. Celia, a telegram arrived for you an hour ago," Enya said. She reached into her apron pocket and handed it to Celia, who sat beside her.

Celia opened it, gasped, and then exclaimed, "It's from my aunt! She wants me to join her in Italy!"

CHAPTER TWENTY-THREE

C ELIA COULD NOT believe she just blurted that news. Everyone stared at her, and the room grew quiet.

"You've got a rich aunt?" Enya asked, her eyes wide.

"Not that wealthy," Celia murmured as she folded the telegram and placed it on the table.

"You're not leaving us?" Tommy said, his voice quivering.

"No, lad. Not for a while. That is if I even decide to go." Aunt Etta said a letter with more details was on its way, including what travel plans to make. Her aunt sounded as if she had no immediate plans to return to London. Well, life could undoubtedly surprise a person. First, Celia had received the money settlement, and now, an invitation to stay with her aunt in Italy.

Celia cast a side glance at Liam. He was stony-faced as usual when faced with a situation that required an emotional response—or any response at all.

"Your fortunes have taken a turn, ducks," Fiona enthused. "Good for you."

"It appears as if more than one of us has had our lives take an abrupt turn," Liam said as he cleared his throat. "As I told you all last night, I appreciate you all. This business does not work without all of you. Your hard work has not gone unnoticed. I know I apologized last night, but allow me to do it again."

Celia's eyes widened. Liam had apologized to the staff last night and told them he appreciated them? Her heart soared.

Perhaps there was hope after all. But why didn't he tell her that this morning? Celia knew why; he couldn't speak.

"I *am* sorry I've been brooding more than usual, but I've learned something about my past that has thrown me for a loop. You've seen Detective Sergeant Mitchell Simpson around before Christmas, and Doctor Drew Hornsby has been here often lately. I discovered in November that they're my half-brothers."

Gasps rose from the table.

"Aye, it was a bloody shock to me and all," Liam continued. "We share a duke father."

"A bleedin' duke?" Fiona cried shrilly.

"The late Duke of Chellenham. He was a nasty piece of work. He has offspring all over the city and beyond, seeing he was a careless, arrogant pillock of the first order."

Fiona shook her head. "All that toff food that came today is from—another half-brother? The new duke?"

"That's the jist of it. I haven't met him yet. There's more of us, the duke's bastards. I'll meet them at some point. Nothing's changed. I'm still Liam Hallahan, faults and all. And aye, I have enough faults to fill a stock pot or two."

Celia glanced around the table. Everyone had stopped eating, and more than one looked dazed. Liam was telling the truth. She was so proud of him that she thought her heart would burst.

"There's more," Liam said in a clear voice. "I've discovered *I* have a son. I learned of it a few months ago. This was a pleasant surprise and I welcome it. It's Tommy."

Loud exclamations rose from the table as all eyes swung to Tommy, sitting to Liam's left.

"It's true," Tommy agreed. "My mum told me before she died. My name going forward will be Thomas Clahane Hallahan." He looked at Liam. "If that's all right."

Liam smiled. "Aye, lad. It's more than all right. I would be proud if you took my name."

"Good heavens," Enya declared. "This is like the plot of a play I saw once."

Light laughter rippled about the table.

"One of those overwrought potboilers, eh, Enya?" Liam teased. "And we all know about pots boiling, yeah?" The laughter grew louder.

Celia's eyes grew wet. This was the Liam she knew existed deep down—warm, giving, occasionally teasing. He'd finally accepted everything life had thrown in his path. Would he accept her now? Would he accept their growing feelings for each other?

"Everyone tuck in," Liam urged. "The food's getting cold. I know I only mentioned it this morning, but does anyone have any names for me, possibly new employees?"

Bruce raised his hand. "I do, Liam. My cousin just started working for the Met Police, and his initial wages aren't enough to keep him, his wife, and their baby comfortable. He wants to know if he can work in the pub three nights a week. He works days with the coppers. I went around and saw him earlier."

"Fiona? When are the busiest nights?" Liam asked as he cut into the fishcakes.

"Well, Friday and Saturday, for sure. And Wednesday for some reason," Fiona answered.

"Bruce, have your cousin come see me tomorrow after his shift. What's his name?"

"Robert Shepherd. He's twenty-five and almost as big as me."

"Brilliant. Anyone else?"

"I've someone," Sally exclaimed. "My older sister, Susanna. She's looking for a job. She's got experience working in in a pub."

"When can she start?" Liam asked.

"Tomorrow night, if you want. I'm sure she'll say yes."

"Well, this is all clicking into place. Tell your sister she's hired, Sally. Morrigan, you can move to the day staff starting tomorrow. You'll work with me in the kitchen until you learn the rhythm."

"Sounds good, Liam," Morrigan replied with a smile. "I'd like to learn about the cooking, and such. I know how to make excellent pork chops."

"Brilliant."

"We need another apprentice!" Tommy interjected.

"True enough," Liam replied.

Timmy raised his hand. "I know where you can get plenty of apprentices—The Strand Workhouse. I was there for three years and knew many boys there."

"Good lad, Timmy. You and I will plan a trip next week, and you can help me select one or two."

Excited chatter broke out around the table. Liam spoke of the large boxes of food delivered, and they decided to offer crab croquettes and cheese puffs to the pub customers tonight at one shilling a plate. His gambling customers could afford it.

After the meal, everyone gathered their dishes and headed into the kitchen. Celia stood and picked up her empty plate. She looked at Liam. "We need to talk," she said.

Liam nodded. "I'll see you in your room in ten minutes."

She entered the kitchen where the boys were already doing the dishes. Morrigan and Sally were loading trays with glass mugs and whiskey glasses, and Bruce and Jack carried a barrel of ginger beer from the cellar. The transition from restaurant to pub was in full swing.

Fiona took her hand. "I hope you stay with us," she murmured. "But I understand if you don't."

"Thank you, Fiona. I will tell the rest of the staff soon of my circumstances. I have much to think about first."

"About Liam, too, I imagine. He's a stubborn bloke. Thanks to you, he's opened up to the staff. He ate breakfast with us this morning, chatting and laughing. It warmed my heart to see it."

"I *am* glad. That warmth and openness have not translated to me, however. Not fully."

"It will, I know it," Fiona whispered fiercely, keeping her voice low so the others would not hear. "Don't give up on Liam. He's worth the trouble, I promise you. He has so much love to give. He's been storing it up all his life. I hoped someday a lovely lady would bring it out of him. *You* are that lady, Celia. You need each other. You love each other. Don't be put off by his dogged efforts to stay detached."

"You *are* wise," Celia replied. "And you and Bruce?"

"As you said, ducks, I will grab happiness with both hands. So should you. Good advice for us all."

Celia nodded and smiled, then took her coat off the hook. Fiona assisted her, slipping it over her shoulders.

"I can do the sandwiches for another day," Fiona offered.

"How about we do them together?"

"Good plan. See you in the morning."

Celia stepped outside. Gentle flurries fell from the night sky. At least three inches of snow had accumulated in the past few days. Once she reached her room, she sat upright on the bed, waiting for Liam to arrive. She would have it out with him tonight. Choices had to be made on both their parts.

LIAM SAT IN his office, looking over the list of food. He had already paid the bills and counted the restaurant income. They did well today. The toff food had helped. One of these days, some aristocrat would wander in, order food, and recognize his personal chef's handiwork. According to Drew, this food came from peerage houses that agreed to participate in the scheme, so no one would likely cause a fuss. But as he'd said before, he could rely on this food. Enough toffs stayed in London during the winter to have a few weekly trays. Come summer, however, when Parliament took an extended break, the upper crust would travel to their country estates, and there'd be no food for him to reuse. Liam opened the safe, placed the money inside, and spun the lock. He'd have to go to the bank in a day or two to make a deposit. Next on his agenda?

Celia.

It felt as if someone had shoved a sharp spear through his heart when she'd revealed that her aunt had invited her to Italy.

Celia should go. She could become reacquainted with her aunt, smooth over their estrangement, recover from her ordeal, and live the life she was born into, the life she deserved. Why would any woman want to share his life? Drudgery, long hours, hardly any profit margin.

Fiona stuck her head in. "Liam, where's the coffee grinder?"

"It was cleaned today. Ask Timmy."

"About Celia… Don't let her slip through your fingers. Tell her how you feel."

Liam growled.

"Give over with that nonsense," Fiona admonished. "She's perfect for you, and you know it."

"She's a countess," Liam snapped.

"I'll wager you my tips tonight that if you ask her, she'd give that life up in a trice. Try it and see. You love her. You know it. Don't muck it up."

Fiona disappeared before he had a chance to respond. *Don't muck it up.* Easier said than done. He stood, grabbed his coat, and headed upstairs. He knocked on Celia's door and then entered. She was sitting upright on the bed.

"How are you feeling?" he asked. "The injury?"

"It twinges a little, but I am healing," Celia replied softly.

Liam entered the room and closed the door behind him. He then grabbed the wooden chair and sat at the foot of the bed. "So, Italy. Are you going?"

"I honestly do not know. Aunt Etta was contrite about the past and appalled at what had transpired in her absence. She is sending a letter with more information regarding traveling to Italy if I wish to join her. I want to reconcile with my aunt. She's the only family I have."

You have family here. But Liam couldn't say it aloud. Not yet.

"What did Winterwood want, or is it none of my concern?" Liam cringed at his snappish tone. "I didn't mean to sound as if I had some claim on you. I'm upset."

"At my leaving?"

"Aye, that," he murmured. "You've become such a vital part of the restaurant."

"And?"

"And a vital part of my life. And my heart. I do have one."

Celia's look softened. "Oh, I know you do. I knew it from the start. Winterwood came to make amends. His wife, the new countess, told him 'to make it right' regarding my situation."

"As he bloody well should," Liam muttered.

"Franklin apologized and said he'd been following the solicitor's advice. I cannot fault him entirely."

Liam crossed his arms. "Franklin, is it?"

"Yes. I forgave him." Her luscious mouth curved into a smile. "Especially after his proposal."

Liam listened, transfixed by her explanation, and, in turn, was heartsick because Celia now had the means to live her own life. She could live as she pleased between the money and her aunt's invitation to Italy. He should never have allowed himself to feel deep emotions because this would always be the result. People left, people died—like his mother and Walter Henning. He should have learned that by now.

But Liam understood these were the conclusions of an emotionally damaged boy. He was thirty years old! *And it is time to step into the light.* He had already made a start with his staff and his son. Now came the most challenging part of all.

"What do you think?" Celia asked, bringing him out of his thoughts.

"I'm pleased for you."

"Did I ask for too much? I figured the amount would equal the dowry I should have had from my uncle and a stipend from my late husband."

"Honestly? You should have asked for more."

Celia laughed lightly, and the pleasant sound reminded him of trickling water in a fountain. Then she sobered. "I do not like leaving things unsaid or unresolved. On the day my parents died, I never told them I loved them. And I did every day before that.

But not *that* day. Instead, I'd acted hurt and disappointed that they were not taking me on the boat trip. It never entered my ten-year-old mind that my parents wanted to be alone. I did not throw a tantrum. It wasn't my way, then or now. I just wish I'd told them I loved them.'"

"You had no way of knowing their fate," Liam said.

"No, but I swore I would never hold back again." Celia met his gaze. "I do not regret telling you how I feel because it is the truth. Why can't you say you love me in return? Unless you do not feel that way toward me."

Her frankness was admirable; he envied Celia's ability to verbalize how she felt aloud. If only he possessed the intestinal fortitude to do the same. He should at least attempt it.

"I'm a brooding bastard, in more ways than one. I always believed that I didn't deserve love. I also don't want you to give up your chance at joining society. You deserve every good thing. You're beautiful inside and out and too good—for the likes of me."

"Liam, don't ever say that. Everyone is entitled to love. I have yearned for that ever since my parents passed away. I did not find it at my aunt's home, and while I discovered the warm camaraderie of friendship with Corrine and Selena, fate pulled us apart. Perhaps it's my lot in life to be alone."

"Everyone here cares for you," Liam said gruffly. "Very much."

"Including you?" He nodded in response. "As I said earlier, I *know* you care. You have from the first. I came to that conclusion swiftly. You gave me shelter and a job. You made me a special chicken dinner and a full breakfast when I was ill, as well as the flummery dessert. You sent telegraphs on my behalf. You took a loss on the gambling debt for my aunt's address and a small settlement. You ended your affair two days after meeting me. Why?"

"I told her that I'd met someone who caught my interest," Liam croaked, his voice laced with emotion.

"Most importantly, you kissed me. More than once. Passion-ately."

Liam's heart thundered in his ears. "Ask me the question again."

"Which one? Oh, 'including me?' That one?" she asked softly.

"Aye, that one. Most especially, including *you*. I've become so anxious, I don't know what to do. What could any lady, a countess no less, want with a cook from an East End eatery, the by-blow of a notorious duke? A man who has been lonely for so long that he forgot how to feel. A man so incapable of recogniz-ing emotion that he failed to comprehend he had a family right under his nose, including a son?" Liam paused, his vulnerabilities laid open.

"You opened my heart and allowed me even to consider that I was worth loving after all," he continued. "I didn't know it until you came into my life like a breath of fresh air. You gave me the strength to take a chance—on love." He stood. "God, how I love you," Liam rasped. "You are—life. Everything. I want you—in my arms, by my side, in my bed, and in my kitchen."

Celia clapped her hands together and laughed joyously. Her eyes shimmered with tears. He had come this far, so he might as well go all in.

"Marry me, Celia. Make my happiness an everlasting reality. Make me whole. For I cannot live without you."

Celia jumped to her feet and ran into his arms. "Yes, Chef!"

Liam laughed, long and loud. His joy was unfettered at last. He spun her around, holding her close.

Celia laid frantic kisses across his whiskered chin. "I love you, Liam. So very much. I think I have from the first. It appears I find grumpy men attractive. I suspected that your sullenness was a protective shell. I *knew* that a passionate man lay hidden within." She pulled back and caught his gaze. "Make love to me."

"Here? Now?"

"Yes. Take me to bed. *Your* bed."

CHAPTER TWENTY-FOUR

L IAM OPENED HER door and peered into the hallway. "All clear," he whispered.

Taking her hand, they ran toward his flat at the end of the hall. Once inside, he closed the door with a quiet snick, then swiftly gathered her in his arms and kissed her passionately.

The kisses grew more frantic as they headed toward his bedroom. His insides were aflame, and so was his desire. Taking her arms, he gently pushed her against the wall, then lifted her right leg to rest on his hip. Liam thrust against her, and Celia moaned.

He wanted to be inside her—now. *But, patience.* A frantic joining had its place, but not here. First, there was Celia's injury. Second, Liam wanted to bring her the pleasure she had never experienced in her marriage. He wanted to be the man who made her come entirely apart.

Liam dove in, thrusting his tongue into her luscious mouth in concert with the thrust of his hips. "What are you feeling," he growled. "Tell me what you want."

"I want," she said breathlessly, "I want—everything. Touch me."

"As my lady commands," Liam replied huskily. His hand tunneled under her wool skirt, making a slow descent up her shapely leg. Celia responded to every slide of his fingertips across her skin with a combination of sighs, moans, and trembling. As he surmised, Celia was passion incarnate, all of it pent up and awaiting release. He located the slit in her drawers and then felt the wetness. *Oh, so ready.* "You're wet. For me."

"Only you," Celia whispered as she caressed his cheek.

He quickly thrust two fingers inside of her, and she gasped. *So tight.* Liam started slow, moving his fingers in and out of her feminine core while brushing the pad of his thumb across that sweet nub. In increments, he moved faster, and Celia responded by grasping his shoulders and digging her nails into him. Her breath came in sharp pants, intermingled with moans of such longing that Liam thought he would spill in his trousers. "Come for me," he urged. "Let yourself go. Look at me."

Celia gasped but did not look up.

"Look. At. Me."

She raised her head, meeting his gaze. "I want to see you fly. Feel it."

"Oh. My God," she rasped. "I've never—" With a piercing cry, she reached her peak. Celia looked beautiful with her head thrown back, a look of awe and satisfaction on her lovely face. She shuddered, her inner muscles clutching his fingers as if they did not want to let go.

Liam laid kisses across her cheek, then captured her lips. After releasing her, he grabbed her rear, lifting her far enough so that he could carry her to his bed. He lowered her onto it, then pulled his white shirt over his head without unbuttoning it. He continued to undress, tossing his clothes in a heap on the carpet.

He stood before her, completely exposed, inside and out. His desire was plain, his love tangible and potent. Celia's gaze leisurely wandered over him, and she smiled. "You are entirely gorgeous." She stepped closer, and when she laid her hand against his chest, it was his turn to moan and tremble. Bloody hell, he was putty in her hands. She touched him all over. Her fingertips left his skin aflame. And when she ran the tip of her finger along his hardened length, he lost all patience.

"Your clothes… Allow me." Liam slowly but swiftly undressed her, and when she stood naked before him, he drank in her beauty. All thoughts of patience left him.

He. Could. Not. Wait.

Taking her hand, he led her to his bed. "Lay on your uninjured side. That's it, love."

He opened his bedside table drawer, located a sheath, and slipped it on. Then he lay beside her, his arm curling about her waist. His erection prodded between her legs, and she lifted her leg enough he was able to seat himself at her entrance. "I'll take it easy, love, because of your injury." Slowly, he thrust inward.

"Yes, Oh, how I have waited for this," Celia moaned.

"Aye, love. So have I." He clasped her breast, his thumb brushing across her nipple as his slides took on a more urgent rhythm. "If it's too much, if I hurt you, tell me," he whispered, laying kisses on her neck.

"More. Give me more."

He pounded into her, the crescendo building. It had never been like this with the few women he'd been with. Not even close. Celia cried out first. He held her closer, riding the wave of her release. Then, he let himself go. Colors burst behind his closed eyes, and every muscle in his body tightened from the overwhelming rush of his climax.

But what amazed him more than the intensity of their lovemaking was the wave of complete and utter bliss that followed.

Liam was in love for the first and last time in his life.

CELIA LAY CURLED into Liam's arms as they tried to catch their breath. How could she describe what had just occurred? It was more than she'd ever dreamed of. Every touch, kiss, and thrust were seared into her memory. "I never knew it could be like that," she whispered.

"Neither did I," Liam responded gruffly. "There's so much more for us to explore, and we'll have a lifetime to take and give pleasure."

Celia sighed. "Liam."

"Mmm?" he murmured lazily.

"I may not be able to have children. You should know that now."

"Because you had none with old Winterwood?"

Celia nodded as her fingers caressed his chest hair. This may not be the best topic of conversation after such rigorous lovemaking, but Celia wanted him to know about it before they continued onward.

"Maybe it was because of him," Liam said. "Even if it isn't, we shouldn't dwell on it. There is no blame involved, and don't ever think it lies with you. Children are not imperative for our future happiness. Besides, I—we—have Tommy. And if we discover that we can't have children? Love, there are orphanages and work-houses aplenty. There is also the foundling home Chellenham sponsors."

"Your duke half-brother?"

"Aye, Damon Cranston. We can adopt one or two if you like. Or not." Liam kissed her forehead. "What I want most of all is *you*."

Celia kissed his cheek. "Thank you for saying that."

"Celia, are you absolutely sure you want this life with me? It will mean giving up your upper-class standing. There won't be much money—"

Celia gently placed her fingertip against his lips. "We have my nine thousand pounds. The interest alone will bring in 400 pounds a year. Perhaps a little less."

"What?" Liam exclaimed. "Bloody hell."

"You want to stay here and run the business?" Celia asked.

"For now. Will I feel differently in ten years? Possibly. Maybe in less time."

"Well, now we have options. Let us say we stay here for ten years. We can use the interest we make to enclose the back staircase, refurbish some of the rooms, perhaps install a small kitchen for our use, and modernize the main kitchen further."

"You've given this some thought?"

"Since Franklin made the offer. I always meant to ask what was on the floor above this one."

"Nothing. Walter lived there, and I had a room there as well. The rest was used for storage. There are stairs to the upper level. It is not as spacious as this floor." Liam pointed to the door on the opposite wall. "Go through there and up the stairs. The brothel was on this floor; the girls lived in these rooms, and the other rooms were for customers."

"Then we have more than enough space to expand and make plans," Celia enthused. Then she sobered. There was still her uncle and cousin. Surely, they would not make any more mischief. What would be the point? She hoped their criminal disruptions were over, especially now that the police were involved.

Liam caressed her arm. "The settlement must stay in your name. It's your money."

Celia placed all thoughts of her uncle and cousin from her mind. She kissed Liam's cheek and embraced him. "That means the world to me. Thank you. I do love you." Celia kissed him deeply, then whispered, "So, when will this wedding take place?"

"You tell me. What do you want?"

Celia thought about it. "As soon as we can arrange it. I want it here, right in the restaurant, and we will have a wedding breakfast. Timmy and Tommy can prepare it with assistance from Enya. We will invite the staff and Drew—" Celia sighed wistfully. "I wish Corrine, Mitchell, and Selena could attend."

Liam smoothed her hair, pushing the tangled locks from her forehead. "We can wait until Corrine and Mitchell return from their honeymoon if you wish."

"It's a lovely thought, but I do not want to wait that long. I want our life together to start as soon as possible."

Liam chuckled. "Good. I don't want to wait either."

"Let's invite Drew over for lunch tomorrow. We will have

him come just before the restaurant opens. I want us to tell him first. We can tell everyone else at the family meal tomorrow night."

"Right you are. Now that we have that all sorted…" Liam gathered her close and then turned over so she was underneath him. "How is the injury holding up?"

"So far, all is well."

"Then I will take it easy. Hand me another sheath."

Celia boldly grasped his erection, eliciting a husky moan from him. "Don't use one. We will be married in a couple of weeks anyway. I want to feel you inside me." She guided him, and with an unhurried thrust, he was seated within. With measured glides, he built the sexual tension, moving a little faster with each pump of his hips. Celia wrapped her legs around him, her fingers digging into his back. After several minutes, they cried out in unison, whispering words of love as they held each other tight.

As Celia slid into that twilight stage of sleep, she smiled as complete joy took hold.

It will never leave me, not as long as I have Liam.

⇥⟫⟫⟨⟨⟨⇤

"YOU ARE GOING to be married?" Drew exclaimed. "When?"

Drew had arrived at the rear entrance at a quarter past eleven. Liam and Corrine swiftly escorted him to the staff dining area for privacy. Then they had told him of their plans.

"Well, we were hoping you would know how to do it quickly," Liam said.

Drew smiled. "Because I assisted in arranging Corrine and Mitchell's nuptials?"

"They took your advice," Liam replied.

"Mitchell and Corrine discovered that marriage at the registrar's office can take up to ten days or more, but only two or three days in a church and with a special license. They opted for the church. I gave them the name of Reverend Wilton, a friend of my father's. He is the vicar of Bow Church in Stratford."

"Oh," Celia replied disappointedly. We were hoping to have the nuptials here. And we want it on a Sunday when the restaurant is closed."

"I am sure James Wilton would travel here any other day, but Sunday is likely out of the question because of church services." Drew scratched his chin. "He could marry you at the church early in the morning before services begin."

"What do you think, love?" Liam asked as he slipped his arm about Celia's waist. The plan sounded acceptable to him.

Celia smiled warmly. "I think it's perfect. We will do it in two weeks. That will give Mr. Eckley time to make a wedding cake for us."

Drew stuck out his hand. "Leave it with me, then. I will contact James Wilton this afternoon. May I offer my sincere congratulations to you both?"

Liam looked at the outstretched hand, and instead of taking it, he pulled Drew into a brotherly embrace. "Thank you— brother."

Drew returned the sentiment, and then they patted each other on the back before parting. "Well met. I *am* pleased."

Celia laughed and kissed Drew on the cheek. "You will come, of course?"

"I would not miss it for the world," Drew replied.

"Will you stand up for us? Fiona will be the other witness," Liam asked.

"Absolutely. I would be honored."

"Do stay for luncheon," Celia urged. "We have mutton with duchess potatoes and roasted carrots."

Drew's eyebrows shot skyward. "That's quite the meal."

"Chellenham sent two huge boxes of food yesterday," Liam replied. "Here, let's get you seated. We open in ten minutes."

After seeing Drew seated comfortably with a cup of tea, Liam and Celia returned to the kitchen. Liam was relieved to have Morrigan assist him now, and he watched in appreciation as she busily stacked plates on the prep table. The kitchen was in full swing when a horrendous crash stopped everyone in their tracks.

"Morrigan, watch the stove." Liam ran through the swinging door into the restaurant to find complete chaos. The two large windows on either side of his corner lot restaurant had been broken. Outside, Liam spotted three men throwing bricks. Customers screamed as spraying glass shards flew in all directions. Some had jumped to their feet, knocking over the wood tables. Food flew across the floor. When the men spotted Liam, they dropped the bricks and ran off in different directions.

"Drew!" Liam yelled.

"There are numerous injured people. I'll tend them," Drew replied.

Liam nodded.

A customer, a young man in his early twenties, stood. "I'll help you catch them, guv."

"Come on then."

Liam, the young customer, and a couple more men fanned out onto Brick Lane. Inside, Liam seethed. This had gone too far. It had to stop—innocent people were getting hurt. As he swiftly gazed up and down the street, the young man pointed toward Chicksand Street.

"There's one of them!"

Liam followed the young man; he had no idea where the other men had disappeared to. Liam and the young man caught up to the perpetrator, whose breathing sounded labored. The customer tackled the brick thrower to the ground.

"Get off me!" the brick thrower yelled.

Liam grabbed his collar and brought him to his feet. He looked like a wily little weasel, probably no more than five inches over five feet tall.

Liam turned toward the customer. "Thank you for the assistance, Mr.—?"

The young man removed his peaked cap. "Paul Tyler, guv."

"Come, we'll get this villain back to the restaurant. Lunch is on me."

"I appreciate that and all, guv. What I want more is a job."

"It just so happens that I'm hiring. Let's go."

Paul grabbed the brick thrower's arm, Liam took the other, and they dragged him back to The Crowing Cock.

While they hurried along the walkway, Liam's thoughts turned to his customers, especially those sitting by the windows. He hoped none had been severely injured. Flying pieces of glass were nothing to laugh at.

As he rounded the corner, his heart sank to see a crowd gathered at the front entrance. They pushed through the mob, keeping a firm hold of the brick thrower, who wriggled and strained, trying to escape.

Liam stepped inside. *What a bloody mess.* This latest stunt could very well kill his business for good. "Please! Nobody leaves until the police arrive!" he yelled. The chattering ceased, and everyone looked toward him.

At that moment, the two customers who followed Liam outside stepped into the restaurant with another man in tow. It was the bloke Liam saw holding the brick.

"We've got him, Mr. Hallahan!"

Well, two out of three was not bad. "Brilliant. Could you please sit him there and hold him?" Liam asked.

"Liam!" Celia ran toward him.

"Here," Liam said to Paul Tyler. "Hold this idiot."

Liam held out his arms, and Celia jumped into his embrace, kissing his face. The crowd grew quiet, except for a few shocked gasps. Liam didn't care. Let the whole world see how much he loved this beautiful lady. "I'm fine, lass," he whispered. With a last peck on the cheek, he released her.

"Tommy's gone for the police. Luckily, Drew says no one is seriously injured, at least so far," Celia said breathlessly. "Morrigan is looking after the kitchen, Hannah and Enya are assisting Drew."

Bruce walked up to Liam. "What can I do to help?"

"Fetch some rope. We'll tie these idiots to chairs until the police come."

Bruce sprinted toward the kitchen.

"Where did he come from?" Liam whispered to Celia.

"He was with Fiona. In her room."

All night? Interesting.

With the suspects tied, Liam shook hands with the men who had assisted him and was about to ask them to please stay so they could talk to the police when Morrisey and his constables arrived.

"Not again, Hallahan?" Morrisey said.

"Aye. This time, we caught two of the three offenders. And we have plenty of witnesses. The bricks are outside on the walkway."

"Northrup, disperse the crowd."

"Aye, Sergeant." The copper put the run to the people lingering about, then entered the restaurant, slamming the door behind him. He then turned the sign so the 'CLOSED' side faced the street. It took over an hour to take everyone's statement, and once Liam apologized to his customers, the least injured ones were allowed to depart. The ambulance wagon was called for two older ladies who'd been sitting by one of the windows. They had glass fragments embedded in their face and hands and needed hospital care. It was lucky no shards had hit their eyes.

"We'll take these suspects to the station to be questioned," Morrisey told Liam.

"I'll tell ya all," the short one yelled. "Some snobby toff hired us."

"We will continue this at the station." Morrisey motioned to the men tied in the chairs. "Take them to the wagon." After the officers escorted the men outside, Morrisey took Liam's arm and led him away from everyone. "You will have to close. The pub, too. You will need that time to clean up the mess and board your windows. I will get to the bottom of this. And today—I promise you. I will come by as soon as I have any information."

"Thank you, Sergeant."

Liam stood among the wreckage, taking in the broken glass, the smashed chairs and food all over the floor. He felt heartsick.

Celia came to stand at his side. "We will clean it up, Liam," she murmured as she slipped her hand in his. "Everything will be well. I have every faith in Sargeant Morrisey."

God, how he loved her. He needed that love and her strength.

"You're so right, love," Liam whispered. Louder, he said, "Staff, meet Paul Tyler." He let go of Celia's hand and pointed at the young man near the door. "He's working here now."

The staff came up one by one and introduced themselves to Paul.

"Want to start work today?" Liam asked him.

"Aye, sir. I do." Paul replied. Liam liked the look of the young man. Earnest, tall and good-looking, Liam could eventually use Paul for serving. But one step at a time.

"Then let's all get to work. But first, Morrigan, is there enough salvageable food for us to share a meal?"

"Yes, Chef," she replied with a smile.

"We should eat before attempting this cleanup. Morrigan, please direct everyone to cook and serve. Paul, Bruce, and I will board up these windows. Tommy and Timmy, you'd best hie off to school."

In the past, an incident like this would have enraged Liam and made him gloomy for days. Not anymore. And not with Celia by his side, along with his restaurant family—particularly his son.

As Celia said, they could accomplish anything as long as they were together.

CHAPTER TWENTY-FIVE

WILLIAM STOOD IN the parlor, entertaining his guests: Mr. Silas Foster and his daughter Lynda. The girl, or rather, the young lady, impressed William. She sat straight, looked him in the eye, and answered his probing questions without hesitation or acting like a simpering girl. She would be perfect for keeping Troy in line. Lynda was solidly built, possessed a good shape, and was tall, perhaps only two or three inches shorter than his son's six-foot height.

Troy had gone out. William had no idea where, but he took advantage of his son's absence and invited the Fosters for early tea while instructing the footmen to pack Troy's trunks and load them on the back of William's Clarence carriage. He did not whitewash his son to the Fosters; in fact, he was entirely blunt, describing in detail Troy's wayward behavior and wicked ways.

"We will soon bring him to heel, eh, Lynda?" Foster said. "Hard work will smash any of those notorious tendencies. I'd say starting as a furnace operator should sweat out all the evil within."

Miss Lynda Foster glanced at Troy's portrait on the opposite wall. "I will ensure he becomes as striking inside as he is outside. I do love a challenge."

Baldwin stepped into the room. "My lord. If I may speak to you a moment?"

"Of course. Foster, Miss Lynda, help yourself to more biscuits and cakes. I shall return shortly."

William lumbered into the hall, closing the parlor door behind him.

"The viscount has returned. He came in a hansom cab and entered through the rear door," Baldwin murmured. "He looks somewhat shaken, my lord. He is upstairs."

"Bring hot tea and more cakes to my guests. I am going to my son's room."

William used a cane today, for he suspected he was developing gout. Taking his time, he climbed the stairs. Stopping for a moment to catch his breath, he flung open the door to Troy's room, finding him looking out the window, which faced the street.

"Watching for the coppers?" William asked.

Troy swung about, a worried look on his face. "If they ask, I've been here all morning."

William's insides twisted. "What have you done now, boy? Tell me, or I will hand you to the police myself!"

"I hired some dock rats to throw bricks through Hallahan's restaurant windows. The blasted idiots were supposed to do it *before* the restaurant opened! They arrived late. The place was nearly full."

Dear God! William fought to keep his temper in check. "And where were you during this chaotic scene?"

"I was in a hansom cab at the end of the street. Once I heard the screaming, I left."

Screaming. Meaning injuries. "You gormless worm. Now you have really done it. You will have to leave. Immediately."

Troy's eyebrows furrowed. "What, the city?"

"The country, you blasted dolt! You are not the first aristocrat to flee England because of the law. It has been done for centuries. You're lucky I have your escape route planned."

"What do you mean?" Troy whispered.

"It means that you will be charged with multiple acts of assault and probably arson! It is not like the old days when aristocrats got away with all sorts. Times have changed. There is nothing I can do for you now. Our solicitor, Signet, says you will be charged with assault causing grievous bodily harm, which means up to sixteen years in prison. And if they can prove intent, it's a bloody life sentence!" Perhaps William exaggerated slightly; Signet claimed that being an accessory after the fact brought a marginally lesser sentence.

Troy gasped. "No, that cannot be right."

"It is! The solicitor would know! He says you will be sent to Newgate Prison. Why, the place is seven hundred years old. Numerous groups are lobbying to have the moldy, damp pile of stones torn down. Many men have died in there, coughing their lungs out. And there are many hardened criminals in Newgate. A pretty boy such as yourself would be fresh meat to them."

"Father!" All the blood drained from Troy's face. William had no choice but to be blunt. The situation was dire.

"Mr. Silas Foster and his daughter, Lynda, are downstairs. You will be leaving with them within the hour. Your trunks are already packed and loaded. You will catch a train to Liverpool, then take a Cunard ship to America. You'll be there in a matter of days. The crossing takes no time at all thanks to steamers. Everything has been arranged."

Troy's eyebrows shot skyward. "America? Jesus, no."

"I am not sending you to hell. Stop being so dramatic. Mr. Foster is wealthy and owns a profitable steel mill in Pennsylvania. It is there that you will marry his daughter. You will also go to work in the steel mill and earn a salary. I will continue your monthly stipend as long as you stay with Foster and marry Lynda. And get an heir off her. With frugality, you will be able to save a pretty penny. Behave yourself, and Foster will leave his fortune to his daughter and you. Provided there are children."

An expression of utter horror covered Troy's pale face. "You cannot be serious."

William ignored him. "I would not recommend trying to run away. Foster's associates here will watch you day and night. And don't even think of doing a runner once you reach America. You will be penniless and never survive, as it is a wild place. Face it, you've gone too far. There is no escape except the path I have opened for you."

Troy's shoulders slumped. Perhaps at last, the gravity of the situation had sunk into his son's selfish brain.

William patted him on the back. "Not all is doom and gloom. You may only need to be away for five years at most. It depends on how long it takes for things to calm down. You will be the earl someday. Then you can return with your wife and children and take your rightful place, hopefully, a more mature and humble man. But until then, you must hide. And you must leave within the hour."

"A wife," Troy murmured.

"A wife is better than a prison sentence," William snapped.

"Not to me. You are doing this to save your own skin and your reputation in society. By banishing me, you are helping yourself."

William sighed. "I will not deny a part of me wishes this for self-preservation, but damn it, boy, I love you, despite your many faults. I will not see you founder in a prison cell. You would not survive incarceration. We both know it."

"I suppose not."

"As to your future wife, Lynda Foster is a handsome young woman with a pleasing personality. She is better than you deserve. It's time to grow up. Now, come downstairs and meet the Fosters, and then you must depart. I will try and stall the police. We can only hope they do not call the train back. They can do nothing once you are crossing the Atlantic Ocean. No son of mine will rot in prison, not while I still breathe!" William concluded dramatically.

Defeated, Troy nodded and followed William downstairs. Quick introductions were made, and William observed Lynda's interest in Troy. To William's surprise, Troy gave Lynda a thorough inspection. Did he see a spark of curiosity in his son's eye? Perhaps he imagined it. Not that it mattered at this point.

It was time to leave. William shook his son's hand. The Fosters and Troy climbed into the carriage and departed.

With an exhale, William returned to his study and sat at his desk for the longest time. An hour ticked by, then another. He would have to curtail his criminal activities for a while in case the coppers started sniffing about. Celia and Hallahan could easily set the police on him.

The sun sank lower in the sky as the afternoon rumbled onward. William knew within his ample guts that this would be his life from now on—sitting alone in a dark room. He had the distinct feeling that Etta would not return home anytime soon. He'd have to write her a heartfelt letter, laying before her all that had happened with Troy, and take his share of the blame for how their son had turned out. William would also have to beg her forgiveness regarding their treatment of Celia. He would also lay his heart bare, for he still loved Etta most desperately. It was on him that he'd allowed her to drift away. Life's regrets had a habit of gnawing away at one's soul in moments of deep reflection.

"My lord. Detective Sergeant Morrisey to see you," Baldwin announced, pulling William from his tortured thoughts.

Morrisey entered with two uniformed police officers. "Where is your son, my lord?"

"Why do you want him?"

"I have a warrant for his arrest for numerous acts of accessory to assault under the Offences Against the Person Act of 1861. These acts were committed during the recent violent incident at the restaurant," Morrisey explained.

"What assaults?"

William only half listened to Morrisey's droning reply. He already knew all the parts of the act because Colin Signet, his solicitor, had explained how the police could charge Troy. All he knew was that the more he asked questions, the farther Troy traveled away from harm.

➤➤➤✦◀◀◀

BY FOUR THAT afternoon, the staff was still laboring to clean the restaurant. Drew left shortly after the injured ladies were taken to St. Thomas's Hospital. He told Celia he would see Reverend Wilton later that afternoon and come by tomorrow with any possible plans for their nuptials.

"Fiona!" Liam called as they finished scrubbing the restaurant floor. "Time for another meal. Let's finish off the toff food."

"Aye, Liam." Fiona took Bruce's arm and led him toward the kitchen, and the remaining staff followed.

Celia turned toward Paul Tyler. "You have worked very hard today. Will you stay for another meal?"

"Gladly, miss. I've never eaten so well."

Liam came to stand beside Celia, resting his hand on her shoulder. The fact that Liam openly showed his affection pleased Celia immensely, but it also had her heart skipping a few beats. She felt his hand, warm and reassuring, on her shoulder.

"Do you have a place to live?" Liam asked Paul.

"Aye, sir. It's not far from here. I live with my sister."

"Come at eight tomorrow morning, and we will discuss your wages and duties. It will be long hours, but meals are included."

Paul Tyler beamed. "Thank you, sir—and miss."

"We use first names here, Paul. We are Liam and Celia," Celia smiled. "Go and assist in the kitchen. We will be along directly."

Paul touched his forelock and jogged toward the kitchen, disappearing through the swinging door.

Celia turned to face Liam, slipping her arms around his waist. "You made a wise choice hiring that young man," she said.

Liam smiled and kissed her on the nose. "I learned from Walter that it's always smart to have a handsome lad waiting tables as it will draw in the lady customers. I may use Paul for that eventually. We'll see how it goes."

Celia laughed lightly. As Liam pulled her closer for a kiss, Bruce entered the room.

"Begging your pardon. Sergeant Morrisey wants a word."

Liam rolled his eyes. "We're always interrupted," he murmured. More loudly, he said to Bruce, "Show him in."

The detective strode through the door and stopped in front of them. "He's gone."

Liam's smile vanished. "What?"

"You had best sit down," Morrisey said gravely. The three of them slipped into a nearby booth. "By the time I took those men's statements, crafted the police warrant, and presented it to a judge, Shinwell had disappeared."

Liam scoffed. "Why am I not surprised?"

"The Earl of Darrington claims his son has left for America to marry a steel magnate's daughter and will go to work in the man's mill. We contacted the railway company, but Shinwell, Mr. Foster, and his daughter had already boarded a ship bound for America. There is nothing I can do. International waters and all that nonsense."

"I cannot believe this, or maybe I can," Celia fumed. "So he is to get away with the lot?"

"It depends what you mean, my lady. Darrington tells me his son will be laboring as a furnace operator in the mill. From what I've heard, that is a brutal job and probably worse than any hard labor he would have to do in prison. It's cold comfort, I know. And I can tell when someone is lying to me. The earl was telling the truth about his son's future."

Liam banged the table with his fist. "Damn them all. What if he returns? Can we charge him then?"

"Although there is no official statute of limitations in Great Britain, many prosecutors do not like to charge a crime after several years have passed. For that certain charge, 'accessory to assault' falls under the Offence Against the Person Act. The most he would get is three years."

"So that bloody pillock can swan back here and take his place in society like nothing ever happened?" Liam growled.

"Unfortunately. I wish I had better news, and I *am* sorry I couldn't get to him sooner."

"We know you tried, Sergeant," Celia replied sympathetically. "I suppose, in a way, Shinwell *is* serving a sort of sentence."

"You are too kind. Oh—" The sergeant reached into his coat pocket. "The earl asked me to give this to you." He passed a thick envelope to Celia.

Celia ripped it open. Inside were numerous pound notes. "Money," she gasped. "And a letter."

"I will leave you to it," Morrisey said as he slid along the bench seat to depart.

"No, please stay," Celia said. "I'll read it."

Dear Niece,

I cannot begin to apologize enough for my conduct, or Troy's behavior. I should have offered you a comfortable room from the start. Instead, I cossetted Troy's shameful manner as I often did many times in the past. But I make no excuses. Perhaps in time, you will forgive my atrocious deeds.

Meanwhile, allow me to make amends the only way I know how. I have enclosed the total amount of Troy's gambling debt along with the interest Mr. Hallahan requested. That fulfills my agreement with him. I have also included an additional 150 pounds for the anguish we have caused you, with another fifty for Mr. Hallahan for the damages caused by Troy's shenanigans. If it is not enough, please get in touch with me, and I can provide more. Again, I sincerely apologize.

Uncle William

"Well, as you said, my lady, it is a sort of sentence. Monetary compensation is usually part of a guilty verdict where damage is concerned," Morrisey said. Then he shook his head. "Shenanigans. Leave it to the upper classes to refer to crimes as such."

"And what about my customers, especially the older ladies who had to be taken to the hospital?" Liam exclaimed.

Morrisey stood and placed his hat on his head. "My unofficial advice? Have the earl offer another settlement to those harmed. And ask for more than fifty pounds for damages. You can claim lost income for the restaurant and pub—trauma for your employees and customers. Threaten to sue him in civil court if he does not pay. That, in my book, is hitting him where it hurts." Morrisey gave them a sly smile. "But you did not hear that from me."

Liam stood and held out his hand. "Thank you for the wise advice."

Morrisey took it and shook. "I wish I could have done more. Good day, Hallahan. My lady."

Liam slid into the bench seat after Morrisey departed.

"Well," Celia said, "This is quite the turn of events."

"Am I shocked that an aristocrat fled the country to avoid lawful punishment? No. Am I surprised your uncle offered money to make things right? My cynical side sees it more as a payment to keep our mouths shut about his criminal life of smuggling and theft."

"And it *is* a payment to remain quiet," Celia sighed. "Honestly, I wish to put the entire sordid incident behind me. However, before we do, we should do as Morrisey suggested and threaten a civil suit. There are the ladies injured, the loss of income, and the stress for everyone."

Liam took her hand. "I will go along with whatever you decide."

"Let me think about it. Meanwhile—" Celia jumped to her feet, bringing Liam with her. "Come with me."

She hurried through the kitchen into the staff dining room. When Celia burst through the door, all eyes turned to her. "We are getting married!" she cried joyfully.

Everyone clapped and came to their feet, smiling and offering sincere congratulations. Many hugs were given. Most of all, what warmed Celia's heart was seeing Liam smile and openly accept the cheers of goodwill. The walls were down, and he had opened his heart at last.

That solidified Celia's happiness and hope for the future even more.

CHAPTER TWENTY-SIX

THE NEXT TWO weeks flew by, and with the rental of an omnibus, the staff traveled to Bow Church and witnessed Celia and Liam exchange wedding vows.

To Liam, everything seemed surreal, like something out of a fairytale that he'd never believed in—until he met Celia. She showed him what happiness truly was, but most of all, love—unfettered, joyous love.

After the exchange of rings and the final blessing, they were off. Due to the restaurant's demands, a honeymoon trip was out of the question, but Liam had tentative plans for a few weeks in the coming summer. Drew had graciously offered them the use of the cottage where Mitchell and Corrine currently were staying in Pevensey Bay on the southern coast of East Sussex. With a few months of intense training, he could leave Morrigan and Fiona in charge and not worry about it.

They arrived at the restaurant, and Liam swept Celia into his arms and carried her across the threshold to the cheers of their friends and people on the street. Once inside, he kissed her as he lowered her to her feet. Liam's breath was taken away when they entered the staff dining room. His friends must have been up most of the night decorating. There were numerous pine boughs with hawthorn and holly winter berries on the wall, including one on the table, with cream-colored candles, which Bruce and Paul were lighting. Surrounding the pine bough display were dried rose petals. Everything looked exquisite, and Liam was genuinely touched that his restaurant family had gone through such trouble.

The table was immaculately set with white china and crystal goblets. Liam cast a glance at Drew. He must have supplied them because Liam did not own such fancy table settings.

Mr. and Mrs. Eckley entered the room, carrying a two-tier cake on a silver stand. It was covered in marzipan with red and pink marzipan flowers.

Celia grabbed Liam's arm in excitement. "It is absolutely beautiful!"

They placed it on the sideboard. "We have more, Mrs. Hallahan. We brought treacle tarts, scones, mince pies, and sugar biscuits."

Celia giggled. "Mrs. Hallahan. Oh, my. How wonderful that sounds."

Liam kissed her hand. "Wonderful, indeed."

"And so are your baked goods, Mr. and Mrs. Eckley. I am so pleased you could join us today," Celia added warmly.

"Now, bride and groom, take your seats here, at the head of the table. Thankfully, it's wide enough for you both," Fiona said. "Enya, Morrigan, Tommy, and Timmy will prepare the wedding breakfast. First, we have cheese, biscuits, fruit, and a lovely apple cider. I will fetch that."

Animated conversation broke out around the table as they passed around cheese and fruit platters. Then, the breakfast was brought forth and laid upon the sideboard: pork sausages, rashers of bacon, scrambled eggs, toast, roasted potatoes and onions, and baskets of pastries.

"Bride and groom first," Fiona announced.

Liam held out his hand to assist Celia in standing. She wore a lovely lavender gown decorated with lace and pearls. Never had he seen her look so beautiful.

Soon, everyone was seated, eating, and conversing. Toward the end of the sumptuous meal, Liam stood, raising his goblet of sparkling apple cider.

"To our family and friends, thank you for your tireless effort in preparing this wedding feast and making all the other arrangements. Celia and I are deeply touched and very appreciative. We have plans for The Crowing Cock. One of the priorities in the spring is enclosing the outside staircase—" Vigorous applause broke out. Liam laughed. "I know, it's deuced cold this time of year. Next, we will renovate the third floor as a living area for Celia and myself. My present living space will be part of it, consisting of a parlor, a small kitchen, and a room for Tommy."

There was more applause, and Tommy blushed at his name being mentioned.

"Timmy will move upstairs into the second-floor empty room next to ours, as he indicated he'd like to stay with us for the long term. Celia and I will be his guardians until he reaches the age of majority. That makes him part of my immediate family and *our* family."

Liam paused as everyone broke out into excited chatter, and congratulations were given to Timmy. He was proud of the lad. Timmy stated he wished to keep his last name of Cagney because it had belonged to his father, and he had loved him. Liam admired that. Timmy also wanted to learn everything about the business and work alongside Tommy, his best friend.

"We plan to be here a few years yet," Liam continued, "And while we are, we will do all we can to make it an even better success!"

Everyone rose to their feet, their cheers echoing in the hall, a symphony of joy and celebration.

"Thank you to my brother, Drew, and my son, Tommy. I am pleased you are part of the family. Lastly, to my lovely bride, Lady Celia Hallahan. You brought sunshine, warmth, and love into my life. For that, I am yours, body and soul. You already have my heart. Cheers to us all!"

Mr. Eckley brought the cake before them, and Liam touched Celia's hand as they cut into it.

"Hope you made a wish!" Hannah cried. Everyone laughed.

Liam looked down into Celia's smiling, lovely face. "My wish already came true."

Celia caressed his cheek and pulled him down for a passionate kiss to more cheers and applause. As they cut the fruit-filled wedding cake and served tea, Liam couldn't wait for the wedding night to commence.

⟫⟫⟫×⟪⟪⟪

CELIA CRIED OUT as she reached her peak, then, after catching her breath, climbed off him and curled up into his embrace. "You have me near worn out already," she gasped.

Liam chuckled. "All we have to do is rest for a while, and I will be ready again."

"It appears I married an unsatiable man." She sighed happily. "Thank goodness."

Liam laughed. "And I married a thoroughly passionate woman. Thank Jaysus."

A knock sounded at the door. "Sorry to disturb!" Fiona said loudly. "A telegram arrived from Italy. I'll slip it under the door. Carry on!"

"Italy?" Celia wrapped a sheet around her and she hurried to the door to pick up the telegram. By the time she returned to bed, Liam had turned up the gas lamp by the bed. She scanned it, and then gasped.

"What is it?" Liam asked.

"Shinwell has been seriously injured at the steel mill. He is paralyzed from his midsection downward. He is not doing well, and my aunt is returning to London immediately." Celia looked up from the telegram.

"Shinwell is in America already?" Liam couldn't believe this turn of events.

"The Atlantic crossing takes only a few days and it has been over two weeks since he left. Shinwell must have gone right to work in the mill." She paused, and shook her head. "Paralyzed. What a turn of fate. I feel terrible."

"Love, you have a kind heart. Your cousin is a villain, and justice has been meted out. Even if he survives, he will never father children, which means there will be no heir for your uncle. Unless the villain managed to get his new bride with child already."

"It *is* a possibility, but a slim one, I assume."

"Is there anyone else to inherit?"

"I don't know much about my uncle's family, but I don't think so. There must not be, because Darrington always mentioned that Shinwell was the only chance for the earldom to carry forward."

"Then your uncle will also pay a price for his criminal life. The earldom dies with him. Good. Do not give those loathsome men another thought."

"You're right, of course." Celia folded the telegram and placed it on the nightstand. "I wish—"

"What do you wish, love?" Liam murmured as he pulled her into his embrace.

"I wish Corrine and Mitchell were here, and I miss Selena. I'm worried about her, Liam. Who knows where she is?"

"First, it's nearly February. Corrine and Mitchell will return to London on March 1st. No time at all. As to your other friend… When Drew and I were in the Devil's Acre, he swore he saw the duchess lurking about the dark alleys."

"What?" Celia cried.

"He chalked it up to extreme fatigue. Let's be honest: why would a duchess be in such an infamous neighborhood? It makes no sense."

"It does sound incredible. But it would be a good place to hide. Who would look for a runaway duchess there?"

"I have a feeling we will discover more, and sooner than you think. Meanwhile, let's sleep, love. We have the rest of the afternoon and night before us."

"Liam?" Celia said softly.

"Hmm?"

"I love you so very much."

Liam's heart soared. He'd never tire of hearing it. "And I love you most desperately."

A future with Celia?

Liam, filled with hope and anticipation, was more than ready to live, love, and experience it all. The future was bright, and he was determined to embrace it with all his heart.

EPILOGUE

Late January,
1899
Devil's Acre, London

Doctor Drew Hornsby had to come to Devil's Acre once again. He could not stay away. Had he seen the Duchess of Barnsdale when he'd visited this rookery with Liam three weeks ago? The possibility had nagged him ever since, enough to compel him to investigate.

With his busy schedule, finding time to conduct a search was difficult. He had a few hours to spare and the weather was not overly cold, so why not?

It was not as if he expected to see her, as Devil's Acre was a maze of crowded rundown tenements, shacks, dark alleys and courtyards. Why would a duchess stay in such a notorious area? The rookery was barely three miles from the Barnsdale residence. Why would she not travel further?

Drew pulled his wool coat's collar upward as he strolled along the broken cobbles. He had left his doctor's bag home, not wanting to draw attention to himself. What were the odds he would see her?

Since he had met her last April on a medical call, the duchess had never been far from his mind. Selena Woodhouse, the Duchess of Barnsdale, was an extraordinarily beautiful woman with golden red hair. In fact, she was one of the loveliest ladies he had ever seen in his twenty-five years. Yes, she had made quite an impression.

The duchess would be easy enough to spot, unless she wore a disguise. Drew scanned the streets. Since it was the middle of the afternoon, quite a few people milled about. He watched each of them carefully.

Around the corner, a woman emerged, carrying two wicker baskets on one arm, while holding a large shawl in place with her free hand. She had it over her head, so he could not see the shade of her hair. She hurried along the walkway in a swift manner, keeping her head down.

Drew had to see what she looked like. He followed her as close as he dared. Then he crossed the street, walking on the opposite walkway, hoping to catch a glimpse of her profile at least.

A loud bang, like the backfire of an automobile, sounded. The lady in the shawl stopped for a few seconds and turned enough toward the noise that Drew got that glimpse he had wanted. It was only for a moment, but enough that their eyes met. One second, two, three... Then she ducked into the alley.

Blast it all, he could not be certain, not one hundred percent, as the lady had a scarf across the lower part of her face. Drew tried to cross the road, but multiple carriages passed each other, delaying his action. By the time he reached the alley, there was no one there.

Gone. Again.

But that would not deter Drew. Not at all.

He would return, and find the duchess, one way or another.

I hope you enjoyed Celia and Liam's story. And don't worry—Drew and Selena will find their own happy ending in *The Doctor and the Duchess*. Coming soon...

Author's Note

Unwanted children in many countries have been abandoned for centuries. In Britain, it wasn't until the Adoption of Children Act of 1926 that adoption gained legal status. Before then, it was informal, if it happened at all. Most children found jobs in factories or apprenticeships; others wound up on the streets. An unmarried woman could not name a man as the father of her child on the birth certificate unless she gained an affiliation order against him, so most children had no idea who their fathers were.

Widowhood for an aristocrat's wife could lead to a woman becoming a propertied lady or impoverished, as was the case with Celia. Most widows were given a small income from their dowry or the estate from rentals or farm income. Celia had neither, nor did her husband leave her any money in his will as women were often not mentioned. It wasn't until the Law of Property Act of 1922 in England that a wife had equal rights to inherit.

As for the illegitimate children to inherit? It wasn't until the Family Law Reform Act of 1969 that children born outside of marriage were allowed to inherit on the intestacy of either parent. Before that, numerous restrictions were in place. For example, a child born from an adulterous affair could not inherit, but a child born from two people who married after the fact could inherit with a change in the law in 1926. It wasn't until 1987 that all restrictions were removed, giving a child born outside of a marriage the same rights as a child born within one.

The tragic boating accident that claimed Celia's parents actually did occur. The S.S. Princess Alice, a steamer passenger ship, sank on September 3, 1878, when it collided with another vessel on the River Thames. Between 600-700 people lost their lives.

Regarding Shinwell escaping his crimes, extradition treaties did not exist between Great Britain and the USA during the Victorian era except for political prisoners. It wasn't until well into the 20th century that further addendums were made, the most recent in 2003.

My fascination with Victorian meals and food practices, which I've meticulously researched, led me to create a chef hero. The Victorian-era cookbooks mentioned in this story are real.

The French-born Alexis Soyer (1810-1858) was considered the first celebrity chef in Victorian England. His cookbook is available for free on the internet. The facts about him and other cookbooks, menus, and recipes have been well-researched.

The 'family' or staff meal at a restaurant has no actual known origin, but it is believed it goes back to the Victorian age. It became more common in the 20th century.

Fried potato shavings (or chips or crisps) first appeared in *The Cook's Oracle*, published in 1817. They were not mass-produced until the early part of the 20th century. In Britain, the Smiths Potato Crisps Company was formed in 1920. The first seasoned chip/crisp came in 1954. In North America, it was barbeque (from the Herr's Chip Company). In Britain, it was cheese and onion (From Ireland's Tayto Crisps).

Thank you for finding my book. I hope you find all my research as fascinating as I did.

Karyn Gerrard

About the Author

A multi-published author from the East Coast of Canada, Karyn Gerrard loves to write historical romances. Tortured heroes are an absolute must. She whiles away her spare time writing, reading romance, and drinking copious amounts of Earl Grey tea.

Karyn's been happily married for a long time to her own hero. His encouragement and loving support keep her moving forward.

Catch up with me on social media:
Website – www.karyngerrard.com
Facebook – facebook.com/karyn.gerrard
X – @KarynGerrard
BookBub – bookbub.com/profile/karyn-gerrard
Amazon – amazon.com/stores/Karyn-
Gerrard/author/B0052XUPQE
Instagram – @karyngerrard

9 781967 169337